WINGS OF STRIFE

SILVER CITY UNIVERSITY

VICTORIA PAULEY

Contents

To those who never felt like they belonged.
There's always a place for you.
Your people are out there.

Author's Note

I'm thrilled to finally share Wings of Strife with you. While this is not a dark romance, the characters in this series all need to overcome their own issues. Some of these issues may hit close to home so please read the list below before diving in.

-This book features an FMC who struggles to fit in. She's bullied and ridiculed for being different (not by the main love interests).

-Instances of prejudice between the different types of angels.

-Open door sex.

-Episodes of PTSD from past trauma with flashbacks of a witnessed death

-Mention of the prior death of a parent.

-A difficult relationship with family.

-Demons intent on harm

Silver City University Map

1

EZEKIEL

I'm numb.

Time trickles by with every frantic beat of my heart, but still Hayliel doesn't wake. The healer has backed off, no longer trying to fix what is so obviously broken.

All of this is my fault.

I tear my gaze from her limp form, unable to look upon it any longer without feeling like I've let her down. And I have. I'm the trained guild intern, after all. I should have protected her.

Instead, she's dying.

This can't be fucking happening.

Without thinking, my eyes shift back to her lifeless body. Raphael and Theo are by her side, comforting her. Comforting one another, too. Fuck. What must they be thinking? Whatever I might have had with Hayliel, her relationship with those two was five times stronger. My foolish belief that I alone could handle Roderick and whoever he was dealing with got us into this mess. It's what will tear her from the two angels I've despised since I saw them having a picnic with her.

I never wanted any of this to happen.

Resolve settles in my gut as I watch them at her side. I can't just sit by and accept that she's dying. Not if there's a chance to save her. I've studied these fucking blades enough that I should know every damn loophole. There has to be *something* we can do. *Please let there be something.*

I take a deep breath, dust filling my lungs, though I barely notice as I mentally sift through what I know about angel blades. They weren't always called angel blades, though I can't recall their previous name. Long ago, during one of the more deadly battles between angels and demons, rumors spread about the glowing black orb in the base of the pommel. They said it was a soul stone, and every soul of an angel slain by a blade lives within it, unable to rest for eternity. If what they say is true, that's what the red swirls are in the dark stone. Churning souls, desperate to reach the eternal resting place they've been denied.

I stare at it, wondering if it's true. Is that what's happening to Hayliel now? If her soul gets trapped there, can we extract it somehow or will she be gone for good?

Shit. This is only making things worse.

A tidal wave of reality hits me, threatening to pull me under in a sea of pain. I can't save her.

I crouch to get a better look at the blade, doing everything I can not to glance at her face. If I do, I'll crumble.

The length of the handle has lines carved into it, and at its base sits the black stone. The markings are most likely runes, but as I focus on them, I notice something is off. None of the runes are complete. Either the creator of the weapon fucked up, or they don't fully understand runes. They're so worn down, though, that it's impossible to tell for sure.

Raphael speaks to Theo in a low tone, reassuring him it's not his fault, and I almost laugh. He can't really think that, can he? How in the world would this be his fault?

"This isn't like last time, Theo. All of us were here, fighting, and I bet all three of us would rather it be us lying there instead of her."

He's not wrong. I would gladly die on her behalf. But what is this talk of last time? I suspected Theo had a past, but I never would have guessed someone died.

No wonder he's got issues.

And this will only make things worse for him.

I take her hand in mine, wincing at the heat of her palm, and finally let myself look at her. She's burning up, far too pale, but I can still feel the thready beat of her heart. "It's time to wake up, hummingbird," I tell her, hoping she can hear me. "Raphael and Theo need you. Hell, *I* need you."

She doesn't move, and even though I swear I just felt her finger twitch, I know it's more likely a muscle spasm than her responding to my plea. The others join in, begging for her to open her eyes or give any sign that she can hear them. She remains still.

This isn't supposed to fucking happen! To the healer, I say, "She should be coherent. Why isn't she waking up?"

"I'm sorry. Wounds like hers have no pattern. If there were some way I could make her more comfortable, I would."

Clinking metal stops me from biting her head off. The clinking grows louder, and I search for the source of the sound. Lieutenant Atlas. He looks rather somber as he eyes the bloodied angel on the ground. He says nothing, yet somehow that just pisses me off further.

"Can you help her?" I ask, desperately hoping for a cure, even though I know there isn't one. *I'm not ready to give up yet.*

He rubs his chin as he assesses her, and for one very brief moment, I'm hopeful. Then he shakes his head.

"I would remove the blade. I've heard leaving it in would only quicken death, as it allows more time for her soul to be siphoned into the stone."

"I disagree, Lieutenant. The blade is the only thing stopping the flow of blood. If we remove it, she'll bleed out." The healer looks like she's ready to hop over Hayliel's body to block access to the blade. And going against a direct superior? She'll likely pay for that later.

He only shrugs. "I was just trying to buy more time. She's not long for this world."

Beside me, Raphael and Theo share a look before turning

their pained gazes on me. Fuck, I wish Azrael was the one who showed up today. He'd understand how delicate our situation is and wouldn't make shitty remarks like that. At least *he* has angel skills.

Instead of leaving, Atlas continues talking. "You're all very lucky to be alive. Someone caught sight of the battle en route to their shift. If they hadn't, it's likely you'd have all ended up in a similar state." He nods to Hayliel's prone form. "Anyway, I sent guild members after the demons that fled. I will do everything in my power to ensure they don't get away with this. You have my word."

"Thanks," I say, though the expression is only a formality. I might have heard his words, but their meaning hasn't sunk in. Raphael and Theo are ignoring the lieutenant. He's completely unharmed from battle, and if we only have so long with our girl, I'd rather spend every last second reassuring her just how much she meant to us.

The healer makes a weird sound, drawing my attention. Her face holds a mixture of confusion and shock that traps the breath in my lungs. I follow her line of sight and notice the blood has stopped flowing around the wound on Hayliel's side. Fear stabs at my heart. If she's not bleeding, does that mean ...

No. She can't be dead. We need more time.

I shift my hand to her wrist, hesitating for a second before I press my fingers to her pulse point.

It can't be.

Her pulse is steady and strong. But how is that possible?

My eyes lock with the healer's, who has Hayliel's other wrist in her hand, likely noticing the same thing as me. With the flow of blood stopped, the healer places her hands over the wound to close it. Golden light flashes from between her fingers, but that's not what any healing I've ever seen looks like.

Hayliel's face has more color than before. She looks almost healthy, if I ignore the blood and blade. Her right eyebrow twitches once, then twice.

Without thinking, I yank the blade from her shoulder.

"What the fuck did you just do?" Raphael says in horror, but his bitching is cut off by something magical.

The gaping hole where the dagger used to be blazes with hues of golden light before slowly stitching itself back together.

She's healing, I say through the connection with Raphael and Theo, but they're already watching. Every wound on her body glows. Some are faint, while the more grievous wounds shine bright enough to blind. Still, we don't look away.

When the golden beams fade, she looks completely unharmed.

"Sunshine?" Raphael whispers, and we all just stare at her. Seconds turn into minutes until the hope I once had begins to fade.

Physical contact. Maybe that's what she needs to come back to us. Taking both her hands in mine, I squeeze. "Come back to us, hummingbird," I say, my voice rougher than intended.

"Please, firefly," Theo adds, his own wobbling slightly.

Then, as if she could hear us between the realm of the living and the dead, her eyes flash open and she jolts upward on a massive inhale.

Alive.

2

HAYLIEL

The sun is blinding, burning my retinas and making me squint, but something stops my hands from coming up to shade my eyes.

I look down to find them held hostage by powerful, warm hands. Zeke's hands. On my other side is a strange woman I don't know. One of her bloody hands covers her mouth as she stares at me in open disbelief.

What the fuck is going on?

My mouth is dry and caked with more dust than anyone should taste in their lifetime. There are no trees around us, only barren, sunbaked dirt. How did I get here?

Theo pulls me into his arms and Raphael piles in too, wrap-

8

ping the two of us up tight. I'm exhausted, so I let myself sink into their comforting embrace. I'm not sure why they're acting like this, but I can't say I hate it.

A gust of wind rushes against my overheated skin, soothing some of my discomfort.

"Thank the Archangels you're alright, sunshine," Raphael says, pressing a kiss to my head. His words don't make any sense. Of course I'm alright. I'm with them. How could I not be?

When they finally pull back, I glance toward the woman in the guild uniform, then to Zeke. Standing just behind him is a frowning angel I don't recognize. A lieutenant, with metal-tipped wings, but he doesn't have the thick brown hair I recall Azrael having. This must have been who I saw earlier during the fight.

The fight!

Memories of our night out crash into me. The house. The barn. Roderick. And two hordes of demons trying to capture all of us.

But we were winning. The guild showed up, and I was heading toward my friends. So why is everyone looking at me like we lost?

"What happened to the demons?" When no one responds, I keep going. "The last thing I remember is getting tackled to the ground. After that, it's just … blank."

Except it's not all blank. I can still hear the taunting remarks of that scarred angel. *Dead little angels don't have power, do they?*

The guys exchange a look, but it's Zeke who finally responds.

"You were stabbed, hummingbird. Several times with an angel blade. We don't understand how you survived, but we're just glad you did."

"What?" My gaze darts between all of them. "But that's impossible."

When no one says anything, I peer down at my bloody clothes. Beneath my shirt, which is lifted on the right side, there's a thin line that shimmers faintly with gold and another near my right shoulder, but it doesn't make me feel any better. As if we needed more unanswered questions, and this time with an audience.

Zeke shifts in my periphery, and the blade he's holding flashes in the light. It's only a quick glimpse, but I can tell from the swirling red and black stone that this isn't an ordinary blade. He carefully sheaths it in the strap on his belt before covering the hilt with his shirt.

The movement is odd. Secretive. Causing a flurry of questions to rise in my throat. The guild is here, a lieutenant directly behind him. Shouldn't we be giving the blade to him?

As if sensing my questions, Zeke shakes his head almost imperceptibly. Fine. If he wants me to drop it for now, I will. But he'll need to answer my questions later.

Behind him, the lieutenant steps closer, scrutinizing me. "For my report, I'll need to know how you ended up here. What were the four of you doing off campus so early in the morning?"

Shit. Has the night truly been that long? The rising sun doesn't lie, yet still it's hard to believe. How the fuck did we end up here, bloody and beaten yet again by those vile creatures?

I yawn, eyes heavy as I scramble to find the words.

Zeke beats me to it, answering like he hasn't spent all night on a high of adrenaline. "It appears we were on a wild goose chase."

The lieutenant perks up. "Oh?"

"We've been trying to uncover information about Hayliel's ancestors so we might understand her, uh, angelic oddities."

"I have discolored wings," I tell him weakly. I may be half dead of exhaustion, but at least I can follow along with what Zeke is leaving out of our story. Without knowing who to trust, it's better to err on the side of caution instead of spilling our secrets out like bile. Something I was foolishly about to do.

Theo pulls me back until I'm resting against his chest while Raphael continues with an explanation. "Clearly we weren't asking the right questions because *BAM*. Next thing we know, demons swarm around us and we definitely weren't prepared for that."

"She deals with enough bullshit from other students, so we kept our investigation a secret. Perhaps if we'd been more open and forthcoming, we wouldn't be in this mess," Theo adds, though his eyes never leave my face.

"I see," the lieutenant says, and I wonder if he really does. Can he tell we're hiding the truth from him? And if he can, what's stopping him from bringing us in for further questioning?

Clearing his throat, Zeke looks almost apologetic as he says, "We apologize for the secrecy, Lieutenant Atlas, but given everything Hayliel has gone through already plus the odd demon behavior I've seen these past few weeks, we thought it best to keep things close to our chest. We hope you understand."

"Of course, of course. And without prying too much, were you at least able to learn anything valuable about her ancestry before things took a turn?" His eyes drill into me until I feel compelled to answer.

I shake my head. "Unfortunately, no."

"Ah. Too bad." He says it with just enough inflection that I can't tell if he's genuine or just saying what he thinks I want to hear, but he continues without another thought. "As for the demons, I've noticed similarly odd behavior. Zeke, have you shared your worries with Lieutenant Azrael?"

"Some, but not all." Zeke appears uncomfortable when he answers, and I wonder if he's worried this might somehow fall down on his friend.

"Well, don't worry about what happened here today. Focus on resting, and I'll see if he and I can come up with anything that might explain these attacks."

"Thank you, Lieutenant Atlas," Zeke replies as Raphael's slate vibrates.

He pulls it out, face grim while he reads. "We need to get back on campus."

Lieutenant Atlas fixes a medal on the lapel of his uniform, wiping off a streak of dark black blood from the shiny surface. If only it were that easy to clean up the mess our city has fallen into. "Great job today, all of you. You," he focuses on me, "are one lucky angel. Whatever they stabbed you with must have been one well-made knockoff. It had everyone here fooled. In the interest of secrecy, I won't mention your wing research, though I admit I'm quite curious about what you'll find if you continue."

"As am I," I tell him. "Thank you." It takes all the energy I have left to keep my mouth shut and not ask him why he thinks the blade is a knockoff. Is that even a possibility? It would explain how I'm alive, at least, but it doesn't explain the manic look of triumph on the scarred angel's face. He truly believed that I'd met my end at his hands.

I watch as the lieutenant leaves us, wondering what it is about him that has me so confused. In reality, it's most likely the fatal wound I somehow survived messing with my mind.

That, and the utter lack of sleep.

Raphael and Theo are arguing with the guild healer about whether they consent to being treated before we leave. They don't, and for some reason, Raphael is adamant that we have to go. Eventually she gives in, but not before making us all promise that we'll get seen by *someone*.

To my surprise, Zeke has stayed quiet throughout all of this. He didn't argue with the guild healer, or even with Raphael and Theo. All he's done is stare at me in a way I can't even begin to decipher.

Is he *scared*?

"Feel like you can stand, sunshine?"

I force a laugh, hoping to hide the fact that my body doesn't feel like it'll do *anything* I want it to at this point. "I'm certainly willing to try."

Raph and Theo pull me to my feet, hovering as if I might collapse any second. They aren't wrong to worry. Still, I can't help but look at it in a positive way. Other than a bone-deep exhaustion and some uncomfortable achiness, I'm feeling pretty good. Much better than I should be, considering the wounds I had just moments ago.

Lieutenant Atlas gathers the guild members and orders them to pack up.

Zeke finally breaks his silent streak, though I wish he'd ask a different question. "Think you'll manage the flight back to campus?"

Honestly? No. There's a better chance I'll pass out in the sky than make it all the way back, but I don't tell him that. "Hopefully. I'd rather not walk or have you three carry me all the way there. But I'd prefer to wait until they leave before we go, if that's okay." Having an audience while I put on my wing jacket and attempt the trip back is really something I'd rather avoid.

"You got it, firefly."

We wait in silence as the rest of the guild members take to the sky, the last of which is Lieutenant Atlas, who throws one last look our way before taking off with his metal-tipped wings glinting against the growing sun.

Knowing there's a mole in the guild only makes me suspicious of everyone. Zeke says we can trust Azrael, but what about Atlas? What about the woman who just healed me?

Despite my aching body, the relief I feel at letting my wings out is damn near orgasmic. Raphael and Theo help me into my flying jacket, taking great effort to be gentle, while Zeke only watches on with that same look on his face as before. I want to ask him about it, but now doesn't feel like the right time.

The hovering should piss me off, and maybe tomorrow it will. But right now, I'm just happy to know that I'm not alone.

My body throbs, limbs trembling, and all we're doing is standing. Fuck. This isn't good. Still, I don't want them to know. I've seen the haunted look on their faces. What happened here scared the shit out of them. *All* of them. It would be cruel of me to worry them further, wouldn't it?

A distraction. That's what I need. "Any chance our little rendezvous went undetected?" I ask Raphael, who's on his slate again.

"Maybe. But the longer we stay here, the lower our chances are. And that," he points to the sky where the sun continues to brighten, cresting over the horizon, "certainly isn't helping."

"Good point."

Theo clears his throat. "Are you sure you're up for this?" he asks, his face pale. "We can find another way—"

"I'm fine, really."

And fuck, I hope it's true.

3

HAYLIEL

I survived an angel blade.

I *survived* an angel blade.

The words play on repeat in my head, but it doesn't matter how much I say them. It doesn't feel real. Not when all we know about them is how they kill our kind. Full stop. No deviation. I even saw it with my own two eyes after Roderick stabbed that man. Could he have survived? Was my running away what killed him?

It's all too much.

As we fly, we keep close to the cliffside, doing our best to remain unseen until we're back in the safety of our campus houses. But I can't focus on any of that when my mind is racing like this. Something nags at me, a comment I overheard at the barn that made it sound like the angel blades were coming from demons. Do they only procure them, or are they somehow mass-producing them? If that's the case, maybe it's not that I survived and more that the weapons were faulty. I guess it's a good thing Zeke didn't give that blade over to the guild after all.

This is all too fucking much.

I can sense their eyes on me. Raphael, Theo, and Zeke. I try to ignore it, but that only leaves me with two options. Go out of my mind trying to piece everything together, or focus on how I feel. Both options suck.

My entire body aches in ways I've never experienced before, from my fingertips to my toes. And despite the cool morning air whipping across my face, I'm so goddamn hot.

It's probably just a fever from the adrenaline. Sure, angelic fevers aren't really a thing, but neither is surviving an angel blade—or three—so the realm of possibilities seems to be up for discussion.

We fly over the shimmering falls, and I catch sight of the dark Fallen house in the distance.

Home sweet home. *Almost there.*

My only focus is on keeping my wings beating and my breath steady, but the harder I try, the heavier my limbs become. I'm so damn tired. It's a battle just to keep my eyes open, let alone stay in the fucking sky.

"Good gracious. You lot are a mess," Professor Castiel says, startling me. His powerful white wings flap with ease as he assesses us. A few tendrils have escaped the ribbon that usually holds his hair back, but otherwise, he looks pristine. "All of you, come with me."

Dread settles in the pit of my stomach as I share a look with the others and pivot to follow him toward the main hall. Fuck. He's going to bring us to Principal Cael and report our leave. As if our night—or morning now, I suppose—couldn't get any damn worse.

Raphael has his slate out, furiously typing. To Dina, perhaps? I search my mind for our bond, wanting to ask him about it, but it's not there. Or rather, it is, but the edges are frayed and the reception sucks. What the hell?

Instead of taking us to the front door, Professor Castiel leads us to a window on the side of the building. He unlocks it with a flick of his fingers before opening it and motioning us inside. Raph is the last to enter, tucking away his slate with a concerned look on his face.

This is Castiel's classroom, which is blissfully empty at the moment. But if he's not reporting us to the principal, then why are we here? All I want to do is curl up in bed and sleep. I don't have the capacity for whatever mental gymnastics he may put us through.

"Would someone like to tell me where you've been and why you all look like you've just survived another attack?" He pauses, taking a second to look at each of us, but no one answers.

It isn't that I have reasons not to trust him. From day one he's been more than fair and supportive, especially to me, but does that mean he's trustworthy? Masks are easy to wear and hard to detect. I try again to reach my friends through the bond, but it's pointless.

Our silence is loud, becoming more uncomfortable the longer Castiel watches us, and I'm about to break it, if only to leave and go to sleep, when Dina barges through the door.

"There you are!" she says, sounding far too jovial for this early in the morning. "I see you survived the rather wild paint night we had. Though if you were going to leave and have a four-way, I wish you'd have told me."

What. The. Fuck?

My jaw falls open in horror, eyes darting toward Castiel because, really? This is the best excuse she could come up with?

"Uh, yeah. I guess we got a little carried away," I reply, sounding entirely unconvincing, even to my own ears.

Castiel looks around our group, one eyebrow raised. "A paint night. That's how you're going to play this off?"

He doesn't buy our shit for a second, and I'm not surprised. We're covered in enough angel and demon blood that we'd have had to be the canvas. I'm just grateful he ignored the four-way comment.

Dina laughs nervously, her mouth opening and closing like she's not sure what to say. None of us are after that.

Something tugs at my mental bonds, telling me my friends are trying to reach me, but as hard as I try, I can't find a solid connection. Pain wraps around my head like a vise, only disappearing when I stop trying to reach them. From the concerned look on their faces, it's obvious they're having a conversation that I'm not part of.

"I'll vouch for Castiel," Zeke says. "We can trust him. And frankly, given what we all survived tonight, we don't really have a choice."

The rest of our group nods, but Castiel holds up his hand. "Wait. Say nothing more. Dina, can you lock the door please, and Theo, could you please do the same with the window?"

While Dina and Theo do as they're told, Castiel heads behind his desk and pulls a candle from the locked bottom drawer. Kind of a weird time to light a candle, but okay. Maybe ambiance is important to him or something?

Once it's lit, he places it on a desk in the middle of the classroom and motions for us to cluster around it. "This is a silencing flame. As long as it's lit, no one outside this room will hear us."

Damn. That's a thing? And he just keeps it in his bottom drawer? Who the hell is this guy?

He pulls a first aid kit from another drawer of his desk, along with an unopened bottle of water. "Now, clean the blood from your skin and tell me what it is you survived."

We each take one of the cotton pads and splash some water on it before scrubbing. Where do we even begin? The attack tonight? Finding Roderick? Before that? It feels like far too much information to share after everything we've been through. And I'm too damn drained of energy to consider the consequences.

"We've been researching my wings."

Castiel nods. "Are you referring to your transformation from gray to gold, or to what caused the demons to turn to ash?"

I bite the inside of my cheek and look at my friends, unsure if I should admit the truth or not. When Theo nods, I let it all out. "Both. For the most part, all we've found are dead ends, but we stumbled onto something else. Strange demonic behavior with angel involvement. That lead brought us nothing but grief tonight when the demons attacked. Thankfully, the guild intervened but ..." I trail off, glancing at Raph, Theo, and Zeke for ... what? Reassurance? It doesn't even feel real to me, and yet I'm supposed to tell another angel about it like it's a fact?

My mouth opens and closes several times, but the words never come.

"What happened, Hayles?" Dina asks with worry in her eyes.

"I ..."

Raphael saves me by saying the words I can't. "They stabbed her with an angel blade. Three times."

All the blood drains from Dina's face, and she watches me with fear in her eyes. I can read the questions behind her eyes as she takes in every ounce of blood on my skin, every tear in my clothes. She wants to know how much longer I have left.

"We thought we'd lost her," Theo adds, his voice raw, like the admission of that was far too hard to say out loud.

Dina swallows, tears welling. "But we haven't, right? There's a way to fight this?"

"I'm fine. Really," I tell her, trying to reassure both of us. Sweat builds on my forehead, the heat in my blood making me wish we could open a door.

The room falls into silence for one eerie moment, then Dina rushes to my side and pulls me into a hug. "Fuck, babe. How is that even possible?"

"Well, since you're here," Zeke says to Castiel, "we were hoping you could tell us."

As unsure as I was about telling him anything, now, more than ever, I hope he has the answers.

He purses his lips, assessing me. "Eventually, I'm going to need the entire story, but it's obvious you need a little reassurance that you can trust me. I get that. As for your question, I'm afraid I don't have a concrete answer. Theories? Yes. But if you allow me, I'd like to reach out to a few of my friends outside the university to confirm my suspicions."

My stomach drops. Telling Castiel was hard enough, but involving other angels, ones we don't even know? That's the last thing I want.

Raphael places a cool hand on my shoulder, and a little of my unease dissipates. "Is that a good idea, though? The more angels who know about this, the less likely the information stays secret. Hayliel has already been through enough."

"I agree. She has. And because of that, I would never do anything to put her in harm's way. I will be as discreet as possible."

There's a tug on my mental bonds, and I try once more to open the pathway. Again and again I try, but each time I fail—and my desperation grows with each futile attempt. I wear the heat of their gazes like a brand.

Fuck this. I push everything I have into the mental bond until it snaps.

Pain erupts in my skull, bouncing around like a game of pinball. The throbbing sensation sends me stumbling into the desk behind me as stars explode behind my eyes.

"Guys," I croak, putting even more of my weight onto my weak arms where they rest against the desk, but I won't be able to hold myself forever. It feels like I'm slipping away. Down, down, down into nothing but darkness.

The ringing in my ears is loud enough to drown out everything. Every sound. Every voice. Even my own thoughts.

Gentle arms wrap around me, and someone runs a finger along my temple, soothing the ache. I don't know how much time passes before the pain subsides, but eventually the murmurs of my friends and the sound of Castiel's voice break through.

"Miss Hayliel, I'm just going to check your pulse. It won't take long."

Castiel stands in front of me. He presses a finger against my wrist, silently counting before offering me a reassuring smile.

"Good. Your pulse is strong and steady. But how do you feel?"

"Achy, and like I could sleep for an entire week." That's the simplistic answer, anyway. The real answer is that I feel like maybe I haven't truly survived anything at all.

"I think that's to be expected, given the circumstances."

I frown, unsure whether I want to fully admit the next part.

Now isn't the time to hold back. "I've been having issues connecting telepathically since. I was trying to reach the bond with my friends when the pain overwhelmed me. Do you think it's gone forever?"

I can't make myself look at my friends, but their concern floats around me like wisps of smoke.

"Your body survived an ordeal today. The aches and exhaustion are part of it, I suspect, and I wouldn't be surprised if the telepathy was too. You and your body need rest." Castiel eyes the others. "All of you do. For now, I want you all to go back to your rooms. Clean up and get as much rest as you can. I'll cover for your morning classes, but you'll need to attend in the afternoon."

"Thank you," I say, my voice weaker than before. At this rate, can I even make it back to my dorm?

Dina takes my hand in hers, offering it a quick squeeze. "I'll grab some food and bring it back to the house. Could one or all of you stay with her until I'm back? I'll bring enough food for everyone."

"Of course," all three of my friends say in unison, even Zeke.

"Good, good. Stick to the skies and use your balconies. The fewer angels who see you in your current state, the better. I'll reach out to my contacts right away, discreetly, of course," Castiel assures us as we head toward the window. Only after we've unlocked and opened it does he add a few last parting words. "You can trust me."

Our gazes lock for the briefest of moments, but all I do is nod.
I really hope we can.

4

RAPHAEL

The flight to Fallen house was more than a little terrifying. Between Hayliel's exhaustion and our inability to connect with her, we had to rely solely on observation and instinct to make sure she made it safely.

But once again, she proved just how strong she really is.

"You guys don't have to stay, really. I'll probably be a while in the shower. Plenty of time for you to go clean up," Hayliel says, leaning against the doorway of her bathroom as if it's the sole reason she's still upright. When we don't respond, she adds, "I'll be fine. You should really go take care of yourselves."

A small smile tugs at my lips. Even after everything she's been through today, she's more worried about us than about herself.

Silly girl. "We know we don't *have* to, but if it's all the same to you, we'd prefer to stay."

Something that looks like relief flashes across her face, but all she says is, "Suit yourself."

With the door shut, it's only Theo, Ezekiel, and I left in her room. Dina should be back soon with food, which should help us all settle a little. If that's even possible.

Zeke looks pained, though I can't see any visible injuries, and Theo appears unsettled. It's going to take work to get him back to where he was before last night. All the progress we'd made on sealing his old wounds has been reversed, leaving them fresher than ever. But for now, there's no point in focusing on the past. We need to look ahead.

None of us speak, not until we hear the shower turn on. There's a sense of déjà vu with the three of us together like this, worried about a girl who has all of us wrapped around her finger. "We aren't going to be comfortable leaving her alone for a while, are we?"

"No," Theo croaks. "I don't even want the door separating us."

"Her loss of the bond worries me. Hopefully, it's just as Castiel said and she'll be able to get it back." Zeke begins to pace as we fall back into silence, the water pounding from beyond the bathroom door soothing the ache her absence causes. *She's only washing up. She's fine.*

Zeke stops his pacing and turns to us. "What if I offered to teach her—and you, if you're interested—what I've learned from combat training with the guild? It would be a bit more sophisticated than the combat class they teach here, more than what I offer to Malik's classes. I don't know, just a thought."

I've never seen him so unsure of himself. Usually he's more arrogant than confident, and all it does is piss me off. Today must have really shaken him up.

"I'm in," Theo says without pause. "I thought I knew enough to defeat those pieces of shit, but looks like I was wrong."

"Me too. But when the odds are stacked against us like they were this morning, I'm not sure any amount of training will turn the tides in our favor." I don't want to be a Debbie downer, but fuck. How many demons attacked us this time? Twelve? Fifteen? More? Having proper training might have evened the playing field, but we're still no match for their damn blades. Not without our own.

For the first time since Hayliel went into the bathroom, Theo looks at me, his eyes the clearest I've seen them all morning. "You know, you might be onto something. I'd forgotten about it until now, but I remember reading about a plant that, if dried out and ground into dust, could weaken demons upon inhalation. Honestly, I assumed it was a myth, but maybe it's real."

Zeke snaps his fingers, looking intrigued. "Now that you mention it, I'm pretty sure I've seen a few guild members with pouches strapped to their belts. I wonder if it holds the substance you're talking about."

I nod, finally feeling like we have a sense of direction instead of being lost at fucking sea. "Then let's see what we can find there. My brother used to talk about this angel who creates protective clothing with runes hand-stitched directly onto the fabric. I'll do what I can to get their contact information."

"That sounds *expensive*," Zeke adds, grimacing. When he sees my expression, he adds, "It's not that I'm against it. I just can't contribute financially to something like that, and I want to set expectations. I want the clothing for her, but I can't afford it."

Watching him, I can tell it cost a lot for him to admit. "Let's just focus on getting information first. We may not even be able to find them."

"Alright." Then as if remembering something, he pulls the deadly blade from the sheath at his side and holds it out for me to examine. "Do the runes look off to you?"

Carefully taking it from him, I focus on the faint lines etched into the handle, but runes aren't really my area of expertise. As much as I don't want to cause Theo more pain by looking at the weapon that harmed so many of his loved ones, we need him.

"Theo, can you tell us if you notice anything strange about the runes here?"

He walks over to us with stiff movements, taking the blade into his trembling hand and inspecting it. His thumb traces an edge several times before his eyes dart up to meet Zeke's.

"I noticed the same thing. It's too hard to tell for sure, given how weathered this weapon is, but I don't think the death rune fully connects," Zeke says, confusing me.

"But what does that mean? Is that why the blade didn't kill her?" At least that would make sense, even if it doesn't explain the glow to her skin or the loss of her mental connections.

"We can't say for sure," Theo says, handing the blade back to Zeke. "Add it to our list of things to deal with after we get our girl back in full."

He walks away, leaving Zeke and I to stare after him. Not that I disagree with him. We're all exhausted, both from the sleepless night, the fight, and the pain of our almost loss. Nothing will come of trying to figure things out today.

Zeke clears his throat. "Sounds like we have a plan then. Since Dina isn't here, I'm going to head upstairs to shower and change. Want me to bring you each some clothes?"

Theo doesn't answer. He's fallen silent again, staring at the bathroom door. "Sure. That would be great. Thanks. If Dina arrives with food before you're back, we'll save you some."

"Appreciate it." Zeke tosses the words over his shoulder as he opens the balcony door. He doesn't step out right away, pausing at the threshold before turning around completely. "Is he going to be okay?"

I look at my best friend and ask myself that same question. "We're all fighting something that others can't see. What happened today with Hayliel was all too real for him, but he's survived worse. Besides, I'm here to make sure he does."

"He's lucky to have you," Zeke says, a sad smile curving his lips. "If there's anything he needs, just let me know." He doesn't wait for me to respond before escaping out the balcony door and leaving me and Theo alone.

The events of last night and this morning have clearly shifted something in that grumpy asshole. Offering support? Leaving us—no, trusting us—to be with Hayliel while also offering to bring us clothes is something I don't think he'd have done even a month ago. Maybe there's hope for him yet.

Now it's Theo who needs me.

I consider my options. I'd wanted to step outside and call Rad—though *wanted* may be too strong a word—but with Theo and I alone, we have the perfect opportunity to talk. He's more likely to be honest with me, and himself, if angels like Zeke aren't looming.

Theo has his ear pressed to the door, his brows drawn tight in concentration. I'm not surprised he's so worried about her. The last girl he saw stabbed by that blade was dead within minutes, and he's still experiencing the effects of that trauma. Even though our girl survived, I don't think his brain will let that be enough to stop the worry.

"Any issues in there?" I ask, placing a hand on his shoulder.

"Probably just dropped something." His words should reassure me, but he doesn't leave his post at the door.

"Come sit with me."

He shakes his head. "I should really stay here in case she needs me."

"Just for a little bit, Theo. If she needs you, she'll call. But if she just needs to break down and cry alone in the bathroom, don't you think we should give her the privacy to do so?"

His eyes are bloodshot when he finally looks at me. All I want to do is tuck him away somewhere so he can focus on his own recovery, but that wouldn't do any good. In Theo's mind, he needs to make things right, and that's the only way he'll feel like a decent angel.

I'm surprised when he steps away from the door and follows me toward the small seating area of Hayliel's dorm. Instead of sitting in one of the plush chairs, though, he throws aside the corner of the rug and sits directly on the floor. Shit. That's a good idea. Until Zeke comes by with a change of clothes for us, we're disgusting.

"I know you want to talk about everything, Raph, but I just can't. There's too much going on in here." He hits the palm of his hand against his head.

"Hey," I say, taking his hand in mine, "we don't have to rehash everything. I just wanted to check in and remind you that Hayliel is alive. She isn't Serah."

He yanks his hand back, freeing it from mine. "But she could have been! And just like last time, I was too weak to stop it."

"None of it was your fault, Theo. Not then, and certainly not now."

"Then why does it feel like my chest is caving in? Every little sound coming from that room has me on edge. What if she's lost the capability to connect with us again? What if there are more severe consequences than we even fucking realize? These awful thoughts just won't leave my fucking skull." He drops his head into his hands, pulling at his hair. "Ever since that awful day at the skatepark, all I've done is train so that if something like that ever happened again, I'd be ready. I've researched and prepared, and what did it fucking get me? Nothing. Another *almost*-dead girl."

My chest aches to see him like this, to hear the personal blame he puts on himself. "We all failed, Theo. You. Me. Zeke. Even her. None of us came fully prepared, despite what we may have originally believed. But I'll be damned if I let it happen again. Whatever rebellion we've stumbled into isn't going away, so it's up to us to be ready for whatever comes next. She's a part of it too, and the last thing she'd want is for you to blame yourself."

Water no longer sounds from behind the closed door of the bathroom. Theo shifts closer, leaning against the wall near the door like a sentry.

Someone knocks on the outer door, and when I open it, a frazzled-looking Dina holding a tray of food and a few bags stands on the other side.

"Sorry I'm late. My dad called. Then a cafeteria worker accosted me for not being in class. The bitch almost denied me food altogether."

"It was your charm that led her to change her mind, wasn't it?" I tease, taking the two bags from her hand and stealing a French toast stick.

She cracks a half-hearted grin and places the entire tray on the coffee table. "Where's Zeke?"

"Upstairs. He offered to bring us a change of clothes once he's done, and I promised not to eat all the food." Her eyes widen slightly but she stays silent, so I continue. "Thank you for this. Theo, food's here."

He looks like he's going to refuse, but he's my best friend, and I know him better than anyone. "Why don't you make up a plate for yourself and one for Hayliel, too? She'll probably be starving by the time she's out."

Sure enough, that gets him moving. I leave them to it, grabbing a few grapes before finally heading out the balcony door to call Raduriel.

The line rings repeatedly, but I don't give up. I wait so long, I've finished the grapes by the time the call cuts off with no response. Shit. Why did I think things would be any different? Surely Mr. Important doesn't have time for his brother. Not that he could know what we'd gone through today, but I thought …

Fuck it. I could sit here and tell myself I won't try again later, but that's only a lie.

I will do whatever it takes to protect my sunshine.

No matter the personal cost.

5

HAYLIEL

Yesterday felt like both a dream and a nightmare, and today isn't shaping up to be much better. I don't even remember going to afternoon classes, though I know I did. We all did.

To make things worse, I slept like absolute shit last night, tossing and turning, unable to get the image of that scarred demon from my mind. Now I'm stuck with another day of pure exhaustion, overheating, and if that wasn't enough, add on ever-present hunger. Sure, it could just be that my body literally fought off the fabled soul stone at the base of that blade and now it desperately needed to replenish fuel, but what if it's something else?

With my luck, the possibilities are endless. Too endless for my liking.

I stop by Professor Castiel's office, hoping he can reassure me. Instead of him, I find a note pinned to his door saying he'll be out for the day.

Out? Has he left to talk to his friends already, or did something else happen? He said we could trust him, and it's not like he's ever given me a reason not to, but I can't let go of my paranoia. It's not just about him betraying us, either. What if him asking questions or taking time away from his job gets him in trouble?

I'm a fucking mess.

My slate is out before I even think about it. I send off a message to the group chat, fear riding me hard as I head to the cafeteria for a quick snack before my next class. The hot breakfast items are gone, but I don't really want something substantial before Wingology. That class already makes me anxious. It's better not to have something heavy sitting in my gut.

I find a pre-made package of nuts and cheese, then swipe my meal card at the cash register before leaving.

Someone shoulder checks me on the way out, making me drop half my nuts and a few chunks of cheese.

You have got to be fucking kidding me.

I bend to clean up the spilled mess, turning to see who the fuck ran into me like that, but only catch the side of their face. Based on the red trim of her uniform, she's from Fallen house. Asshole. She doesn't apologize or even acknowledge the blow, just continues going like nothing happened.

I'm half tempted to call her on her shit, but honestly, I'm too tired to deal with conflict. There's enough of it going around in my head. I don't need to add any more.

Well, either she's a bitch, or her day's far worse than mine, and neither of those are things I can change.

My slate pings with a message.

> **Theo**: I wouldn't worry too much, firefly. Realistically, it makes sense that he'd want to talk to his friends in person. The questions we have aren't really things we should write in a letter or send in an email. It's good that he's doing this himself, more secure.
>
> **Raphael**: Plus, that guy is OLD. And he couldn't have survived that long without being practical.

Their words settle the fears in my core. They're right. It's a good sign that he's gone in person. And as long as he comes back—no. I won't go there.

I finish the rest of my snack as I head to the arena for Wingology class. I've been avoiding Professor Uriel's insistence on another counselor meeting, though I'm not sure how much longer I'll be allowed to put him off. Hopefully, he doesn't take his annoyance out on me in today's class. I laugh, because that would be a miracle. When *hasn't* he taken something out on me here?

I get changed into my flight clothes in record time, ignoring the other students like I usually do. Not because I'm rude or antisocial, but I get into far less trouble if I stick to myself and keep quiet.

The mid-morning air feels cool against my heated skin as I step into the arena to join the other students who have already changed. As I approach the block of bleachers we usually sit at for class, everyone grows silent. Fucking great. What the hell is it this time?

Instead of worrying about it, I ignore the gawking, find my seat, and look around. The arena has a different setup today that looks oddly familiar. When Theo, Raphael, and I were at the park for the Archangel's Feast, they had some sort of competition. I remember because there'd been a family arguing about it. Not that I stood around witnessing it, and maybe I should have. A leg up would be nice right about now.

True. But if I stayed, I wouldn't have gotten to visit Remiel's prayer tent. Whatever the outcome today, I wouldn't change a damn thing about that day. It was worth it ten times over.

Professor Uriel steps up, and the class falls silent.

"Today we'll be working on flying maneuvers. You may have noticed the setup behind me. I suggest you study it. We will begin today's class with a demonstration from me on how to complete the obstacle course, and then everyone will have the chance to try it. I will time each of you so I can track your progress over the next few weeks. I expect all students to have their wings out for the duration of class." His sharp eyes train on me as he finishes, and I wonder if maybe I should have skipped class.

The number of fucks I give today are terrifyingly low. Something that will probably get me in trouble if I'm not careful.

All around me, students let their wings free until I'm surrounded by a healthy mix of black and white wings. Anxiety spikes, restricting my lungs, but I take deep breaths to calm myself. I wish I had at least one trusted friend in this fucking class. Maybe then I could put my wing jacket on and at least blend in a little.

Once my heart is back to a normal rhythm, I take a deep breath and let my wings escape. I keep them tight to my back, not allowing them to expand, even though the motion is uncomfortable. Yet despite my best efforts and the clouds above, they still sparkle enough to pull the attention of my classmates.

Professor Uriel steps up to the starting line and turns to speak. "Pay attention to my movements. Watch how I weave for optimal speed."

He presses a button along the side before moving into a half-crouched position. The sound of a shot goes off, and then he moves. He's fast, his white wings almost a blur as he flies down the track at breakneck speeds, taking sharp corners with the grace of a practiced warrior.

I don't *want* to be impressed, but damn. The asshole is fast.

When he gets to the finish line, it doesn't feel like I know the obstacle course any better. Maybe if he had taken it slow, explained his tactics, I would have been able to follow along and learn. From the stunned silence around me, I doubt it's just me who feels that way.

Professor Uriel peers up at the clock, smirking at his time. When he turns, damn near preening under the sounds of the fawning students, our gazes lock and his eyes narrow in a way that sets me on edge. He looks down at his slate, reading off a few names, but I drown him out.

Until he says mine.

My legs move without my consent, and before I realize it, I'm standing at the starting line with three other students. The only familiar one is Marina, a Pure angel I've spoken to a few times, though I wouldn't exactly say we're friends. The other two are Fallen, and while their features are familiar, I don't think I've ever spoken to them.

We get into our starting positions, and Professor Uriel presses the button to begin the countdown.

Strategy races through my mind. I'm better off taking my time, learning the obstacles first before trying to blow through them at top speed. And, if that keeps me out of the limelight, all the better.

Boom.

The starting shot rings loud, and suddenly we're all moving. It's a straight line at first, and I hold back as the others pick up speed, getting closer and closer to the ninety-degree turn at the end.

Around the bend is a series of strategically placed walls followed by another sharp turn at the end, but I don't have time to worry about what's beyond that because I'm at the first turn.

I let everything fall away until it's only me and this damn course. Avoiding the walls is easy, and at my slow pace, so are the turns. When I reach the last stretch, I swallow hard. There are only a few narrow pathways to fly, and each one has machines that close up and crush whatever's between them.

Speed will be important here.

My heart slams against the cage of my chest as I plan the best route. Everyone else has already made it to the finish line, but I don't let that bother me. Not when I'm trying to figure out how to avoid getting flattened. Metal clashes on metal as the machines open and close in a steady rhythm, and I let it move through me until it feels as though it and my heartbeat are in synchronization.

With one big inhale, I advance toward the last obstacle. My palms are sweaty as my wings hurdle me through the first machine without issue. The next one is off to the left, so I pivot, but I push too hard and now I'm not lined up with the machine. It takes a few seconds to get myself in position, but I eventually make it through that one, too. Only one more left.

The distance between the hurdles isn't much, not enough to pick up the pace, and the machine opens and closes at a different rate than the first two. If I time this incorrectly, I'll shatter my wings. How is this even allowed? Angels are bound to get hurt, their wings destroyed.

Did the university sanction this? It wouldn't surprise me if this was something Professor Uriel chose just to watch his students suffer.

My limbs grow shaky as fear wells up inside me, but I push it down, tucking it away into a box in my mind and closing the lid. I can do this. With a final burst of speed and two immense flaps of my wings, I'm flying toward it. Metal clashes from behind me, and I know I only have seconds to make it through this machine or else I'm a goner. But the distance is too great.

This machine is longer than the others, and I don't have time to get out.

As if in slow motion, the machine walls close around me and it feels as though I might suffocate.

No, no, no!

There isn't enough space for me to flap my wings in here, but I make small movements, anyway. Just a little bit farther.

I finally make it through the machine, but there's no time to celebrate, not when I notice the tip of my left wing is still between the metal walls, and time has run out. I expect a rush of pain to go along with the sound of metal clashing, but I don't really feel *anything*. Only a soft compression around my wings.

What the hell?

As soon as my wing tip is free, I dash toward the finish line, not caring what my time is. How did I just survive that? Is it the same reason an angel blade didn't kill me?

"Your time is abysmal at best," Professor Uriel calls out to me. "And if those machines had been real, you'd be out of commission with a shattered wing. Pathetic."

"Real?" I sputter, not following.

"The university wouldn't allow an obstacle with real danger, despite my valid arguments." Under his breath, he adds, "I should have known putting you first would uncover that little secret. Now the entire practice is in jeopardy."

I can't even believe this guy. He's such a fucking dick. Here I am, crashing from the adrenaline of thinking my wings were about to get obliterated, and he's upset that I revealed the truth? My hands shake, breath unsteady, as I do my best to ignore him and calm my nerves.

He calls out another four names, his hand hovering over the button to start the course, but he doesn't press it. "I don't want the knowledge that these machines won't hurt to deter you from doing your best. And if I detect any of you doing so, rest assured there will be consequences. Got it?"

Students shout their agreement, but Professor Uriel still doesn't move. "And one more thing." His shrewd gaze lands on me for a single heartbeat before it advances to the other students. "Once the course starts, you *do not* stop. In an actual situation, you likely won't have time to get your bearings. This is no different. Begin!"

I watch as student after student passes the finish line. Some don't make it through the hurdle at the end without getting caught in the machines like I did, which at least makes me feel a little better. On Cadriel's first attempt, he'd passed by me with some scathing remark, but I stopped listening the moment he opened his mouth. I know better than to listen to him.

Karma must have finally caught up to him because he didn't

even make it through a third of the course. He'd taken on too much speed and ran face-first into one of the walls around the first turn. The crunch of his nose breaking is something I won't be able to forget. He's a dick, but damn. It was hard to watch. Of course, his injuries weren't severe enough that he couldn't insult me on his way to the infirmary. Assholes will be assholes, I guess.

After everyone makes it through one round of the course, Professor Uriel brings us back to the start and tells us to practice. These laps aren't timed, though the rules still apply. No stopping. Do better.

I have to stop myself from rolling my eyes at this guy's shitty attitude as I step up to the starting line again. When I make it through the course this time, I think I was faster, though I still couldn't finish without getting a wing caught in that last machine. There has to be something I can do differently.

My muscles ache, unused to getting such a workout. I guess the years of keeping them hidden, only using them when absolutely necessary, is coming back to bite me in the ass. But the pain is good. It means I'm growing stronger.

And I need to be stronger to make it through what's coming.

While I wait for my next turn, I hear a group of Fallen talking as if I'm not even there.

"We're supposed to believe she killed all those demons at the well? Yeah, right," a girl with a hawkish nose, pierced on both sides, says to her friends.

"She can't even make it through the obstacle without getting squashed. There's no fucking way," her friend says, a guy with a mohawk who might have been attractive if it weren't for the sneer on his face. "Not that I want to believe that Pure bitch Seraphina, but maybe she was on to something. Gray wings, gold wings, it doesn't matter. She's a monstrosity that doesn't deserve to be here."

Their words cut me far deeper than the angel blade had. I shouldn't let it bother me, not when I've heard it a million times before, but this is different. These are Fallen, the angels I always thought I could rely on, and now they're turning their backs on me.

Tears threaten to spill, but I can't let them see how much it hurts. That will only fuel them.

Professor Uriel approaches, his lips pursed. "It would appear we have several more items to discuss in your next counseling session. You do realize those are required, don't you? I would hate for your place at this school to be put in jeopardy."

As fucking if. Does he actually expect me to believe he'd be upset if I was kicked out? Not after the way he's treated me.

"Things have been hectic recently. I'll make time soon," I tell him, but it's a lie. I have no intention of being alone with him again.

"Good. Your course time worries me. It might even be the lowest I've seen in my tenure here. I'll need to see a significant improvement in your final score in order for me to feel confident in your continued success here."

He should really just come out and say it, seeing as I can

read his intentions plain enough already. With or without my attendance at his counselor meetings, my place here is in danger.

"Of course, Professor."

He moves on to speak to another student, berating him on his time loud enough for others to hear. It should bring me some solace that he's not just picking on me, but it doesn't.

When it's my turn to fly the obstacle course again, I almost don't want to.

Fuck, I wish I could connect with my friends right now. They'd lift my spirits and tell me I'm a badass, but I've been too scared to try again since what happened in Castiel's office. I close my eyes, picturing Dina, Raphael, Theo, and even Zeke. All of them believe in me. And I think—no, I *know*—they see more in me than anyone else does.

Including myself.

When the gun blasts, I bolt. After two tries at this thing already, I feel more confident. Or at least that's what I'll tell myself over and over again until I believe it.

Even if I don't fully make it through that last obstacle, it's not the end of the world, right? Progress is progress. That's what I should focus on.

This time I look at the clock when I cross the finish line. Out of the four angels I raced with, at least I didn't come last this time.

The professor calls for one more group, and I walk off to the side to watch on. To my left, a mixed group of Pure and Fallen angels talk in hushed tones. I have no doubts about what they're discussing, and even though I can't hear their words, I step further to my right until I'm blissfully alone.

Except, I'm not.

"Protector, my ass," someone says, though I can't see him. "That angel can't even protect herself from getting crushed in a fake obstacle course."

If someone replies, I don't hear it. Part of me wants to turn around and figure out just where these fuckers are, but I don't. Somehow, it's worse if they know I'm standing right here, listening to every word they say.

The guy scoffs indigently. "We're treated like shit for our black wings, and yet somehow, that train wreck gets special treatment. She's just as fucking Fallen as the rest of us."

"No, she's beneath us. That bitch walks around here like she's royalty, but after today, the only monarch I see is Queen Shit of Turd Island," an unfamiliar female voice says, and I swallow past the knot in my throat.

If the Pure hate me and now the Fallen do too, I'm not sure I can take it. Fallen House has been my refuge. It's my safe space where I know I'll escape from the angels like Seraphina, Cadriel, and even Professor Uriel. How many more Fallen feel this way? Is it everyone?

My breaths turn shallow as I struggle to take in enough oxygen. All my life, I've felt like an outsider, but at least then I had my parents, Dina, and our Fallen friends. They always just *understood*.

I've never felt more estranged in my entire life.

Maybe I don't belong anywhere.

I'm too lost in thought when Professor Uriel starts speaking. He says something about the obstacle course being part of our final exams in a few weeks.

If everyone hates me, will I even make it that long?

The changing room is loud with whispers and comments from the angels around me, but it's like I'm on autopilot. I just need to change and get out. It's too crowded. Too warm. It feels like I'm slowly suffocating in here.

And as I leave the changing rooms, and head away from the arena, I can't shake the eerie sense that something is very, *very* wrong.

6

HAYLIEL

The cafeteria swarms with students. It's too damn crowded today. Or maybe it's only me who thinks so.

Since Wingology class, I haven't been able to shake the feeling of total worthlessness. Raphael and Theo sit on either side of me, with Dina directly across from us. Their presence helps quiet the unwanted thoughts, but it doesn't get rid of them entirely.

I'm lost in my head, trapped there by nothing more than my own fear and ineptitude.

A figure approaches our table, spiking my adrenaline as I worry what the next insult will be from him. He might be a Fallen, but he's also someone I feel I can count on, at least a little.

Zeke pulls out a chair, ignoring the obvious look of shock from a few of the other Fallen in the cafeteria. He never sits with us. He never really sits with anyone. So what's he doing here now?

"Are you sure you want to do that? Seems to be causing a bit of a stir," Raphael says, his cautious gaze roaming the cafeteria.

Zeke sighs. "I'm here, aren't I?"

He makes a good point. If there's one thing we all know about Ezekiel Oren, it's that he doesn't do a damn thing unless he wants to.

Our eyes lock, and I try to decipher the emotions I find swirling inside their green depths. Worry, maybe, and a hint of something that looks a hell of a lot like longing. That last one could just be annoyance, though. It's too hard to tell with him and the many masks he hides behind.

"Well, I'm glad you're joining us." And I am. We haven't really hashed out our shit, yet the fact that he's here—especially on today, of all days—goes a long way in mending old wounds. I may never learn why he turned me away so cruelly all those months ago, but maybe we can find some solid ground for our friendship to grow on.

And sure, maybe I still feel this carnal fucking pull toward him, but that doesn't matter. *Yeah right, Hayles. Keep telling yourself that.*

A few angels walk by in their Fallen trim-lined uniforms, gawking at Zeke. I recognize the guy in front by his mohawk, and he doesn't even try to keep his words low as he talks to his friends. "Why the fuck is our house leader consorting with the riffraff?"

The hawk-nosed girl from class is with him too. "Maybe she can control angels once she's fucked them. Might explain the entire table."

Mohawk guy barks a laugh. "Like, she's cute and all, I guess, but I don't stick my dick into beasts."

Zeke's fists clench, but so do Raphael and Theo's. They're seconds away from getting up and telling this asshole what they really think, but I stop them.

"Drop it, please," I whisper before taking a bite of my sandwich. "They gave me shit in Wingology class too. Just ignore them."

"What do you mean?" Dina is the first to ask.

"It's just been a long fucking morning. First, someone ran into me before class, then I had to listen to Cadriel in Wingology, and to make matters worse, the Fallen now seem to hate me." I pull a bit of crust off the bread, popping it in my mouth, and do my best to focus on steadying my breathing. My emotions are too fucking strong today.

"The Fallen don't fucking hate you. I'm here, aren't I?" Zeke says, trying to reassure me.

"You are, but you heard their reaction for yourself. And honestly, that was tame compared to some of the shit they said earlier." I pull at the collar of my uniform. Archangels, it's hot in here. What the fuck is happening to me?

Raphael's usually bright smile is gone. "Let me guess. Useless

Uriel did nothing to stop them."

The hint of a grin tugs at my lips. *Useless Uriel.* Now that has a ring to it. "He didn't, but I'm not sure he even heard what was said. His focus was pretty singular on that damn obstacle course. Although, he did make some offhand remark about how my ability to continue at this school relied upon my attending the counseling sessions and doing better on that course, so it's not like he wasn't an asshole all on his own."

"I fucking hate that guy," Theo says, shocking me. He's usually so calm, so neutral. To hear him actively hate someone is a pretty big deal.

I reach out to squeeze his hand. "Look, it's fine. It's not like the comments are new. And sure, I'm upset that the Fallen seem to have turned their backs on me, but I have you guys and that's enough for me. Now, can we change the subject?"

Theo squeezes my hand back and nods. "We can. Are you still worried about Castiel?"

I sigh in relief and relax only slightly. "A little. The last thing I want is someone else trying to help me and getting hurt or in trouble."

"He'll be fine. I'm due back at the guild in a few days, so if he's still gone, I can double check the logs and make sure we haven't had any reports involving him." Zeke pushes the food around his plate, but doesn't eat any, and I wonder if maybe he's uncomfortable sitting with us.

One thing at a time, Hayles. One thing at a damn time.

"Do you still think you'll be able to collect some of those

things we talked about?" Theo asks him.

Clueless, I ask, "What things?"

"Things that shouldn't be said out loud with so many angels around," Zeke answers. If I didn't know any better, I'd think he was completely unruffled, but I know his tells now. The twitch in his jaw and the disinterested gaze see far more than he lets on. "But yes. I'll do my best to gather what I can and also push Azrael more for answers. I'm sick of him keeping me in the dark."

So they aren't going to tell me shit, it would seem. Though I suppose they have good reason not to, given the number of angels around us. Most of whom don't particularly like me. "Whatever it is you're looking for, please be careful. If there's even a possibility that you'll be caught, it's not worth the risk."

Zeke flashes a small smile at my obvious worry. "I'll be fine, humm—Hayliel. Theo, have you figured out anything more about that other thing we talked about?"

I don't miss the way he almost called me hummingbird, but I can't give him shit on that because I'm once again lost. What other things have they been talking about, and *when*? Before now, Zeke actively avoided us. Hell, he disliked Raph and Theo with all the passions of an endless flame. But now they're talking? Strategizing?

I must have entered an alternate reality.

Theo shakes his head. "I'm still trying to find the book. No luck at Knowledge house yet, but I'm almost certain we have a copy at home. Are you still willing to train us?"

The book? Willing to train? Did Zeke offer to teach all of us how to fight like the guild? Fucking hell, just how much have I missed?

"Don't think I'll forget this entire confusing conversation later. I expect someone to loop me in eventually. And soon." I purposefully meet each of my friends' eyes, imploring them to take my words at face value because I mean it. As worthless as I might feel, it's only made worse when they keep me in the dark.

"We will. I promise, sunshine."

A few students walk by and we shovel food into our mouths to appear at least semi-normal. One of them, a Fallen guy with big ears, does a double take of our group. When he notices Zeke among us, his face falls, and he whispers, "So disappointing."

Trying not to let it bother me, I avert my eyes to anywhere else in the cafeteria and just so happen to spot something even worse. Seraphina sits in the corner with her friends. The look she gives me is full of hatred, probably pissed off that her last attempt at separating me from Raphael didn't work.

There really is no place for me, is there?

When the area around our table is less crowded, Zeke finally answers Theo's question. "I'm still willing to train, yes. And the sooner we start, the better. Because I help Malik with his combat classes, he gave me a private training room for the semester. We should be able to meet there without raising suspicion."

Dina's eyes light at the mention of Professor Malik. A while ago she mentioned he'd be the teacher she'd hook up with if she had a choice, and something tells me there's a bit more to it than that.

She folds her arms on the table and leans in. "This whole talking in code thing while students glare at us isn't fucking working for me. Can we use that room Malik gave you as a meeting point or at least eat lunch in one of our rooms to talk all of this shit out instead of whispering in public? Other than *things* and *books,* I really have no idea what's going on."

"Amen, sister."

Zeke looks thoughtful as he says, "Maybe. But a private room offered to me to work out in is a far cry from a safe space to talk about *other things.* We may want to consider another option."

Raphael places a hand on my thigh, and the warmth of his palm grounds me. "According to Raduriel, there's an attic at the top of the tower. I'm trying to get in touch with him for something else, but I could ask him about that too."

"Wait," I say, completely taken aback. "What do you need from your brother?" Their relationship is strained at best and has been for a really long time. I can't think of a reason that Raph would willingly set aside their issues to call him. Not on purpose, and certainly not by choice.

"He has information that could help keep you safe. All of us, even. So I have to try."

I place my hand over his where it rests on my thigh and squeeze. Just when I think I'm at the edge of my rope and there's not a place in this entire city where I belong, he makes me believe otherwise. They all do.

As much as I want to ask for more information, I understand

what they're saying. Here isn't really the best place for it. And Dina's right. We really do need a safe, private place to talk openly.

An idea floats around in my head, but I'm not entirely sure it's possible.

"What is it, firefly?" Theo asks. If it were anyone else, his level of perception would bother me. But with him, all I feel is safe. Guarded.

"It could be nothing but ... that house we were in the other day. It had protection runes. Whatever location we decide on as a meeting place, could we put our own runes or wards up? Something to make the area even more secure."

"That's actually not a bad idea," Zeke says, nodding. "Theo and I should be able to help, though I'm not sure how much they'd work on school buildings. It's possible they have protections already in place to not allow silencing runes. But if we have a few location ideas, we can definitely test them."

Raphael pushes his tray away and leans in. "Well, we have the tower attic and your training room. Does anyone have another suggestion?"

Silence falls at our table as we think, which works out well because lunch time must be almost done. Students get up from their tables and head toward the exit. We'll need to do the same soon, too.

"What about the cave near Somersault Falls?" Zeke asks, looking more than pleased with himself.

"A cave seems a little damp and dingy, doesn't it?" Dina

replies, and I can't stifle my laughter.

Zeke throws a dark look my way. "What?" I laugh some more. "She's got a point."

"If we can't ward the others, it might be our only option. Unless you want us all to meet in your room?" Zeke raises an eyebrow at me, and I'm about to take the bait of his challenge when Dina chuckles.

"Oh, hell no. I love you, babe, but I'd rather not risk having to watch my best friend get dicked down by those three every time we meet." She shoots them a glare.

My cheeks flame with embarrassment, and as much as I want to check their expressions, I'm too scared to look. Raphael and Theo have been more than fine to share between the two of them, but Zeke? Whatever truce they have is new enough that I'm not sure it could withstand something like *sharing*.

Raphael rolls his eyes. "No one will be forced to watch anything. If the others don't pan out, we'll spruce up the cave until neither of you recognize it as such. Deal?"

"Alright. I'll scope out a few places after class this afternoon. It'll be nice to feel useful for a change." Excitement bubbles at the prospect of having our own special place. There's still a lot to do, but the hope is enough to make me forget the bullshit I've gone through today.

Theo grabs my free hand, pressing a kiss to my wrist. "I'd prefer if at least one of us were with you, given the shit the Fallen have put you through so far today. Please don't go off alone."

I want to tell him I'm fine, that I'm not some weak little girl who needs protecting. Aside from Dina and my parents, I've been doing this shit alone for as long as I can remember, but I don't have to anymore. I just need to let them *in*.

Smiling, I nod. "I'll make sure someone is with me."

"And then you're resting, I mean it," Dina says, standing and offering me a stern look.

"Yes, Mom," I tell her with a giggle.

I haven't quite figured out how I'm going to handle everything that life seems to throw my way, but with friends like this at my side, it feels like I can make it through anything.

7

EZEKIEL

I walk through the lobby of the Guild as if I'm not half an hour early and planning to snoop and steal. My pace is unhurried, normal.

Irene nods at me from the front desk. I return the gesture, just like I do on every shift. Nothing out of the ordinary.

I promised Hayliel I'd check the logs to see if anything's come up about Castiel. I'm not expecting to find anything, but if checking will bring her comfort, then I'll do it. Hell, there isn't much I *wouldn't* do for her. Something one of those assholes talking shit in the cafeteria learned the hard way. If things continue the way they're going, I'll be kicking a few more asses before the week is over.

It's a terrifying revelation, feeling so strongly about someone, knowing you'd rock the entire world if it meant their happiness. I've tried my best to deny it, those feelings, but after witnessing Hayliel damn near die right before my eyes, things have changed.

I've changed.

Before I can make it to my locker to drop off my bag, Azrael calls my name. "Zeke. Come with me, please."

Thoughts race through my mind, but I don't let them get out of control. This could be any number of things. He hasn't said a word to me about the attack or Hayliel's miraculous survival, so maybe he's finally speaking up about it. Or this could be him finally shedding some light into that dead body I sent him to collect.

There are a million things he *should* want to discuss. And about damn time, too.

I follow along without question, keeping my mask firmly planted. Or it is, until I realize where he's taking us. The weapon and accessories locker. *Does he know what I'm planning?*

My expression doesn't shift when we enter the room, and I'm about to ask him what's going on when he breaks the silence.

"It's good that you're here early. Otherwise, I was going to have to leave without you."

"Leave? Where?" Is he following a lead from the dead body and *finally* keeping me in the fucking loop?

He unhooks a multipurpose weapon from the rack and tosses it to me. "If luck is on our side, we may have found a demon hideout. Our goal is only to scope it out and call for reinforcements if needed."

Disappointment sits heavy in my gut. It's not that my blood doesn't sing for the opportunity to watch those asshole creatures suffer after what they did to Hayliel, but I had hoped it was something else.

Why are we going on a scouting mission, though? The more I think about it, the more this entire thing just seems strange.

"Isn't that a bit beneath you, Lieutenant?"

He glances at me over his shoulder, a deep laugh rumbling up from his chest before he turns back to the cabinet. "I am in charge of the interns, am I not? This will be a good experience for you."

Something in the cabinet beside him catches my attention. Row after row of protection charms sit behind the glass doors. If Azrael wasn't here, I'd grab what I need and add them to my pack, but it would seem I won't be that lucky today.

A door closing startles me from my thoughts, and I watch as Azrael tucks a sunblade into the sheath at his side. It's not the first time I've seen one, not by a long shot, but that doesn't lessen the impact. The steel is perfectly sharpened, with sunfire glowing from the etched markings down the center.

If he's bringing one with us today, he must suspect we'll need it. Which seems odd for a scouting mission.

Before we leave, he grabs one more item. A pouch like the one Theo and I are sure must be a tool we can use on the demons.

"What's with those, anyway?" I ask as he tucks it into one of the many pockets of his uniform. "I've seen other lieutenants with them, but don't know what it's for."

His face hardens, something I rarely see from him. "And for good reason. We limit the use of these to rare circumstances and *only* where necessary."

"But why?"

"Just trust me, Zeke. And leave them for the lieutenants."

Confusion wraps around me like smoke. Did I hit a nerve? Azrael rarely avoids answering my questions. Even when he keeps me in the dark, it's usually followed by some reason or another, so what's causing this shift, and why is he keeping this from me? *He's been keeping quite a few things close to his chest lately.*

I let it drop, even though it pains me to do so. But it's not like I'm giving up. If Azrael won't give me any information on what's inside those little sacks, then there's even more reason for us to find out for ourselves. We'll just have to be extra careful.

Clouds fill the sky as we fly out, sticking toward the mountains. The air is thick with moisture, a sure sign of rain to come. Azrael hasn't given me any information about where this supposed hideout is, but I don't like that we're heading toward the university. We sure as hell don't need a horde keeping so close to school.

To take my mind off the constant worrying I seem to do now, I ask a question that I don't expect an answer to. "Any leads on that dead angel from the Fallen district? Last I heard, you were examining some of his belongings."

Azrael looks like he'd rather be having any other conversation, and when he sighs, I swear I can hear his displeasure. "This case is sensitive. I know that isn't what you want to hear and that you feel I've kept you in the dark, but I promise it's for good reason. All I can say is that I'm following a lead based on the items I found. It's safer for you, and for the information I'm attempting to dig up, if no one knows."

Blood pumps harder through my veins as my anger rises. "But you can trust me. Hell, you wouldn't even have this information if it weren't for me. Can't you—"

He shakes his head. "I'm sorry, Ezekiel. I can't. Not yet. The moment it's safe, you'll be the first to know. I promise."

I fly a little faster, though it's futile because I have no fucking idea where we're going, but I just need a moment alone to process this rage. With my eyes closed, I picture Hayliel's warm smile, and the anger subsides, though only slightly. What would she do if she were in my shoes? I don't even have to think about it before I know. She'd be annoyed, but she'd find a silver lining somewhere and focus all of her energy on that.

I've always trusted Azrael. So if he says he's following a lead and that it's a sensitive case, that should be enough. It must be or else I'll go mad. Besides, if part of the reason he's keeping information from me is for my own safety, can I really be upset? My father would do the same thing, and I wouldn't think twice about it.

That's got to be it. He's keeping his cards close to his chest, not just about that dead angel but also, I'm guessing, about the attack on us near the Fallen district. His overprotective nature is annoying, to say the least, yet I can't fault him for that.

It might be silly for him to worry about me when I can take care of myself, but it's certainly not spiteful.

When I've calmed down, I slow my pace and join Azrael in flight once more. He says nothing about my little outburst, and the tension between us fades.

Moments later, he stops, hovering in the sky as he points to an outcropping of rock below us. "There. Do you sense anything?"

The place is oddly familiar, though I'm not sure why. I close my eyes and focus on my other senses. A soft breeze rustles my feathers. Thunder booms from somewhere in the distance. Azrael's metal-tipped wings tinkle gently. But otherwise we're alone.

I open my eyes and scan the rock again. "If there ever was a horde here, they're gone now."

He nods. "Precisely my thoughts as well. Let's get closer, but keep your guard up."

The moment my feet touch the rocky mountainside, I see them. Four statues, or at least what used to be four statues. Now they're shattered.

"Demons did this?" I ask, incredulously. We stand on the offering grounds, a place where angels come to deliver their goods for the Archangels' Feast. The place Hayliel recently visited with her parents. Was it like this when she came? No. Surely she'd have mentioned it if it were. Others would have as well. That must mean this is new.

Azrael crouches beside what was once Remiel's statue. "That is my assumption, yes."

"This is too close to the Archangels," I say, more to myself than him. "Demons grow more and more reckless, but why? What is it that gives them such confidence?"

"My guess? Based on recent events, it's most likely our proven inability to stop them." He turns his attention to the ruined statues and the ground around them, and I try to put my questions to the back of my mind so I can join in with his investigation.

Back at the guild, I struggle to write up a report on our findings.

While we didn't find any active demons, it was clear they'd been there. Angels don't bleed black, and the few drops of black blood we found near the statues were proof enough. Part of me wishes we would have run into them, if only to enact my revenge. I want to see them pay for what they did to Hayliel. But even I know my emotions would only have clouded my judgment.

As I note the location in my report, I wonder if they'll notify the Archangels of just how close demons are venturing into Silver City. Do they already know how aggressive they've become? Do they even care?

I sigh. Running a hand down my face, I do my best to push aside the questions and doubt. My window for grabbing those amulets is almost gone. The sooner I finish this damn report, the sooner I can snatch them and get out of here.

Ten minutes later, I've documented every detail and sent the report directly to Azrael's slate for approval. I make busy tidying up my already spotless desk, wasting another eight minutes in case he has any comments or suggested changes. Under normal circumstances, I wouldn't bother waiting around for him to approve it, but the extra precaution will help ease my mind. I don't need anything getting in my way.

I'm about to give up when his reply comes in, thanking me for the detail and telling me to enjoy the rest of my day.

If he suspects anything from me, he certainly doesn't show it.

The weapon and accessories locker is empty when I arrive. Luck must really be on my side today.

On silent feet, I head directly for the cabinet with the protection amulets. There they sit, lined up neatly just like they were before, but instead of grabbing them right away, I close my eyes and listen.

Someone is walking around, but they're far away, and I can barely make out a voice, but it's not close enough for me to worry. I should be in the clear.

The handle of the cabinet is cold, and it soothes my hot and sweaty palms. This needs to go down without a hitch. I don't know what will happen to me if I'm caught, but my internship here is too valuable for me and my friends.

Friends. A bark of laughter threatens to escape, but I hold it back. If someone told me a year ago that I'd become actual friends with Pure angels, I'd have called them a liar. But now, even knowing Raphael and Theo's wing color, I don't think of them as Pures. They're just angels. Friends. Ish. Friends-ish.

The happiness drains from my face when the cabinet door won't open. I try again, pulling harder, but it doesn't budge. What the fuck?

There's a black rectangular scanner. Shit. These are locked. I must have missed it earlier when Azrael used his card. My own card hangs heavy against my hip, begging me to scan it and see if it will get me what I need. I pull it up and—

"If you're hoping to take something from there, you're going to need a lieutenant's key card."

I whirl around to find Lieutenant Atlas's daughter leaning against the wall, watching. The girl who's already seen far more than I'd have liked. How the hell did she get in here without me knowing, and why the fuck is she poking her nose where it doesn't belong?

Ignoring her words, I change the subject and hope it's enough to derail her. "I haven't seen your father today, so no, I don't know where he is."

"That's a pity. He could have helped you get into those cabinets." She steps closer, looking entirely out of place in a loose-fitting black pantsuit with her wine-colored hair slicked back.

I roll my eyes. "I'm not—"

"Tell me what you need and maybe I can help."

Ugh. This angel is really starting to get on my nerves. What the hell is she even doing here, snooping around when she's not even a guild member? It's not like she can get into the cabinets herself.

"Or," she adds before I can respond, "you can keep silent and leave here empty-handed. The choice is yours, Ezekiel."

The lump in my throat grows, but I swallow past it, anyway. I forgot she knew my name. What are the chances this same damn angel keeps finding me doing shit I shouldn't be doing? Though I suppose she never ratted me out after our last run-in, so maybe I can at least trust her to keep her mouth shut. Besides, it's not like I can get into the cabinets myself. Whatever I tell her is all just words.

I take a deep breath, unsure that I'm making the right decision. "I need six amulets and one of those pouches."

"See? That wasn't so hard." She waltzes past me to the cabinet with the mysterious pouches. From her pocket she pulls out a keycard, swiping it against the scanner and grabbing one of the bags.

She tosses it to me without a second thought, and I rush to catch it. The way Azrael talked about this shit, I don't trust what's inside not to explode if it hits the ground.

When I'm certain I've got the thing secured, I ask, "Whose card is that?"

"Oh, this?" she waves it around, stalking toward the cabinets with the amulets. "It's my dear old dad's."

I freeze. She's using Lieutenant Atlas's card? Dread settles in my gut at the same time that fear ignites in my veins. Does he know she has it? Will this lead back to him somehow? What the fuck had he been thinking to trust her, a non-guild member, in the first place? But even as the thoughts cross my mind, I know what I'd been thinking. There are angels counting on me to acquire these items, angels I care about. This whole *friends* thing is really messing with my head.

She turns, ignoring the look of horror on my face, and passes me the amulets. I'm putting them into my bag when I notice there aren't six here, there's seven. "You grabbed one too many."

"No, I didn't." She takes the extra amulet from my grasp. "This one is for me. I gave you a pass last time I caught you creeping about where you shouldn't be, but I hate being kept in the dark. This time I want in. Whatever you're doing must be dangerous, or else you wouldn't need this shit. And I just so happen to thrive in dangerous situations."

"Fuck no," I try, but she just keeps talking.

"When can I meet the lucky recipients of those amulets?"

I don't answer, unsure what to say. How the fuck do I even end up in these awful situations? I could push back, but that has risks, and what we're doing is far too important to fuck up. Telling her has its own risks, but she's already kept one of my secrets. What's one more? I just have to hope the others see it the same way.

She sighs loudly, clearly done with my indecisive ass. "Look, I might not *want* to threaten you, but I will. Let me—"

I throw my hands up in the air in defeat. "Archangels' balls! Fine. If it'll shut you up. We're meeting on campus at SCU this weekend. I'll let you know the details once they're finalized."

It almost feels like a betrayal. My friends and I have spent the better part of a week finding a secure place for us to meet, and we finally found one. We're doing everything we can to ward and protect the secret location, and I'm about to put everything on the line to avoid an even greater risk. How has my life come to this?

I throw the bag, filled with stolen items, on my back and turn to leave before she realizes we haven't exchanged numbers, but I don't get very far.

She clucks her tongue. "A for effort, Ezekiel. Give me your slate."

It was worth a shot.

Reluctantly I pass it to her, though she doesn't seem to notice. She taps away before passing it back to me. Not only has she added her contact info under the name Mira, but she's also messaged herself from my slate. *Great.*

She looks at her own slate, smiling when she sees the message from me. "Well, that settles things. You can trust me, dude, but if you try to keep me out of this, I'll show up on campus and start running my mouth to anyone who will listen."

The sad part is, I believe her. Who the fuck is this chick and why is she so obsessed with joining in on a plan she knows fuck all about?

Instead of asking her that, I head toward the door and say, "I wouldn't dream of it."

"See you this weekend, Ezekiel," she calls after me, but I don't respond.

The sky is beautiful when I make it outside the building and take off in flight. The sunset lights up the world in a kaleidoscope of red and orange that usually threatens to steal my breath. But I find no joy in the view tonight.

All I can think about is how the fuck I'm going to explain what I've just done to the others.

8

HAYLIEL

irds chirp as I walk the path between the thick canopy of trees that stand tall in front of Fallen house. It's a little thinner than when I walked it that first day with Professor Castiel, but the scent of wood and moss still brings a smile to my face.

It falls when I think of Castiel.

Apparently, he's back on campus, and has been for a few hours now. I can't hold off going to see him any longer. Raphael and Theo offered to come with me, though it was more of an insistence. They don't want to leave me alone for fear of what the now disgruntled Fallen might do, but I live at Fallen house. The opportunities to do me harm there are rife. Maybe I should have agreed and let them come with me, but their focus is needed elsewhere.

I glance toward the tower and sigh. The attic space we looked into as a private area for our friend group was beautiful. A little dirty and worn, but it had the potential to be incredible. Unfortunately, both it and the weaponry building were already so heavily protected by the school that adding more wards just wasn't an option. That left the obscure cave near the base of the falls as our secret HQ. It might smell of damp earth, but it will do.

Besides, the room Zeke has in the weaponry building will still serve as a private area for us to train. Without attempting to dig a larger area in the cave or lug training materials in, we'd have to make do using something a little less protected. As long as angels don't realize what we're up to—receiving guild training to survive and take down demons—we should be fine.

I wonder if Zeke would have offered to come with me to see Castiel too, if he hadn't left for the guild after lunch.

A door opens, jostling me from my thoughts, but when I glance up, the back doors of the main hall remain closed. To the left, I spot someone exiting the infirmary. The Fallen angel strides toward me with his head down, but something about him is familiar. He looks up, our eyes locking. Black and blue bruises ring his eyes, standing out against his ashen face.

Recognition clicks, and I realize this is one of the assholes making comments in the cafeteria last week, but what the hell happened to him? Blood covers his shirt in a way that tells me it poured from his nose. Either he's clumsy, or he got in a fight with someone far stronger.

He averts his gaze, speeding up as he continues past. That's odd. He sure as shit didn't behave like that in the cafeteria.

Letting the strange encounter go, I continue on to Castiel's office and take the longer, less populated route. I'm in no mood to deal with shitty students, or worse, cruel professors.

Honestly, whatever issue the Fallen now have with me is getting out of hand. In the last week, I've been *accidentally* bumped into or tripped more than once, and they're becoming bolder in their nasty remarks. It's clear I did something to piss them off. I just wish I knew what.

Do they know what happened with Roderick in the Fallen district or outside of it with the demons? Even if they do, it's not as if I did anything wrong. In fact, I almost fucking died. Surely that should earn me some god's damn grace.

Despite the warning in my gut to leave it alone, I refuse. One way or another, I'm going to get to the bottom of it. *Besides, what's one more thing added to the list?*

Professor Castiel is alone when I make it to his office, though his face lights up when he sees me.

His brows crease, and I realize that maybe I'm not masking my expression as well as I thought I was.

"Is everything alright?"

My laugh is self-deprecating at best. "Somehow, the answer to your question is both yes and no. I'm glad you're back. Do you bring any answers with you?"

He shakes his head, and my hope plummets. "Nothing concrete yet, I'm afraid. But don't lose hope. That friend I went to visit is positive he has a book that might help."

"Well, that's promising, at least," I tell him, doing the best mental imitation of my parents and trying to find the silver lining. It feels as though we've read every damn book there is, so if Castiel's friend thinks he has something, I'll try to trust it.

"It is. When we parted ways, he was heading straight for his ancestral home. The moment I hear back from him, I'll seek you out."

"Thank you. I'll strive to work on being patient."

Professor Castiel chuckles. "No need, Miss Hayliel. Come see me anytime. I'm here to help with whatever you need."

I smile and turn to leave, but I don't get very far. As much as I wanted to make sure he was unharmed and see if he had any answers, that's not the only reason I came. Before I can second guess my decision, I'm standing in front of his desk again.

"Actually ... there was something else I wanted to discuss with you. I've been having these hot flashes lately. They're becoming more frequent, and I'm getting a little worried."

"Hmm, I could see how that would be concerning. Have you noticed any other symptoms or side effects other than the heat?"

Have I? I let myself consider everything I've felt since surviving that deadly blade, but nothing stands out. "I don't think so. So much has happened that honestly, it's too hard to tell."

"That's completely understandable. And the bond? Are you still having issues?"

I look away, not wanting him to see my weakness. Not that it really matters, given what I'm about to tell him. "I haven't really tried again since your office. I'm not ready to face that it might be gone forever."

"Ah, but are you also not ready to face that it might not be?" When I finally look up at him, all I find is understanding. "Refusing to try doesn't just mean avoiding bad outcomes, Miss Hayliel. It also means missing out on the good ones."

He's right. Not testing the bond again because I fear what will happen is only making things worse. How will I know it's truly gone if I don't try? It's not like me to give up so easily, not with how my parents raised me, but things have felt so damn out of my control for so long that I didn't see the point.

Now, I think it might be worth giving it another try.

"Thank you. For everything, Professor."

"You'd have realized it, eventually. I only gave you a nudge."

I say goodbye and leave with an extra skip in my step. Today might not be the day I test out my mental connections, but I will eventually. And even though I'm still worried, there's hope too, and an acceptance that at least I'll know for sure.

Pulling out my slate, I check the time. I'm supposed to meet Raphael and Theo at the weaponry training building. It's a little earlier than planned, but I doubt they'll mind.

As I head down the hall from Castiel's classroom, I pass by Professor Uriel's room. The door is open, and I can't halt my feet as they bring me closer. Tilting my head forward, I peek inside.

I'm shocked to find the bloody and bruised guy from earlier sitting with the professor. What's he doing with Uriel?

Someone slams into me from behind, shoving me to the side where my head bounces painfully against the wall.

"Get out of the way, you waste of fucking space."

Stars dance behind my eyes, blurring my vision so I can't see who just ran into me, but I don't miss the telltale red lining of their uniform.

This is getting out of fucking hand.

I don't know how long I stand there, leaning against the wall. No one comes to check on me. Not the bruised Fallen and certainly not Professor Uriel. At least that's a blessing.

Anger and hurt simmer inside me, mixing into an explosive concoction.

My conviction to stay the fuck away from Uriel solidifies into something almost tangible. If he can't choose which side to be on—either the helpful teacher or the uncaring one—then I'd rather not have a counselor, anyway. And if the Fallen want to continue assaulting me, then I'll sure as shit be ready for the next one. No longer will I just roll over and take it.

I keep my head down as I take purposeful steps toward the weaponry building. This anger and pain that's growing inside of me needs an outlet before it consumes me.

The door to Zeke's private training room is closed when I arrive, but I enter the four-digit code he gave us and it unlocks easily. Without a sound, I open the door and step inside to the short hallway at the entrance of the room.

Raphael and Theo's erratic breathing immediately meets my ears, doing all sorts of things to my insides. Without seeing them, my mind makes up all kinds of scenarios as to why they might make such noises.

I don't want them to know I'm here yet, hoping for a single moment of privacy to just take them in. Closing the door softly, I tiptoe to the end of the hall and peer around the corner. What I find takes my breath away.

They attack each other with ferocity. Sweat glistens on their naked torsos, their muscles bunching tight as they give the fight everything they have. The sight has me caught in a choke hold, unable to look away, not that I even want to. My heart races as my mind conjures up visions of several ways I could get them sweaty like that. How would their grunts differ if they were from pleasure instead?

"Are you enjoying the show, sunshine?" Raphael asks, jolting me from my illicit daydream.

Our eyes lock in the wall of mirrors on the opposite side of the room from where I stand, but it doesn't last. Theo takes advantage of Raphael's distraction and tackles him to the soft mat.

He doesn't keep him down long, but I almost wish he would. The sight of Raphael pinned beneath Theo does things to me. Strange things. *Tingling* things.

"I could watch this all day," I tell them, meaning every word.

Raphael's eyes darken. "I'd rather you join."

They both get up from the mat and head toward their belongings. Theo stays quiet, tossing a water bottle and a towel to Raphael.

They drink their fill, but before they can wipe the sweat away, I stop them. "Leave it. I rather like the sweaty look on you guys."

Heat pools in my core as they both stare at me with unadulterated want.

Theo throws the towel down and says, "Why don't you go change so you can join us?"

I consider my options. I could head to the private changing rooms attached to this one. That's most likely what they expect me to do. Or I could drop my things right here and change where they can see. Where they can watch.

"Alright," I say cheerfully, heading toward the changing rooms.

They get back on the mat and begin another round of training so they don't catch on right away when I drop my bag on a bench and untie my sneakers. They don't see when I remove my socks or pull my hair back into a ponytail. But when I unzip my jeans and pull them down my thighs, all sounds of sparring ceases.

I pretend not to notice at first, though I feel their eyes scorching a trail over my bare legs as I pull a loose pair of shorts from my bag and put them on. Before I take off my shirt, though, I glance in their direction. "No need to stop on my account."

Except they don't resume their sparing, and that knowledge fuels something wicked inside of me. With their eyes on me, tracking my every movement, I feel powerful. They watch as I pull my shirt off, left only in my favorite sports bra—a pretty turquoise piece with a zipper down the front and crisscross design along the back.

When I step onto the mat, it's as if I've stepped into a bolt of lightning. Electricity dashes across my flesh until I feel invincible. I wonder if they feel it too.

Neither man exits the sparring mat, and I realize why. "Two against one, huh?"

Raphael's eyes darken, causing goosebumps to rise on my arms. "I think you can handle us both just fine, sunshine."

I stifle a groan at his innuendo.

They don't wait for me to get settled, but they don't go hard on me, either. This is a training session, after all. I duck to avoid Raphael's grasp, then somersault away from Theo. Running away might not be the best option, but I don't know how the hell I'm supposed to watch two beings at once and still plan attacks. Having eyes in the back of my head would be fucking awesome right now.

But this isn't like any fight with the demons would be. They sure as shit don't look at me the way Raphael and Theo are right now. Like I'm the cure to what ails them, and after searching across the entire world for it, they aren't willing to give it up for anything.

We circle a few more times. I avoid most of their grabs and fake swipes, but sometimes if I'm not quick enough, the tips of their fingers graze my arm, my back, my belly. Every time a part of my body comes into contact with theirs, it feels as if I might die without more of it.

I trip over my own feet while trying to avoid Theo's long arms and fall right into Raphael's trap. He wraps his long fingers around my throat, gentle but firm, and pulls me into him for a searing kiss that has my toes curling. His lips demand more from me. All of me. As if he's traveled across a frozen wasteland and the heat of my mouth is the only thing that can cure his frostbite.

Theo steps up behind me, pressing his body into my back. I reach behind me until I have one arm looped around Theo's neck and one arm wrapped around Raphael's. Connected to them both.

Slowly, I break the kiss with Raphael, turning between them to search for Theo's mouth. His lips are soft yet demanding, consuming every waking thought as his kiss devours my entire fucking being.

I let go of every ounce of pent up emotion. My anger toward Professor Uriel. My disappointment at the behavior from the Fallen angels. And my fear that I'll never connect with my men again.

I'm nothing but a churning ball of need and want, and nothing matters but the sensations I feel in this moment. Cherished. Wanted. Needed.

Cared for.

9

HAYLIEL

R aphael strips off my clothes while I'm lost in Theo's kiss.

Having them pressed against me like this, with their warm, sweaty bodies covering mine, I'm going out of my mind.

Delirium. In the best possible way.

"Tell us you want this. Us," Raphael says, slowly unzipping my bra. There's a desperation in his voice that almost has me undone.

Theo leaves my lips to press kisses across my jaw and down my neck, toward the opening in my bra Raphael just created.

"Gods, yes. I need you both. I'd never survive if I lost either of you." The words escape, unbidden, but I don't regret them. I need Raphael and Theo to understand just how absolutely smitten I am. They have to know that I'd never choose between them. I couldn't.

"Only our deathbed or your say so could keep us from you, firefly," Theo says, placing kisses against the swell of my breasts until I ache with need.

I wonder if they realize that I'll never send them away. Not now, not tomorrow, and certainly not years into the future. As for their deathbed, I don't even want to consider it. Recent events have taught me that things can change in the blink of an eye, so I plan to fight for every ounce of happiness while I can.

"You're both far too dressed." I stand completely naked between their half-clothed forms, feeling like the center of the entire fucking galaxy.

Theo only chuckles once, this deep, husky sound that lights a fire in my veins, then I'm in the air, my legs wrapped around his torso and the hard line of his erection pressing against my bare center.

I suck in a sharp breath and grind against him, completely oblivious to what he's doing until I find myself lying on my back on the mats in the center of the room. Beneath my head are three fluffy towels folded into a makeshift pillow. I'm in paradise.

A small giggle escapes me that quickly turns into a moan as Theo grinds against me, the friction feeling so fucking good and yet not enough at the same time.

Raphael is beside me in an instant, completely naked and beyond gorgeous. How the fuck did I get so lucky?

His lips are on mine, tearing apart my soul with an

earth-shattering kiss that has my limbs trembling and pussy drenched. Only when he pulls away do I notice the curly-haired Adonis settling between my legs.

"How wet is she for us, Theo?" Raphael asks, his eyes blazing.

But Theo doesn't answer right away. He runs a finger from my clit to my achingly empty pussy, pressing the digit inside me for only a second before pulling out and holding it up. It glistens with my wetness.

"Oh, she's wet," he says, then sucks me off his finger. "But I think we can do better."

"What do you think, sunshine? Are you up for it?"

Theo blows gently against my pussy, distracting me and making me damn near beg.

"Do your worst," I say, teasing, but from the looks on their faces, I wonder if maybe I'll regret those words.

They move languidly, in no rush to make me come, and somehow their easy-going behavior only heightens the sensations. Raphael lavishes my over-sensitive nipples with attention, while Theo makes long strokes against my pussy with his tongue, pressing it inside me before trailing it back up to my clit.

On his next trek down, he stays there, fucking me with his tongue while Raphael makes gentle circles on my clit with his finger. I'm on the verge of an orgasm when they shift their touch just enough to stop me from coming. *Assholes.*

Raphael's laugh is almost diabolical. "How wet is she now?"

Theo does the same test as before, but this time when he presses a finger inside me, the slickness is audible. Heat rises to my cheeks, but I'm not embarrassed. I just need to come.

"Getting there," he says.

"You hear that, sunshine? I think he's having fun getting you wetter and wetter, don't you think?"

"Yes, but." The words come out as a whimper.

"But what, firefly?"

"I want to touch you both, too." The last word turns into a moan as Theo resumes his work on my pussy, but Raphael doesn't let me off the hook.

"If you want to pleasure me, baby, all you have to do is ask. I've been wanting to fuck that pretty little mouth of yours for weeks. Will you let me?"

Images of Raphael taking what he wants from me almost sends me over the edge, which only causes Theo to back off. Does he have a fucking orgasm sensor or something? Fuck!

I nod, mouth watering with the need to lick the drops of moisture from Raphael's tip. For a second, I think we'll have to switch positions in order to accommodate, but he straddles my head, placing one knee on either side of me, and I realize he's about to call all the damn shots.

It only makes me want him more.

"Do you trust me?" Raphael asks.

"Always. Now just fuck my mouth already, Raph. I need to taste you."

His eyes darken as he brings the tip of his cock to my lips, allowing me to swirl my tongue around it and suckle just enough to make him shudder.

Before he thrusts any further, he peers over his shoulder at Theo and says, "I think our girl deserves a prize. Why don't you give her one?"

As Raphael moves, fucking my face with slow movements, Theo does the opposite. It's like *he's* the one who can't bear to continue teasing *me*. Not that I'm complaining. How can I when he strokes my clit with his tongue and pumps two fingers inside me.

Thank the Archangels that Raphael can take what he wants from me because I'd never be able to focus enough on sucking his dick while Theo does all *that*.

I tangle one hand in Theo's hair, the other cupping Raphael's balls as my orgasm builds to a dangerous level. All of their earlier teasing only added fuel to an already raging fire, and the heat of it threatens to send me to my death in a blaze of flame and smoke.

When I moan around Raphael's cock for the third time, he thickens in my mouth, a string of curses leaving him.

"If you keep doing that, sunshine, I'll never last."

He doesn't realize that's what I want. I'm so close to oblivion, and I want him to come with me. I want Theo there too, but I can't suck both their cocks at once, at least not in this position.

I moan again, my hands moving to grip Raphael's ass, holding him in place so he can't escape. When he curses again, I'm gone. Lost in bliss as a scream bubbles up from my throat, muffled by his cock. My back tries to arch off the mat, but I can only go so far with Raphael above me. Then, with Theo still paying lavish attention to my clit and enhancing my climax further, I taste it. Hot and salty, Raphael's cum fills my mouth as he shudders and groans. I swallow it down, not willing to waste a single drop.

"I didn't realize you liked the taste of my spunk so much, little sun," Raphael teases. "But just because I can't fuck you now, doesn't mean I'm done with you."

I lick my lips, loving the way he's looking at me. Like I'm about to receive the best sexual payback of my entire life. "Is that a promise?"

Raphael doesn't bother answering. Instead, he kneels at my side and plants a fiery kiss to my lips that has my nipples pebbling and my pussy begging to be filled.

When he finally lets me go, Theo—who somehow found the time to shed his clothes—positions himself between my legs. I revel in the feel of his massive cock pressed against me. *Yes. This is what I need.*

As if he heard me, Theo takes us back to the floor, holding close to my head so I don't hit it on the soft mat. He treats me like I'm precious, something to be cherished, and fucking hell, I'm starting to believe it.

Through the kiss, I roll us over until Theo's on his back and I'm straddling his hips. Raphael watches us, his cock thickening again. Even a half-hard cock won't keep him away, though. He comes up behind me, and just as I'm lining up to sink onto Theo, Raphael stops me.

He presses against my back, wrapping an arm around my hip and dipping between my legs. "Not yet, sweet sunshine. I want to make sure he'll fit." Without waiting for a reply, he pushes two fingers inside me, pumping and flexing them until this intense pressure builds inside me and I feel like I'm about to lose control.

His fingers make sloppy, wet sounds as they piston inside me until I can't hold back the pressure anymore. "Oh gods," I moan as a gush of liquid drips from my pussy onto Raph's hand and down to Theo's pierced cock.

"Fuuuuuck," Theo groans, smearing my arousal across his hard length and toying with his piercing.

I feel Raphael's smile against my shoulder. Pleased with himself, he removes his fingers and finally lets me sink down onto Theo's cock. Just like the last time he was inside me, it takes a moment for my body to adjust to his thickness. I still don't even understand how that monster thing fits inside of me, but I'm damn glad it does.

Distracted by my stretching, aching pussy, I lose track of what Raphael is doing until I feel his fingers *there*. He circles the tight ring of muscles with a finger coated in my arousal, so it glides over smoothly. *No one's ever touched me there.*

"Shit, firefly," Theo practically groans out, his voice gravelly like he's barely holding back. "You've got my cock in a vise grip. Whatever you're doing, Raph, our girl seems to like it."

A soft, breathy moan escapes me despite the herculean effort I put into keeping quiet.

Raphael only chuckles, continuing his soft exploration. "No one has touched you here before, have they, sunshine?"

I try to speak, but the words won't come out. All I can do is shake my head.

I catch sight of us in the mirror and suck in a sharp breath. Is this truly what we look like? Theo lying between my legs, looking up at me with something akin to intoxication. Raphael kissing my neck, his hand moving steadily at my backside. And then there's me.

My face is flushed, nipples pointed and hard. I look *hungry*, just not for food. It's these men that I yearn for, including one who isn't here. Would Theo and Raphael let him join? Where would he fit in? But I already know where. A smile tugs at my lips as I picture him beside me, making full use of my mouth.

In the mirror, I see Theo shift his head. He's no longer looking at me, staring somewhere beyond, but before I can turn my head to see what's caught his attention, he pumps his hips up a little. Goosebumps race across my skin as my eyes roll back.

"We'll take it slow," Raphael says, "and when you're ready, we'll take you just like this."

He spits, spreading the saliva around my tight hole.

"Mmm. Fuck, sunshine. When you're ready for us, we'll fill you to the fucking brim."

On the last word, he adds pressure to the finger that's been toying with my ass, pushing it inside me. I gasp, the feeling of fullness washing over me.

"You okay, baby?" Raphael asks, and all I can do is nod. I doubt I'd make any sense if I tried to speak right now. "That's it. I knew you could handle this. Us. You look so goddamn good at our mercy."

As if the two of them planned this, they work together. Theo pumps into me in opposite strokes to Raphael's fingers until I'm tumbling head first into sensation overload. It's somehow both too much and not enough at the same time.

I lose track of everything but the feel of them. So much so that I don't even realize that someone's pulled me down until I'm lying on Theo's chest. My pleasure builds into something wild and uncontrollable.

So. Close.

You're so fucking perfect, Theo says, his usually soft voice rough in my head.

I barely register Raphael spitting again until he adds a second finger to my ass. It burns at first, but that only pushes me closer to oblivion.

You're doing so fucking good, sunshine. Raphael's praise tugs at my heart, adding another sensation to the mix already coiling inside of me.

So. Fucking. Full.

Somehow, Theo thickens inside of me, and it sends me over the edge on an earth shattering scream. The sound is muffled against Theo's warm chest, but his own groan comes out shaky and intense, which only extends my orgasm. I did that to him. Me.

Theo brushes the hair from my face, where a few loose strands of my ponytail stick to my damp cheeks. Have I been crying? Shit. He holds me almost reverently, while Raph rubs a hand up and down my back and slowly withdraws his fingers from my ass.

I must spasm around Theo's softening dick because a shudder runs through him and all I can do is sigh. I should probably get up and let him do the same, but I'm absolutely boneless.

"How do you feel, firefly?" Theo asks, pressing a kiss to the top of my head.

"Hmm? So, so good," I reply sleepily, nuzzling his chest like I could burrow in deep and hibernate there. Maybe that's not such a bad idea.

Raphael comes back, hiding his perfect dick beneath his shorts. "I hate to break up the snuggle fest, but we should probably get you cleaned up before anyone catches us like this."

Shit. Zeke. This is his private fucking room.

Raphael is right. We need to get dressed before he stumbles in. I'm realizing his tough guy act might just be that. An act.

The last thing I want to do is hurt him.

Theo rolls us over, then pulls out of me with a careful slowness that steals my breath and makes me want to start our little fun all over again. Immediately, Theo's cum leaks from me, but Raphael is there with a warm, damp cloth to clean it up.

"If we were anywhere else, sunshine, I'd be bending you over and filling you up too, just to watch it drip from your perfect pussy. But we have to get dressed and then we're going to celebrate."

Images of me, spread eagle on the bed with their mixed cum seeping from between my legs, has me gasping. I'm so stuck on it I almost miss what he said after.

"Celebrate?"

We have a lot to be thankful for, Theo says through our mental connection, and my jaw practically unhinges.

I want to cry or scream, bounce around in joy because holy shit.

My mental connections are back!

10

EZEKIEL

My mind won't shut off on the flight back to campus.

How the hell am I going to explain what happened with Mira to everyone? It's not as if I had a choice, not if I wanted the pouch and amulets. But will they understand? Will Hayliel?

Just thinking her name has my lungs constricting as images of her on the ground, the handle of a blade protruding from her shoulder, fills my vision. No. I won't think of that. I can't.

Things between me and her have been good lately. I won't say that I owe it all to Theo, because fat fucking chance of me ever admitting that, but I can't deny that his words made an impact. I also can't deny that changing my attitude has made a big difference in my relationship, not only with Hayliel but with her Pure boyfriends too. Maybe we're all meant to be friends after all.

Assuming they forgive me for getting tangled up with some outsider.

I land outside the weaponry building, tucking my wings away and waving to Malik, who just exited the front door.

"Are you planning to join your friends?" he asks with a grin.

Shit. I guess he found out I'm not the only one using the room. He must have heard them in there, sparring. "I am. I hope it's alright that I'm sharing my training room with them. We wanted some place private to meet and enhance our form. We're taking it seriously, I assure you."

"Oh, I definitely understand the need for a private space." He chuckles. "Just be careful. Group activities like that often lead to uncomfortable situations and I'd hate to see you in the middle of one."

What the hell is he talking about? "Uh, sure. Yeah, I will. Thanks, man."

"Have fun!" he calls over his shoulder before taking off into the sky.

Well, that was weird.

Brushing it off, I enter the silent building. I'm grateful there are no other students training now. There's enough on my plate to worry about without adding useless small talk to the mix.

The light in the private room is on, which doesn't surprise me. I knew they'd be training tonight. It's why I hightailed it here to give them my shitty news. The old me probably would have avoided the entire conversation until the last second, but I'm trying to do better. Be better.

Except when I step through the door, I halt in my tracks. Heavy breathing and soft moans fill the space, the sound nothing at all like what I expected to hear during combat training. This is far too sultry for a workout.

Part of me wants to turn around and leave, and even though my mind screams at me to do just that, my feet have other plans. When I make it to the end of the short hallway, I see them.

A naked Hayliel riding Theo with Raphael on his knees behind her. Pain erupts in my chest as I watch them, hear them. Fuck, even smell their pleasure.

As if sensing me, Hayliel glances my way in the mirror and I swear my shocked gaze meets her half-lidded one in the reflection.

She doesn't look surprised to see me or even embarrassed. *She doesn't care about you, remember?*

Seeing them like this after everything ... it fucking *hurts*. The sting in my chest builds and builds, spreading out until the ache is damn near unbearable.

That they would do this here, knowing I could walk in and catch them, is almost as painful as actually fucking catching them.

Hayliel looks away then, her gaze dropping to Theo, not caring at all that I've caught them or that I'm standing here having my bloody, beating heart obliterated.

I try to ignore the voice in my head, but it's too loud. Too insistent. *She wants them, not you. You've always known this.*

Turning on my heels, I storm out of the room clutching onto the slivers of the broken organ that barely manages to beat beneath my ribs and don't look back.

11

HAYLIEL

I sit next to Theo in history class, with Castiel sitting in his usual spot at his desk.

It's nice to have him back, for more than just my fear for his safety. Selfishly, I'm happy to have him as an ally, someone I know won't put up with any bullshit from the other students. That, mixed with having Theo next to me and an interest in the subject matter, makes this one of my favorite classes.

Castiel checks the clock on the wall, then presses a button on his slate and stands. Mine pings immediately, and I open up the attachment he'd sent to everyone. A packet that contains information about our final assignment, along with example articles for reference.

"The end of term will be here before you know it. I never liked big weighted exams when I was a student and that hasn't changed, so I'm giving you all an assignment instead. During class, we'll go through several articles highlighting extraordinary angels. Ones who have made a significant change for our society. Today, we're focusing on a piece written about the Archangels. Take a few moments to read through and then we'll discuss."

I open the attachment and immediately start reading, curious to learn more. The Archangels are kind of legends for us. They're the saviors of our entire city, if the stories are true.

The article is old, dated a month or two after they overthrew God and saved angel kind from a fate worse than death. It starts off a little cheesy, setting all four Archangels on a pedestal. Still, I'm intrigued. Reading on a little further, the author dives into Mikhael, the unofficial ruler of the Archangels and possibly the strongest of them.

> *Archangel Mikhael leads with a kind heart and strong will. He had been the closest adviser to God, something our other three leaders never held against him. In fact, he rarely ever made a decision without consulting the others first, signifying a true partnership among the four of them. Even now, as we move into a time of peace and prosperity, Mikhael is the face of our rulers. With him, he offers us strength and warrior energy, instilling confidence and courage into every one of his sub-*

jects. For this article, I tried to learn the truth of his abilities, hoping to find out if there is any merit to the rumors of his healing aura, but he would not comment on such a thing.

The article holds me completely captivated, and as much as I try to reflect on what I've just read, I can't stop from moving onto the next paragraph. This one is about Auriel, the Archangel I'm most familiar with, as he's who my family has made every single feast offering to since I was little.

Archangel Auriel uses his powers to ignite faith into the hearts of all angel kind. With his flame-topped staff, he draws out the wicked thoughts and evil acts from our minds, leaving only joy and serenity. It is said that our new-found peace is greatly in thanks to him, for even sitting so high above us in the Archangels' Sanctuary, his power can reach all of Silver City.

It's no wonder my parents have always favored him. They were the living, breathing embodiment of optimism, seldom letting any dark thoughts enter their mind. Perhaps it's their faith in him that allows them to be so positive. Hopefully, he doesn't take it as a slight that we switched it up this year. But after what Raphael, Theo, and I did in Remiel's prayer tent, I had to gift him something. A little zing of excitement courses through me as I realize he's the next focus.

> *Archangel Remiel is the epitome of hope. Thanks to his ability to glimpse the future, he's highly intuitive, but it also means he keeps himself more secluded than the others. If you're ever lucky enough to meet him, you'll find he carries a book with him at all times. This is where he draws the visions that come to him. I asked if he'd show me a page but he shyly refused, explaining that the visions he sketches are too sensitive to share, and that if anyone but him got hold of that book it would be a catastrophe.*

I would love to see his sketches, if only to witness his talent. They would have to be good enough to clearly depict what he sees, which makes me think his ability to draw must be a sight to behold. But it's not like I'll ever meet them. You won't catch me racing for the chance to win a meet and greet with our great rulers, and given how much shit the other students have caused me lately, I don't even know how much longer I'll be allowed to stay here. Shit. I need the Archangel Auriel to come ignite a little faith in me right now.

The article moves on to the Archangel I know the least about. Shubael.

> *Archangel Shubael is known as the ruler of trea-*

sures. He sorts through the items received during the Feast and helps disperse them to angels in need. Thanks to the nature of our offerings, Shubael can determine who made what offering, and even which Archangel it was submitted to, which helps them decide as a group who might be a suitable candidate for commissioner or other high-ranking titles. Earning his favor can be beneficial.

I read the last line again, wondering if maybe my parents made a mistake in choosing Auriel. Had we and all the other Fallen given our offerings to Shubael, would we still be in this mess? I ponder on that thought for a moment before Castiel clears his throat.

"You should all have had a chance to read through the article, but if you haven't, I encourage you to finish it after class. For now, I want to hear your thoughts. What did you think?"

The quiet girl who sits at the front of the class raises her hand. "It sucked me in. Even though I already knew some of what they wrote, it still felt new and exciting."

Castiel smiles, nodding in agreement. A long-haired guy in the third row speaks, his voice low but audible enough to be heard from where I sit next to Theo. "I wonder if Archangel Auriel can purge our school of a certain parasite who can't seem to take a hint."

Theo looks like he wants to jump up and pummel the guy, but Castiel silences the entire class when he points to the door and says one word. "Out."

"W-what?" the boy asks, incredulously. "But why? I'm only saying what we're all thinking."

"I was clear about my stance on bullying from the beginning, and I will not tolerate your baseless comments in my classroom. You're dismissed. If you want a passing grade, I expect you to fix your attitude before coming back."

The rest of us are silent as he packs up his belongings, shoving them into his bag while his whole body trembles. More than once, he looks back toward me, glaring daggers in my direction, and I don't miss a few grumbles from the other students around him, either. Oh boy.

When he's gone, Castiel claps his hands. "Now, where were we? Right. The author was able to discover something captivating about all four of these beings that make them stand out from the rest. Do you know why that is?"

"Because they're the Archangels?" a guy from the second row asks, his manbun looking far nicer than anything I've ever been able to manage with my own hair.

"Good guess, but no. It's because every one of us has something that makes us unique, and that isn't a bad thing. Each of us has a talent or quirk that makes us different and sets us apart from others. It's what this report focuses on, as well as the others we'll go over in class, and it's what will determine your final grade."

The girl from earlier raises her hand again, her voice trembling a little when she says, "We have to write about ourselves?"

"Not this year, though that will come. For now, I want you to pick an angel from history. It can be anyone except for a parental figure. Then, you'll need to research them and write an article that focuses on who they are and what distinguishes them from all others. You have two weeks to select your angel and email it to me, along with your reasons for picking them. Choose wisely."

12

THEO

Over the last few days, we've gotten into a steady routine of classes, working on wards and runes for the cave, and training. At least, most of us have. Ezekiel has made himself scarce lately, except to work with Dina directly. It's clear he's avoiding us, though this time I understand why.

The worst thing happened. He caught us. Walked right into what should have been a safe space for him and found the three of us fucking like wild rabbits. Oddly enough, he hasn't said shit about it to anyone. He didn't throw us out immediately and ban us from returning. He just left.

Shit. I need to talk to him soon.

We haven't let his absence stop our progress. Without him

there to impart his guild-trained combat on us, I've taken the opportunity to get started on dagger training with Hayliel. She's been pretty sad with Zeke's cold shoulder behavior returning, but learning how to wield knives has definitely helped keep her mind off it. It helps that she's taken to it like a pro, too.

Gagiel and the others have joined in a few times, which proved to be an excellent distraction for Hayliel to keep her mind off things. It's nice to see them growing stronger, more confident. Knowing they're learning to protect themselves makes her happy. It gives her a sense of purpose, something she desperately needs right now.

Today, finally, is the day we've been working our asses off for. Our little slice of cave paradise is fully warded and ready for us to use.

"Ugh, I'm definitely not interested in feeling that every time we come here," Dina says with a shudder.

I nod, letting the need to flee diminish as I stand inside the cave.

Thanks to Zeke's knowledge and my research, Dina was able to ward the area near the entrance to create a strong urgency to flee for anyone passing by. It's not perfect by any means, but it's the best we could find to keep others away.

At first glance, the space looks just like any dingy old cave, and that's exactly what we want angels to see. Zeke had found a special rune that would mask the contents of the cave in the unlikely event someone other than us stumbled inside. It wasn't foolproof, not if someone was eager to discover our secrets, but once again, it's the best we could do in a pinch.

Unfortunately, we haven't figured out how to personalize the runes so that they don't apply to us. I know there's a way. I just can't find a book that details the *how*. It's like the Archangels removed all traces of pertinent information when they had Silver City's books redone. Still, the discomfort and initial confusion were worth the private place for us to meet.

Now that we know it's safe, we can start making the inside a little more cozy and a lot less evil lair.

"Zeke lugged me here last night to add a few last-minute runes. Protection, healing, and one that somehow manages to keep that damp cave smell at bay."

As Dina speaks, I walk around the cave, touching the spot on the wall where they painted the original mask rune until it falls away, along with the moldy scent of the cave. Near the ceiling, six areas begin to glow brightly, lighting up the area.

"Did you do that, too?" I ask, but she shakes her head.

"No, but maybe Zeke did? I left after we couldn't get the silencing rune to work, but he wasn't ready to give up yet. It'll definitely come in handy, though."

"You're not wrong about that."

Hayliel and Raph show up next, each carrying a large box.

"Fucking hell, that's strong," Raphael says, shuddering through the ward repulsion as he drops the box to the floor. He moves to help Hayliel with hers, but I beat him to it.

"It's going to take some getting used to, that's for sure," Hayliel agrees. She pulls me in for a kiss that turns scalding hot, fast, but we don't let ourselves get carried away. Not yet, at least.

"What's in these?" I ask them, eying the boxes.

"*Someone* went on a shopping spree, and even though I helped him lug everything over here—inconspicuously, I might add—he still refuses to tell me what's inside." She glares at him but can't hold it for long before she's smiling.

Raph wraps his arms around her waist, burying his face in her neck. "Be patient, little sun. You'll find out soon enough."

"Good thinking with the lights, Zeke," Dina says to the scowling house leader. It's too hard to tell if the expression is because of the discomfort caused by the words, or if it's just his natural prickly demeanor.

His eyes land on me, then move to where Raph and Hayliel are cozied up beside me. Something that looks a lot like pain flits across his face, but he hides it quickly.

"Zeke! I'm glad you're here," Hayliel says, pulling out of Raphael's embrace and walking toward him. "How did it go at the guild?"

That pained expression is back on his face, and I can tell he's avoiding making eye contact with her. Shit. He keeps looking away, glancing at the door and then back to his bag on the floor. I can't make heads or tails of what's going on with him, but he seems pained and skittish. The first one I can understand, but the second gives me pause.

"Fine. I was able to grab enough for all of us." He pulls six amulets out and passes them around.

"Who's that one for?" Hayliel asks when he's given each of us our new protection amulet.

Zeke runs a hand through his hair, glancing at the door again before he says, "Castiel, if he proves himself worthy."

I share a glance with Raphael, caught off guard by Zeke's thoughtfulness. Castiel is a Pure, and we can both attest to how fucking hard it's been to get him to trust us. Our relationship with Hayliel has definitely made that harder, but his aversion and distrust of all Pures in general hasn't helped. It's nice to see him coming around.

"That's really nice of you, Zeke." Hayliel places her hand on his forearm and he just stares at it, that pained expression back on his face. Poor guy is clearly struggling.

He steps back, cutting off the physical contact which I know pains my girl. His next words cause the hair to rise on the back of my neck.

"I have to tell you guys something, and before you freak out, I need you to know that I did everything I could to avoid it."

What the hell did he do now? Raphael says through our mental connection, and I can't help but wonder the same thing.

We all just kind of stare at him, waiting for him to continue, but it's like he's waiting for something. A burst of rage? Disappointment? Permission to continue? It's hard to tell.

Finally, no longer able to take the suspense, Dina breaks the silence. "Whatever it is, dude, we trust you. Just spit it out."

"I got caught sneaking around at the guild."

"How does that work? You still have the amulets," Raphael says, looking confused.

I'm just as lost, but my mind goes down a different path. "Caught by who?"

"Just a girl. Daughter of a lieutenant. I'm fairly certain she isn't a member of the guild, though she hangs out there enough, so it's hard to tell."

Raphael shrugs. "Okay, well, she let you leave with everything, so what's the problem?"

Zeke rubs a hand down his face and sighs. "It's not the first time she caught me snooping around. She also saw me coming out of the file room, or at least coming from that hallway. I played it cool then, but she saw through my shit. The good news is, I don't think she ever told anyone."

"And the bad news?" I ask, unsure if I want to know the answer.

"Well, this time she caught me in the act as I was trying to access the locked cabinet with the amulets inside. She demanded to know what I was looking for, not so subtly threatening me if I refused to tell her. I didn't see that I had a choice, so I just told her I needed a couple of amulets. She used her father's key card to access them."

Raphael folds his arms across his chest. "I mean, it's not great, but that doesn't sound as bad as it could've been, so why are you acting so weird?"

"Because she took an extra amulet for herself and forced me to invite her here."

Dead silence fills the space. We just spent the last week making this place secure and safe from outsiders, and already he jeopardized that.

"I'm sorry. What?" Raphael says, his eyes a stormy-blue.

Zeke groans. "I know, I know. It's fucking stupid, but I didn't have a choice, alright?"

Raph steps toward him. "This is way more than just *stupid*, Zeke. This could put everything at risk!"

"Don't you think I fucking realize that? I didn't go out of my way to get caught, Raphael. It just happened."

Before things have the chance to get physical, Hayliel steps between Raph and Zeke. "Everyone needs to calm down. Yes, this isn't ideal, but we can't change it now. All we can do is plan. So, what do we do now?"

Zeke nods. "She sent me a rune, one she assured me would help prove her loyalty."

"And you trust her?" Raphael asks with a laugh of incredulity.

Ignoring him, I ask a question of my own. "What kind of rune?"

"She hasn't fucked me over yet, has she? Besides, we have the amulet and the pouch of whatever the fuck it is we're hoping will help us against the demons." He grabs his slate, swiping through until he finds whatever he was looking for. "This is what the rune looks like. I couldn't find much about it online, but from what she said, it's a judgment rune and we'll need to add a drop of our blood to the paint."

"Because that's not fucking suspicious," Raphael mutters, and while I agree with him, it's definitely not the time.

"If you're that worried, then keep your blood in your veins and shut the fuck up."

The air around us chills, dropping several degrees as tensions mount. I understand where Raph's coming from, but everything I've heard so far makes me believe we can trust her. Why else go to all this trouble?

"Can I see that?" I ask Zeke, wanting a closer look at the rune on his slate. He hands it to me without question and I survey the thick lines. It's not one I recall seeing before, but that doesn't mean much. We've been trying to find out more about Hayliel's wings for months and we haven't gotten anywhere. Information tends to disappear in Silver City.

"You can have my blood," I say, handing him his slate back.

"Mine too," Dina agrees.

Raphael looks at me like I've just kicked his knees out. *I'm sorry. I think this is worth trying.*

Hayliel watches Zeke, who still can't look her in the eye before she shrugs. "If it works, maybe it'll help us trust Castiel's motives too, right? I'm in."

"Great," Zeke says dryly, like he hates that it's come to this. "It's settled, then. If we work fast, maybe we can have it ready before she arrives."

Dina grabs the small can of paint we've been using to mark the other runes around the cave and pours some into a small cup. We all prick our fingers, letting a few drops of our blood mix with the paint, and then Zeke draws the image on the stone near the entrance.

When he finishes, Raphael assesses the symbol. "What exactly does the judgment rune do again? How will we know it worked?"

Zeke shrugs, which only pisses Raph off more. "No idea. Mira just says we'll know."

Raphael scoffs. "Right. Let's all just put our faith in this mysterious Mira angel and ignore the threats and secrets she's holding over your head."

"That's enough, Raph. Let's just focus on the things we can control right now," Hayliel says, surprising all of us. My friend looks hurt, but a small touch of Hayliel's hand has him shaking it off. Zeke, though, looks floored by her sticking up for him.

Fuck. I really need to talk to him about what he saw the other night. I would have done so sooner, but he's been avoiding us like the plague. As much as I think it's silly, I can understand it. This entire time he's felt like Hayliel chose us over him, so walking in on our little love fest, especially in his personal training room, probably didn't help matters.

I won't let him leave this damn cave without having a conversation.

Zeke's slate dings, and I watch the emotions flit over his face. Resignation, worry, and finally, fear.

"Mira's on campus. She'll be here any minute."

13

HAYLIEL

Mira.

The name is beautiful, and likely so is she. As hard as I try not to think about it, my mind can't help but conjure images of this badass, gorgeous angel who's far more on Zeke's level than I am.

He's been acting weird all week. Staying away from us as much as possible and even avoiding eye contact with me. Now he's even more fidgety, barely bothering to look anywhere aside from the floor. Is it because of her? Are they together or something?

It shouldn't bother me. Things between Zeke and I have finally gotten to a place of friendship, or they did before this odd change in behavior, and even though the greedy woman inside of me wants more than that, I don't know if he'd be interested. I certainly can't imagine him sharing me with Raph and Theo, so can I really be upset if there's more between him and Mira than he's letting on?

Shit. Who the hell am I? This isn't like me at all.

Footsteps approach from beyond the cave entrance and I hold my breath, my hands turning clammy.

This is it.

A tall woman walks in with hair the color of wine and an air of confidence about her that almost makes me envious. The new rune we just finished painting glows an iridescent blue before fading back to normal. What the hell does that mean?

"Zeke! I see you put the rune to good use. I'm impressed." Her voice comes out unexpectedly raspy, but not in a bad way. "Hopefully this means you'll trust me now."

Zeke grumbles something, but the angel cuts him off. She definitely takes no shit.

"It's nice to meet you all. I'm Mira Harlow. Whoever made that deterring ward, kudos. It's strong as hell." She shakes her hands like she's trying to rid the feeling.

"That would be me. I'd feel better about it if we didn't have to deal with the damn thing, too. I'm Dina."

"I can help with that," Mira offers with a smile.

Raphael clears his throat, eyebrow raised in suspicion. "Really? You can stop us from feeling the effects of the ward?"

"Yup. And you are?"

"Raphael."

Dina claps her hands together, clearly excited. "As much as I want to figure out *why* you'd offer to help, I'd rather we fix it more. Maybe you can help us with our other ones, too."

"I'm with Dina on this one. Nice to meet you, I'm Theo."

Mira gives him a smile, revealing a pretty dimple in her cheek that makes me want to hate her. Except I don't think I can.

She walks over to me with the stride of a runway model. The bracelets on her arm jangle, and I can finally read the word on her shirt. *Fake.* Let's just hope it's not a sign of who she is as an angel.

"Something tells me you're the glue that holds this group together. Is that true?" she asks, her gaze quizzical.

I'd be offended that Zeke hadn't already talked about me if it wasn't painfully clear he didn't tell her about anyone. "Uh, I don't know about that. I'm Hayliel."

She leans in, her voice lowering so only I can hear. "Well, don't worry, babe. I'm not here for any of your men."

My eyes widen. "I'm not—"

"Oh, so it's like that? Interesting. Regardless, I'll stay in my lane."

It takes me a moment to get my shit together. How the hell can she tell I have men she needs to stay away from? We've barely spoken, and it's not like she walked in on me with any of them. Did Zeke tell her? Is he included in my lane, the one she just promised to stay out of? Archangels, I'm a mess.

"So, what are we all doing here, exactly?" Mira asks.

Raph laughs. "You mean you don't know?"

She shrugs. "Mr. Secrets over there wouldn't even invite me unless I threatened him," she pouts, "so no. I don't know shit."

Theo places a hand on Raphael's shoulder, a not-so-subtle nudge to keep his cool. "Can't really blame us for keeping the cards close to our chest then, if you're going around threatening angels, can you?"

Leave it to Theo to tell it like it is. He has a way of airing out all the bullshit and getting straight to the point, all the while seeming to have a perfectly normal conversation. It's a talent I wish I had.

"No, but I didn't snitch when I caught Ezekiel waltzing around near the file room, and I just walked through that entrance without becoming paralyzed. I figured that was proof enough for you to trust that I'm not a threat."

Paralyzed? Is that what the rune will do to someone with ill intentions? Shit. Maybe I should put one of them at my parents' house. Eventually, we'll need definitive answers as to what exactly it is that rune does, but for now, we have a choice to make.

Everyone turns to me, and I feel a soft whisper against the bond with my friends, but I don't allow it to connect fully. I already know what they're going to ask. How do I feel about letting Mira in on our plans? But it's a tricky question. There's something about Mira that reminds me of my friendship with Dina. That she clued in on *something* between me and the guys, and even offered reassurances of her lack of interest, had done far more in the trust department than I'd care to admit.

She could have easily gone to Zeke's superiors or even her father and told them all about the suspicious shit she'd caught him doing. Our plans would have been royally fucked if she had. And while I know that most angels don't do favors for strangers without wanting something in return, it doesn't change the fact that I'm grateful she kept her mouth shut.

I think about everyone I've trusted so far. Raph, Theo, Zeke … Gagiel and his friends, and even Castiel, though that was still a work in progress. So far, none of those angels have betrayed me. Maybe trusting my gut isn't such a bad idea.

I make eye contact with Raph and shrug, hoping the others will understand my gesture.

"We're here because of me," I tell Mira, realizing I didn't exactly have a plan for what I was going to say.

Fuck.

My words spark her interest, but she doesn't rush me. She gives me space to find my words, and damn, if it isn't refreshing. "A little while ago, my wings randomly transformed. We've been researching to find out what the hell happened, but that's led us down a dangerous path with secrets, lies, and demons. Now we're trying to figure out what they're planning so we can save the city before it's too late."

There. I think that's enough information to give her the gist without us being here for hours while I go over every detail. If it also gives us a bit more time to get to know her better, well, that's just icing.

Her smile grows even wider. "No shit! That's cool as hell. How can I help?"

I stare at her, positive that I must have heard her incorrectly, but she says nothing more. Only stands there looking like she'd hit the jackpot. That's it? No further probing or demanding of answers, just a willingness to help? Huh. I definitely didn't see that coming.

The rest of us share a look, but it's Dina who strides toward Mira. "Come with me." She squeezes my hand as she walks past, then to Mira she adds, "You fix the wards and I'll fill in some gaps about our situation."

14

EZEKIEL

Dina leads Mira outside the cave, chattering on about why we selected the wards we did and the issues we've had to make them work. Soon they're too far away for me to keep eavesdropping.

Well, Mira hasn't completely ruined everything, so that's something, I guess. Though I know the others aren't very pleased with me. It's not like I wasn't careful. That girl was just snooping around all the damn time. How was I supposed to know she'd keep following me?

Hayliel and Raphael open the large boxes in the corner. One contains a small table and chair set which they begin putting together. The more I look at it, the more familiar it becomes.

Is that the same set they have in the Power house library? His family is rich, so it really shouldn't surprise me. They open the second box, which I *think* holds a bunch of bean bag chairs? I don't see any beans though, just an excited Hayliel at whatever's inside.

That they haven't badgered me with their disappointment hasn't gone unnoticed. Raphael wanted to wring my neck earlier, so I don't doubt that it's coming. Everyone might be putting on a calm, cool, and collected act, but that won't last forever.

Sure, I've gotten a few looks, but nothing close to what I expected to happen.

Banishment, maybe. Booted from the group of angels I never wanted to work with yet now can't imagine being parted from. I hate it.

Even still, it's hard being in the same room as them. Hayliel and her boyfriends. She seems completely unperturbed by Mira's presence, laughing at something Raphael said. I guess I should be happy about that. It's not like I want her upset. I just thought we'd finally gotten to a good place, one that could develop into more than just friends. Playing her boyfriend clearly made me delusional.

After what I witnessed in the training room, the way she looked straight into my fucking eyes while getting railed by *them* and didn't say a single fucking word, it's clear as fucking day. She doesn't want me. Maybe she never has.

What did you expect? A fucking invitation? She prefers Pures, dude.

I do my best to ignore my bitter inner voice. Raphael and Theo are more than just Pures. I realize that now. But I'm only a man wallowing in his pain. It's easier to think of them as monsters than admit I've been the problem all along. The only one to blame for her lack of interest is me.

I look away from the happy, laughing pair and straight into Theo's watchful gaze. Shit. How long has he been there?

He doesn't give me much time to wonder. "What's really bothering you, Zeke? I know it's not just this Mira shit."

Does he though? He couldn't, not unless Hayliel told him what she saw and fucking hell, I couldn't survive being another joke to them. She wouldn't have done that, though. Even if she didn't want me, I've learned enough about her these past few months to know she doesn't go out of her way to hurt someone. Which means Theo doesn't know, and I sure as hell don't want to bring it up.

Besides, if I say the words out loud, it'll just make them real. I'm not ready for that.

Instead, I deflect like an asshole. "What, like we're best buds now? Pass."

Hayliel's voice cuts through the tension, but the worry in her voice only sets me further on edge. "We'll be right back. Just need to collect a few more things. Will you be alright here?"

And there it is. She's worried Theo isn't safe with me. Another blow to my raw heart.

"We'll be fine," Theo tells them, and neither of us speaks until their footsteps are nonexistent. He barely gives me a moment to relax before he's on me again. "You're hurt. I get it. But fucking hell, man. Stop bottling everything up and start talking. I know you saw us the other day."

The beating thing in my chest cracks. He knows how unwanted I am, how pathetic I must be for even still showing up here. My pain turns into anger.

I keep my voice neutral, trying not to cause a scene because that would only make things worse. "She tell you that, huh? Won't talk to me about it, but she'll certainly go to you. Why am I even surprised?"

"What? No. She has no idea you were there." Theo looks genuinely shocked, but I don't buy it.

"That's bullshit. I know she saw me, Theo. You're just trying to cover for her." I turn away from him and face the wall, my anger only a cloud to cover the gaping hole of hurt in my chest.

Theo doesn't leave me be though, the asshole.

He steps closer but doesn't touch me. "I'm not fucking covering for anyone. I'm the only one who saw you, Zeke. And if you'd have stayed instead of running off, you would have seen that I waved you in."

More than anything, I want to look at him if only to read his face. Is he being honest? Is this entire thing caused by my insecurities? I want to believe him, more than I want to fucking breathe, but the scared, betrayed little boy inside of me can't.

I keep facing the wall, not wanting Theo to see my face. "But why? That would have brought an unfortunate end to whatever you had going on." My voice wavers, despite my best efforts to hold it steady. Fuck! I hate that he's witnessing my weakness.

"I disagree. And the why is obvious, isn't it? I tried to wave you in because that's what Hayliel would have wanted. How come you can't see that?" His voice isn't accusatory or angry like I expected. No, it's worse. Concern laces his words, only serving to slice through the already torn up organ in my chest.

My mind whirls with things I can't comprehend. Would she really have wanted me there, with the three of them? And Theo would have embraced me, maybe not with open arms—and given their state of undress, I definitely wouldn't have wanted that—but enough to let me join their love fest? Because that's exactly what it was. Love.

None of it makes any sense.

Theo touches my arm then, his warm palm seeping through my raging thoughts. "She's nothing like the girl who hurt you, Zeke."

His comment has me whipping around, my eyes burning. He can't fucking know what my ex did to me. How could he? "What are you talking about?"

Theo straightens his spine like he's preparing for me to fight him. "Someone hurt you. It's why you act so hot and cold with Hayliel, and I suspect it's why you dislike Pure angels as much as you do. But Raphael and I aren't those Pures, and Hayliel would rather wound herself than see you hurting."

I want to be angry at him for seeing so much. Maybe punch him or act out so he'll stop staring at me with that damn look on his face, but I can't. All I can do is search Theo's eyes, looking for any sign of an ulterior motive or secret plan, but he seems genuine. *He* clearly believes what he's saying, so why can't I?

Inhaling deeply, I do something I've never once considered doing before this moment. I let myself be vulnerable. "I want to trust what you're saying, but it's not that easy."

Theo barks a laugh. "None of this is easy. Not for you or me or Raphael. And certainly not for Hayliel. We're all fucking dealing with shit, Zeke. Wouldn't it make things better if we dealt with them as a team?"

He waits for me to respond, but I keep silent because I've been an absolute fool. It's the second time Theo's brought clarity to my life, shoved my face into the mess I've made as if I were an untrained dog pissing in the house. I've been a selfish idiot, not willing to see that I'm not the only one hurting. These angels, my *friends*, are going through shit too and all I've done is pile on.

"The three of us care for her, and it's obvious she feels the same. If I've learned anything this semester, it's that our lives aren't guaranteed. We owe it to ourselves to make every moment count and spend as much time as possible with those we care for, don't we?"

I stare into his eyes, letting his words ignite the hopes and dreams in my soul. Watching Hayliel almost die put things into perspective for me. It made me realize there are no guarantees in this life, and if I want something, I need to act. That had been the plan before witnessing Theo, Hayliel, and Raphael going at it like wild dogs. I thought I'd been showing up before, putting in effort, but I'd really just been a coward, hoping she'd figure it out without letting myself be vulnerable and making my intentions known. Now, with Theo's words playing on repeat in my mind, I realize that maybe there can be space for me in her heart if she knows that's what I want.

Before I can respond, there's a commotion from outside.

Hayliel rushes inside, followed by Raphael, Mira, Dina, and finally Castiel. The rune glows blue when he passes through, just like it did for Mira. He looks frazzled and unkempt, a far cry from his usual appearance.

Everyone turns to him when he drops words that have the world turning upside down.

"Miss Hayliel, I've found it. I know what you are."

15

HAYLIEL

Is this a dream?

I pinch myself, wincing a little when it hurts, but it does as intended. This is real. Castiel figured out why I'm different, but am I even ready to find out? What if everyone else was right all along and I truly am spawned by the very creatures who almost killed me?

I'm not sure I could handle that.

Subtly, my friends drift toward me, pushing a sense of calmness through our mental connection. I try to let it settle within me and shove the other thoughts away, the ones where they leave me when they find out I'm a monster.

Shit. Where the hell is my parents' optimism when I need it?

"Do we really think it's a good idea for everyone present to hear this?" Raphael asks before Castiel can unravel my history. He nods to Mira in a way that's less subtle than if he'd just said her name.

As expected, Mira notices. "I've kept his secrets, *your* secrets. And besides, I gave you a rune to literally showcase who you can trust, which I walked through unharmed, I might add."

Castiel's eyes widen. "Ah, so you're the reason there's a banned rune etched near the door?"

"I am, though I'm starting to think it was a waste," Mira mumbles.

"Not a waste, my dear. It's precisely what's needed. This runic symbol detects intended harm. Any being who crosses through an area marked by this rune will be judged. If they mean no ill will to those that created the mark, they are free to pass, which you saw from that blue glow when I walked in. But if they mean to harm you, the rune will glow a dark maroon and the perpetrator will be immobilized."

I stare dumbfounded at Castiel. "Immobilized?"

He smiles. "Yes. Vines will sprout up around them, with thorns coated in a paralyzing substance that will wrap around the evil doer and keep them still until you can figure out what needs to be done."

"Holy shit," Dina says, the excitement at the prospect of taking down our foes so easily clear on her face.

"Indeed. When the Archangels took over, they banned that rune. They wanted to present a united front amongst the angels and have all of angel kind band together in peace."

Peace. It feels like such a foreign concept, but it ignites a burning question in my gut. If the Archangels knew how bad the in-fighting is now, would they step in to stop it?

Startling me from my thoughts, Theo touches my arm. "Since the information Castiel has is about you, I think it's only fair that you decide if Mira can stay to hear it."

I study her, still not knowing the real reason she's here, but unable to ignore what she's done for us so far. Mira doesn't balk at my perusal, only stands still. "She kept our secrets long before even knowing what they were. Besides, the rune marked her as safe. She can stay."

"Thank you," she says, lips tipping up slightly. "I won't let you down."

I don't know what it is exactly, but I feel her truth in my bones.

Castiel claps his hands once. "Now that we have that settled, Miss Hayliel, are you ready?"

"I think so." Nerves wrack my body, though I try to keep the fidgeting at bay. I'm about to find out what I've been searching my entire existence for, yet it's not at all like I expected it to be. I always pictured discovering it alone, somewhere in a dimly lit library with only myself and my history. This is better. Surrounded by friends and the angels I love. While *I* may not be able to handle it if I'm truly spawned from demons, I'm slowly coming to realize that I don't think my friends will care that much. And that is true, unconditional friendship.

With a clearing of his throat, Castiel begins. "I believe you're what's called a Seraphim. I suspected as much when your wings first changed, but I felt even more confident once I heard about your hot flashes—"

"Hot flashes?" Raphael asks, looking confused.

"—and about your miraculous survival against an angel blade."

Mira's mouth falls open. "Now wait a damn minute. You survived a blade? But I thought that was impossible ..."

"Our Hayliel is full of surprises," Theo adds, nudging me softly, but I can't focus on anyone else's shock but my own.

The relief that flows through me is a tangible thing, surrounding me like a warm, cozy blanket. I almost can't believe it. "I'm not spawned from demons," I say, collapsing into one of the small chairs Raphael and I built earlier.

"Quite the opposite, actually," Castiel reassures. "In terms of power, Seraphim are ranked above Archangels but below God. Because of how powerful they are, it's rare to have more than one Seraphim alive at once. There's only one instance of such a thing happening, and it changed the course of angelic history."

I should feel pleased, but the way he says the words makes me think it's a far darker story than I might hope. "What do you mean?"

"A very long time ago, there were two powerful Seraphim. A pair of siblings, one boy and one girl. As they grew, so too did their power. Eventually, God began to feel threatened by them until one day, he snapped. He moved against the Seraphim and anyone who stood in his way. It took all four of the Archangels to stop him, but not without casualties, including the last two Seraphim in recorded history."

As Castiel speaks, my heart breaks for the two siblings. The word Seraphim bounces around my head, ping-ponging through my mind until I remember where I've seen it before. There was a book in the library with pages ripped out that mentioned this type of angel. Is what happened with God the reason all mention of them has been removed from history, because they can't be trusted? Maybe I haven't escaped my fate of being a monster.

"Was there any truth to God's suspicions? Were the Seraphim trying to take over?" Theo asks like he plucked the very thoughts from my mind.

"That I don't know. I only met them once when they were young and both seemed kindhearted. Like you." He says that last point to me, and I wonder just how much of my worry is plastered on my face.

"Do we know how they died?" I ask, wondering how such powerful beings could be taken from this world.

"Not exact details, no. But as far as I know, only God could kill a Seraphim, so I would suspect one of their last acts in this world was helping to save Silver City from tyranny."

If that were true, then why aren't they celebrated as the Archangels are? Why isn't the story more widely spread? It makes no sense.

"With no God around, does that mean she's truly immortal?

And if so, is that why she survived the blade and not because of the faulty runes?" Raphael asks, causing my heart to squeeze. It's a scary thought to consider. True immortality would be incredible, but not alone. I couldn't survive living forever if it meant being without my friends and family. That would be a fate worse than death.

The second part of his comment finally registers. "Wait. What do you mean, faulty runes?"

Raph and Theo share a look, then Theo shrugs and says, "The dagger we pulled from your shoulder looked off. Some of the runes didn't fully connect. We couldn't tell if it was old and faded, or if something else was at play."

I read between his words easily enough. They think the demons supplying the angel blades are messing with them, but if that's the case, what about the one I saw Roderick use to kill that guy? Because he absolutely died. And besides, it was demons that attacked me with the blade. Why would they use a faulty blade? It doesn't make sense.

Before Castiel can answer Raphael's question, Zeke asks one of his own. "If you suspected what she was all along, why didn't you say anything?" My hard-headed, grumpy house leader looks more angry than usual, but this time his ire isn't directed *at* me, but *for* me.

Castiel sighs. "I can only speculate on her mortality, I'm afraid, but I can comment on the runed dagger. It isn't the runes that make it deadly. It's the material used to make the blade. Shards of a very powerful scythe. Even if they messed with the runes, on purpose or not, that thing would still kill any one of us except for her. As for the rest, there are many reasons I didn't speak up about my suspicions. To start, there has been no record of Seraphim since the siblings died, so how Miss Hayliel possesses the gene is frankly a miracle. And besides, I was under the impression that they have golden wings as soon as they develop."

Zeke rolls his eyes. "Fine. Say I believe that excuse. Why wouldn't you have at least mentioned it after her wings changed? You knew how hard she was looking, how much pain she was in not knowing what she was. Keeping that knowledge to yourself was cruel."

Butterflies flutter to life in my belly as Zeke defends me. Even with the distance he's kept lately, it's nice to know he still has my back.

"If I had gotten her hopes up and been wrong, that would have been far more painful for her. What happened near the well could have been a fluke from your transformation, a one-time thing only. It's only when you told me about surviving an angel blade that I felt confident."

"And yet you still needed confirmation from a stranger, someone outside our group who now knows the truth," Zeke grumbles, growing more annoyed with the professor.

Castiel, ever the mature angel, doesn't seem to notice. "A necessary evil, yes. Phiel is trustworthy. He's a recluse by choice, but he knows how to keep his mouth shut. Regardless, knowing what I do now, I'm sorry that I didn't share my suspicions with you earlier, Miss Hayliel. I hope you'll forgive me someday."

I smile, not having even an ounce of space in my soul for anger. Not today. "There is nothing to forgive, Castiel. I understand what Zeke is saying, and I even feel those exact same things, but you're right. If I had known what you suspected and then it was wrong, I would have felt so much worse. The fact is that we know now. Finally, after all these years, I know who I am."

"I've always known who you are, babe," Dina says with pride in her voice. "You're my best friend and the greatest angel I know. The difference now is that we know *what* you are. You're still you. Don't forget that."

Tears well in my eyes as I nod at my oldest friend.

"When I was little, my grandmother would read me stories before bed and there was one I always insisted on hearing," Mira says, grinning as she recalls the memory. "It was a story about a golden-winged angel with the power to heal others and harness a blade made of pure sunfire. I always thought it was made up, just a story to bring hope to little girls like me, but maybe it was real."

She stares at me with open adoration, like I'm the one her grandmother used to read about, but I'm nowhere close to being a beacon of hope. If what her story talked about is true, then maybe someday I can be.

To my surprise, she doesn't ask to see my wings, which only makes me like her more. Why can't more angels be like her? Instead, I'm stuck at a school filled with creeps like Professor

Uriel or cruel bullies like Seraphina and Cadriel.

"Castiel, do you recall when the last sunblade was made?" Zeke asks. His question causes me to pause because I know exactly where his mind is going. But there's no way, right?

My mind whirls in a million directions as I wait for Castiel to answer.

"Picked up on that, did you?"

"Can you elaborate for those of us who aren't quite following?" Dina asks sheepishly, and I can't help but laugh.

Castiel chuckles too, then nods. "Sunblades are created using sunfire, which only the Seraphim can harness. They have what's called the smiting touch and can summon sunfire at will to kill demons with a single touch. Imbuing any weapon with sunfire will make it strong enough to kill those creatures too."

Holy shit! I can make more fucking blades!

"That must have been what I did at the well when those demons turned to ash. It sure as hell would have come in handy earlier, say before I got fucking stabbed, though."

"Hey," Theo says, placing a comforting hand on my arm. "We can't change the past. We can only move forward."

He's right. I can't do anything about the things that have already happened. I can only look ahead, and maybe, if I can create more sunfire imbued weapons, then we'll stand a fighting chance in winning this war with demons.

"How good are the chances that someone here knows how I can do the whole harness and imbuing thing?"

"Not so fast," Castiel says before anyone else can speak. "We need to be careful."

"Be careful?" Zeke scoffs. "We're at war with demons and we're *losing*. Things are so bad some of our own kind are on *their* side. The time for being careful has long since passed."

Castiel sighs. "Acting rashly won't help you win any wars, Ezekiel. In fact, doing so will most likely get you killed. I'm not saying you shouldn't make those weapons, but you don't yet have all the facts."

I shoot Zeke a look, hoping he'll get the hint and just chill the fuck out for a minute. "What can you tell us?"

"God believed those sunfire imbued weapons could harm more than just demons. From what I've heard, he was positive that if they were infused with enough sunfire, they could harm even him."

Theo grimaces. "So what you're saying is if this information gets into the wrong hands, or even makes its way to the Archangels, they might have the same reaction as God did."

I shrug, not having heard enough to keep me from at least trying. "Then we keep doing what we've been doing and be discreet. I agree that it's risky, but if I have even a sliver of a chance to help us fight back against the demons, I'm going to do it. We all saw what those creatures did to the students at SCU, and I know firsthand what their deadly blades can do to us. I'm a lot of things, but a coward isn't one of them."

Zeke, who had been silently pacing, stops. "I agree with Hayliel. And when you succeed in making more blades, we can't just waltz in and supply the guild with some. Not until we figure out who the mole is and just how much leverage they have."

"Wait. There's a mole in the guild?" Mira asks, looking alarmed.

Castiel raises an eyebrow, realizing he and Mira are the only two who seem surprised. "This is news to me as well."

I slap my hand to my forehead. Whoops. I guess we never really spilled the beans, did we? "Sorry. With so much having happened, we must have missed filling you in. The short story is that demons and angels are working together, though the cause for their partnership is undetermined. We know the guild is involved because of conversations we overheard between a demon and an unknown angel, though we suspected it before then."

"And during the attack at SCU, one of the guild's secret armories was broken into, and that's pretty much impossible to do without someone on the inside," Zeke adds.

I rack my brain, trying to determine if that's the gist of everything we've been through so far, but it's too hard to tell.

"Well shit. That's not good." Mira laughs. "How the hell are any of you passing classes with all of this going on?"

"By the skin of our teeth," Dina says dryly.

"This is grave indeed and might explain why the guild was less than helpful during the attack," Castiel adds, looking concerned.

Zeke nods. "That's my suspicion as well. I assume whoever the mole is paid several angels to make fake reports and clog up the call systems. It's why when I called my father, or even

Lieutenant Azrael, no one answered. Apparently, everyone was seeing demons that day."

I shudder at the thought, not wanting to relive that awful day on campus. Sure, it might have brought my transformation on and finally led me to know what I am—something I still can't believe to be true—but it still haunts me.

Mira looks like her mind is a million miles away, so I'm surprised when she speaks. "Knowing all of this, I have to agree with Hayliel on creating those blades. Does that mean you can summon sunfire at will, or? How does that work?"

I wince, not wanting to admit defeat, but knowing I can't lie. "I, uh ... haven't quite figured that bit out yet. It happened once, but honestly, I thought the transformation itself was the cause."

"Hey," Raphael says, pulling me in for a quick hug and placing a quick kiss on my forehead. "We've uncovered another piece of the puzzle now. You'll figure it out in no time, sunshine. Just you wait."

"Speaking of figuring things out," Castiel says, "Have you attempted to connect through your mental channels yet?"

My cheeks flame as I think about what me and the guys were doing when we discovered the mental pathways were unblocked. I sure as shit won't tell Castiel it was during a three-way in the weaponry building.

To make matters worse, Dina jumps on the questioning train, and all I want to do is hide. "Wait, it's back? When did this happen?"

"Yeah," I damn near squeak. "The other day."

As if sensing my discomfort, Zeke changes the subject before anyone else can continue their inquisition. "So we continue with what we've been doing then. Combat training, digging into what the fuck's going on with demons and angels, and now discovering how to summon your abilities. All the while remaining inconspicuous. Does everyone agree?"

Right. Sounds like a piece of cake.

A round of agreement goes up, including one from Mira. I feel bad for her. She can't have known the shitstorm she was walking into when she stumbled upon Zeke doing sketchy shit. I wonder if she regrets it.

"Look, I know I'm new and I don't even go here, but I'm all in. If you'll have me, of course." It's the first time since meeting her that she's looked apprehensive.

I glance from Zeke, to Dina, to Raphael, and then to Theo, but before any of us can agree, Castiel speaks.

"I don't know who she is or why she's here, but if she passed through that door without issue, then you can trust her. And given everything that's going on, it wouldn't hurt to have an extra ally."

He's right. We need all the help we can get.

16

HAYLIEL

"**B**itch."

Instead of reacting, I make the valiant effort to ignore Seraphina's words as I walk by her in angelic powers class a few days later. Except we aren't in our usual classroom for today's lesson. We're in the arena.

I make it without so much as a blink in her direction while Raphael has no issues putting her in her place. But it's not with words or aggression. No. He pulls me down into his lap a few rows ahead, cups my cheeks, and kisses me like we're alone. Like he has every intention of finishing what he's just started.

My internal heat and the beating afternoon sun have nothing on the warmth that erupts in my body at his touch. When he pulls away, I don't try to get up.

"You know she's not going to take that well," I say, nuzzling his nose with my own.

"That sounds like a her problem, sunshine. I'd rather go home to my awful family than be near her for any period of time. Besides, if it takes a little PDA with you to understand that I'm off the market, that's a sacrifice I'm willing to make." He places an open-mouthed kiss on my neck, sucking a little before pulling away and holy fucking shit. The things this man does to me.

"Thank you all for meeting me here," Professor Isidora says with a smile. "I know this meeting place might seem unusual, but the work we're doing today can sometimes be unruly, so we thought it best to move to a more open area."

"If we're using our powers to fight, I call dibs on the mutant!" a guy in the back says. Within seconds, a storm cloud builds over his head and water pours from it in fat droplets, soaking him to the bone.

Whoa. What the hell was that? I share a glance with Raph, who looks like a golden retriever with far too much energy. He must know what's coming.

The guy splutters and wipes the water from his eyes, but Professor Isidora has moved on. "Use of your powers against another student is off-limits. If I find any of you breaking that rule, the punishment will not be one you enjoy. Have I made myself clear?"

Still wide-eyed, everyone nods in agreement.

She smiles. "Good. The power I'll show you today is one we won't spend much time with. It's unpredictable and much harder to master than the others, but having a basic understanding is still imperative to your progress at this school. Now, pay attention while I show you one of our more volatile powers. Weather manipulation."

Oh shit. That's a thing? I sneak a peek at Raphael and find him already watching me. *After today, I'll be able to make you wet in more ways than one, baby.*

I snort a laugh at his comment, knowing full well he already creates a storm of emotion inside me. It'll be fun to see it come to life outside my body as well.

Professor Isidora goes through the instructions on how this power will feel different than the others we've learned so far. Because of how unstable weather is in nature, what we create is hard to summon and even harder to control.

"It will likely feel weird to call on this power at first. That's completely normal. Ground yourself and dig deep into the wells of your ability. Find that core of energy and coax it to do your bidding." As she speaks, she weaves her hands through the air, creating little gray clouds above her head in a tiny circle that she pushes out until they surround her in droplets of rain without a single one touching her. It's magnificent. "Take turns working with your partner to summon a small rain cloud. I don't want to see any lightning or hear thunder. No snow or hail. Just a rain cloud. Start small and build up. I'll make my way around to see how everyone is fairing. Begin."

Raphael stands us both up before gripping my hand and tugging me to an emptier part of the arena. I don't miss that we're several groups away from Seraphina, thank the Archangels.

Holding onto my chin, he tilts my head up. "Do you want to go first?"

I shake my head. I'd rather watch him try first. Even if he fails, at least I'll know it's not just me.

"Alright," he says, brushing his thumb along my jaw. "But don't think I'm letting you leave here without giving it at least one attempt."

The stern set of his jaw is in stark contrast to the laughter in his eyes. I think he could convince me to do just about anything. Maybe that should scare me, but it only makes me feel alive.

I watch as he closes his eyes, arms extended in front of him and palms spread. This man is entirely too handsome for his own good. A breeze ruffles the blond hair at his temples, but it doesn't look like he notices. It's almost as if he's in a trance. Becoming one with the core of his power. Can I do that too?

Then suddenly, so quick that if I blinked, I'd have missed it, something flickers above his palms. I watch the space like a hawk, willing myself not to look away until I spot it again.

There, forming just above the palm of his hand is a puffy white cloud. It almost looks like cotton candy, and I'm half tempted to grab it straight from the air but hold myself back. As it grows bigger, the white darkens until I'm staring at two gray clouds, each the size of a watermelon.

Holy fuck.

His eyes open, meeting mine at the same moment that rain begins to fall from the clouds he just made. I'm struck by just how talented he is. Pure family aside, his power seems to come so fucking naturally to him. Part of me is jealous, but the other part is so fucking glad. It means that whatever the future holds, I know he can protect himself.

"You're incredible."

He lets the power dissipate until the clouds fade away into nothing, and he shakes the wetness from his hands. Professor Isidora mentioned snow earlier. If I can learn to manipulate the weather, then maybe I'll be able to experience the wonders of the cold, white powder. Apparently, Earth is covered in it. Or at least in some areas. Humans make what they call snow angels. I'd like to try that sometime.

"Now it's your turn. It really does feel strange at first, but let yourself get used to it before you try to build anything, alright?" He kisses my forehead and then steps back to give me space.

I repeat his stance from earlier and close my eyes, searching for that well of power. Finding it is easier than I expected, but the glowing orb at my core is hard to miss. I wonder if Raphael's looks like the sun, or if it's only because I'm a Seraphim. This must be where my infernal heat comes from. Maybe this will help me summon sunfire. It's worth a try, considering nothing else has worked so far.

Reaching out internally, I stroke the orb and let the odd sensations wrap around me. It's not painful, exactly, mostly just bizarre. Kind of like when I went to the park as a kid and would swing upside down while all the blood rushed to my head. Finally, things settle and I picture a cloud forming atop my hands, just like Raphael's did.

His voice filters through my mind then, echoing as if it's in an open chamber. *That's it, sunshine. I see it!*

Excited, I push a little harder, hope spiraling inside me, but instead of the clouds growing, they collapse. Fuck.

I sense another presence but don't bother opening my eyes. Raphael is here. He'll protect me. And something tells me I'm so close to getting this right, I don't want to lose my concentration.

"Valiant effort, Miss Hayliel," Professor Isidora says. "This time, try having your arms stretched wide at your sides, palms curved a bit like you're holding a cup. Exactly! Now, again."

Maybe it's just me, but it seems like this position made my core of power grow twice the size, but I have to be imagining it. I brush the thought away and try once more to bring forth a cloud full of rain. Wind whips my hair, but I keep my eyes closed, feeling the moisture in the air forming above my outstretched hands.

"Oh my," Professor Isidora says, and Raphael mutters my nickname, but still I keep my eyes shut and focus. It's only when a drop of rain hits my cheek that I open my eyes.

The space above my hands is empty, but dark clouds fill a once clear blue sky and rain pours from above. Was that from me?

Raphael whoops as the droplets fall harder, soaking my

clothes and hair. He twirls me around and kisses me. His lips are wet from the rain, and he tastes like a summer storm. Bright and refreshing. His tongue sweeps across mine, sending sparks of lust straight to my pussy. I need him. I need him now.

"Ahem."

My eyes flash open and I meet Professor Isidora's curious gaze.

Right. We're in power class and probably shouldn't be wet-humping in the middle of the arena.

Raphael and I break apart, putting some much needed distance between us, and blue sky peeks from between my scattered clouds. Of course, it would have brightened when I kissed Raph. He's light and hope and everything that's good in the world.

"I'm sorry, Professor. I don't know how—"

The streak of lightning comes out of nowhere. One second there's a flash and the next I'm lying flat on my ass with pain arching across my chest.

"Hayliel!" Raphael is by my side in a second. "Are you okay? Please, please, please, tell me you're okay."

"I'm fine, I think." I press a hand to my chest, wondering if I'll find a gaping hole there, but other than a dark spot on my soaked shirt, all seems normal.

Things move quickly after that. Professor Isidora instructs Raphael to take me to the infirmary. Her eyes hold an angry glint as she turns her pissed off expression toward Seraphina. Of course she's behind this. That bitch has had it out for me since the beginning, and it looks like she's no longer content to glare and stir things up from a distance.

"I swear to the Archangels, if she doesn't get in trouble for this stunt I'll be having fucking words with Principal Cael." Raphael fumes as we walk, but despite the obvious anger and fear, he never once lets me go. At least one of his hands is on my body at all times, and I can't say I hate it.

I must still be in shock because it feels more like something I saw than something that happened directly to me. Having to tell the angel at the front desk that I'd been struck by lightning felt like a joke, but the soreness in my chest tells me it's real.

The healer takes me to a private room and tries to have Raphael wait outside, but I turn that shit down fast. She doesn't argue, though she doesn't necessarily look pleased either. I get it. I doubt every angel companion would be as respectable as my Raph, who practically melts into the wall when the healer instructs me to take off my top so she can see the extent of the damage.

He doesn't say a word, but I feel his eyes on me like a caress. He's worried, but he also wants to finish what we started in the arena. The feeling is mutual.

"You're one lucky angel, that's for sure," the healer says once I put my shirt back on and sit on the edge of the examination table. "And you said lightning struck you? Hmm. There must have been something else nearby that took the brunt of the energy, because normally you'd be a wreck. Aside from some bruising on your chest and ribs, there's no serious damage. The bruises should heal by tomorrow, but I'd recommend you take it easy for the rest of the day just to be safe. And no more electricity play, do you hear me?"

She gives us both a stern look before leaving. Wait. Does she think we ... Laughter tumbles up from my throat as I realize exactly where she thinks this little wound came from. Sex and electricity. Now I'm intrigued. Maybe once we forget about this silly mishap, my guys would be willing to explore with me.

"How do you feel?"

My gaze meets Raphael's. He's looming over me, brow furrowed as his eyes roam over my body, looking for any sign of injury.

"You heard the healer. I'm a little bruised and beaten, but I'll survive."

"Archangels' balls. I can't ... fuck." He gathers me into his arms and breathes in the scent of my wet hair. "I'm not sure how many more times I'll survive watching you get hurt."

"Trust me, I'm about done with it, too. But I'm sorry. I—"

"Don't you dare apologize." Pulling back, he cups my face in his large hands, thumbs gently caressing my cheeks. "None of this is on you. It's on them. The assholes I want to obliterate from this city so they can never try to take you from me again. Because without you all the color would fade from this world. I would cease to exist, sunshine."

My eyes sting as his words absorb into my soul. "It's the same for me with you, Raph. I would die before I let anything happen to you, and apparently I'm damn near unkillable, so you're stuck with me."

He kisses me, but it's not gentle or meek. It's hunger. Desire. Need. All the things I'm feeling but doubled.

"Fuck, baby. I need you," Raph groans, fumbling with his pants.

I help him pull them down, freeing his jutting erection and wrapping my hand around it. "Please," I whimper. He slides a hand beneath my skirt, pulls my underwear aside, and shoves two fingers inside me.

A growl leaves him when he finds me wet and waiting. Desperate for him. His other hand grips the side of the exam table so hard his knuckles turn white. "I'll try to be gentle, but I don't—"

"I can take it. Just fuck me already."

My bright, funny angel doesn't hesitate. He pulls his fingers out, rubbing my wetness along the length of his cock before plunging it inside me to the hilt. He pumps into me with long, quick strokes. I stifle my moan, not wanting anyone to hear us and barge in. It's just him and me.

His thrusts turn so ferocious, all I can do is sit there and take it. I lean back on my elbows for leverage as he grips my thighs and holds me steady while he fucks the breath straight from my lungs. It doesn't matter that we have to be quiet. I can barely breathe through the sensations of pleasure, let alone scream.

"Are you close, baby? Please tell me you're close."

A strangled "Mmm" is all I can muster before stars dance behind my eyes and it's like the entire galaxy implodes within this room.

"Oh, fuck," Raph groans as he goes over the edge with me. He doesn't pull out right away, both of us content to just sit here joined like this. Outside of this room, reality is waiting for us, but in here we can pretend things aren't so shitty.

"I can't lose you, little sun," Raph whispers.

"Neither can I." I kiss his chest. "I've got a training session with the others soon. Why don't we go get a head start and—"

"Oh no, no. You're taking a rest day. Doctor's orders. And if I have to tie you down, well," his smile turns wicked, "it will be my pleasure."

17

RAPHAEL

The sky is dark when I fly from Power house to Fallen house.

There's not another soul awake below me, but I'm okay with that. A yawn threatens to escape and I let it out as I land just outside the front house doors, stretching away some of my tired fog. Things have been nonstop in the week since Castiel told us what Hayliel is. Between classes, research, and combat training, none of us have had a moment to relax.

Training has been fun at least, though I hate to admit it with Ezekiel as our teacher. Mira and Castiel have done their own lessons, and it's surprising how much they know. Castiel makes sense. He's been around longer than dirt, but Mira is a mystery. We found out recently she's a Pure—likely the reason she hasn't joined the Guild herself—and despite her father being a lieutenant, it still shocks me that she knows as much as she does. The forbidden rune, how to disarm someone while barely breaking a sweat. It's impressive.

Still, I can't figure out what exactly she's getting from helping us. Whatever it is will eventually come to light. Secrets don't stay hidden forever.

I pull out my slate, and there's a text from Theo telling me he's on his way. I consider calling Raduriel again despite the early hour. He's been avoiding my calls, and although my dear mother tells me he's been pulled away for work and that I should leave him alone, I rarely do what she tells me. I tuck the device away, not wanting to deal with more disappointment when he inevitably doesn't pick up.

We're running out of time, and I need his contact. I guess the joke is on me for ever thinking I could rely on him.

Hayliel's been working hard at trying to summon and harness sunfire, but it's only made her exhausted. Knowing that, I probably shouldn't be knocking on her door at the ass crack of dawn, but we practically forced her to bed early last night.

I knock again, and then a third time when I catch sight of Theo coming up the stairs and Mr. Grumps descending them. I have to get over my shit with him, but fucking hell, he doesn't make it easy. Scowling all the time, like everyone in the world has disappointed him. Get in fucking line, dude. You aren't the only one.

"She hasn't answered?" Theo asks, rapping his knuckles on the door three times.

"No. She's probably out cold. Poor thing is exhausted."

"She sleeps like the dead," Zeke says, stepping between us and pulling out a key. He unlocks the door, then opens it, gesturing for us to go inside.

I want to ask him how the fuck he knows what she's like when she sleeps, but I keep my mouth shut. There's a history between them. Theo and I haven't missed it, but until she's ready to tell us, I have to respect her silence. Even if it kills me.

We sneak inside, and Zeke shuts the door softly behind him, bathing us in darkness. The curtains to the balcony are drawn shut, the bathroom door partly closed, and Hayliel is tangled up in the sheets. One of her feet sticks out from the mess of blankets as she sleeps on her side, arms curled up around her neck. Fucking adorable. I want to crawl into bed beside her and never leave.

Theo and I approach her form on the bed, but Ezekiel stays back. I don't buy his act though. Something tells me he'd die to slip into bed next to her.

"Wake up, baby," I whisper, smoothing the hair from her face. She burrows into my hand, mumbling my name on a sigh.

She whispers Theo's name next, causing a grin to spread across his face. "I'm here, firefly." He rests his hand on her thigh, and I watch in utter desperation as she lets out a small whine, licking her lips like she wants far more than a platonic wake up call.

You and me both, sunshine.

Letting my urges win, I lean in and press a gentle kiss to her lips, but when I pull back, it's not my name on her tongue.

"Zeke." She says his name like a plea, one the asshole house leader doesn't miss. Theo only smirks, tossing a glance Zeke's way that screams, 'do you believe me now, fucker?'

Instead of seeming pleased, he looks stunned, like he has no sweet clue what he should be doing.

Huh.

Maybe he's not as confident—or arrogant—as I once thought.

He snaps out of it, moving robotically toward the balcony and throwing open the curtains. Not that it does any good, seeing as the sun isn't up yet. Poor guy just needs something to do.

While Theo whispers words to our girl, my mind wanders to just how much has changed with Ezekiel since our little chat in his room. Or, at least it *had* until he flipped the switch and went back to his bullshit hot and cold behavior. Theo says the guy is going through more than we realize and I should cut him some slack, but that's far easier said than done.

"Oh," Hayliel says, panic rising in her voice as she shoots up in bed.

"Shh, it's alright. We're only here to kidnap you," I tease, gripping her hand. She looks between me and the guys before her gaze settles on the clock beside her bed. The groan that escapes her throat is almost erotic, and I have to force my dick into submission because a sleepy Hayliel is fucking hot. Every version of her is.

"No one should be awake at this hour," she mumbles, tossing the blankets off of her like it physically pains her to do so.

"Oh, quit your complaining," I tell her, helping her out of bed and chuckling when she shoots me a tired, angry glare. She's fucking cute as hell.

She grabs a few items of clothing before disappearing into the bathroom, keeping the lights off.

While she's gone, I sit on the edge of her still warm bed. Hung on the wall are new picture frames. The photos inside are from our day at the photo parlor. There's one of just her, looking like a badass warrior, but the rest are with all three of us.

Seeing our faces mixed in among her family has joy bubbling up in my chest.

Hayliel finally emerges from the bathroom dressed in a pair of loose pants and a tank top. Zeke helps her into her wing jacket. She puts it on without asking where we're going, and none of us offer the information either.

A yawn forces itself free, which she barely covers with her hand.

Theo taps his bag. "I have a thermos full of coffee. You can have some once we get to where we're going."

"Do I have to share? At this hour, I might need the entire thermos to myself."

Theo only laughs. "We'll see, firefly."

We leave from her balcony and fly through the darkened sky,

over the beach and ocean. Hayliel follows along in silence, a questioning look on her face, but she doesn't say anything.

Below us, the water roils angrily, but from all the way up here, it's almost picturesque. There's something about the ocean that captivates me. Its depth seemingly endless, full of unknown creatures and hidden secrets just begging to be explored. Still, I wouldn't give up being able to fly to breathe under water.

It doesn't take long for the island Castiel told us about to come into view.

Hayliel sucks in a breath when she sees it, the sound stolen by the wind. "What is this place?"

"Paradise," I yell over the wind whipping by us while we fly. Even though Castiel described it to us, the sight of it amazes me, and I wish I knew what Hayliel was thinking. Does she feel transported to another realm, just like I do? Does it feel like the worries and troubles in her life are somehow diminished out here, as if they're nothing more than pebbles sinking to the vast ocean floor?

We land on craggy rocks that make up one of the three mountain peaks set in an almost perfect triangle. When Castiel said this would be the perfect spot for us to implement our idea, I didn't believe him, but now, seeing it with my own eyes, I know he was right. Apparently this used to be a training grounds of sorts, long before the Archangels took over. Now it's entirely abandoned.

"It's beautiful," she murmurs, twisting around three hundred and sixty degrees to get the full view.

Theo, Zeke, and I do the same, taking in the salty air and mixture of green, grays, and browns of the surrounding landscape. "We thought it might help to practice flying maneuvers away from the rest of the world. What do you think?"

Tears well in her eyes, but they don't fall. She just grins like a fool and nods. "The only thing that would make this better is caffeine."

"Holy shit. Slow down, sunshine!" Hayliel's black wing jacket lies crumpled in a pile on the grass. Her golden wings shimmer as the sun crests the horizon, but she's moving so fast it looks more like a lit sparkler at midnight, leaving a trail of sizzling flares in its wake.

Without the pressure of Uriel and her classmates, she's much faster. Like wickedly fast. Unbelievably fast. It's hot as fuck.

She lands beside me with the biggest grin I've ever seen spread across her face. Happiness shines from her in waves, surrounding me as she wraps me in a hug so tight it steals my breath.

"Are you having fun, little sun?"

Theo and Zeke land before she can respond. They'd taken up residence on one of the other two mountain tops so that Hayliel always had one of us close by. She gives me one last squeeze before pulling away and looking at the others.

"This is by far one of the best days I've had in a long time. Thank you."

"It was nothing, firefly. We're just glad to be here with you,"

Theo says, returning her hug.

When they separate, she immediately beelines for Zeke, who looks shocked that she'd include him in her thank you tour. His face settles into something serene when he rests his chin on the top of her head. Shit. I can't deny the hold she has over all three of us. Not that I'm willing to just accept him into the fold and forget all the fucked up stuff he's done. At least not yet. He's got a lot of shit to make up for.

Hayliel stretches, and I have to stop myself from drooling. Her eyes light up for a second before she turns to Zeke and says, "Hey, I meant to ask you something earlier. Why don't you ever use weather manipulation? They would have taught you last year, right? We all saw what Seraphina's little stunt did to me, and apparently I was lucky to get off as unscathed as I did. I bet a little lightning strike would help a ton in our fights against demons."

She makes a valid point. Why wouldn't he use every power at his disposal?

He shrugs. "It's not a power I feel particularly gifted in, given the lack of practice. Besides, the guild advises us not to use it. It's unpredictable and volatile, and has caused more harm than good in the past. Honestly, the fact that Seraphina managed to strike you dead on is surprising. It's a lot harder than it looks."

"Ugh. I hate that she's skilled," Hayliel grumbles, and I must admit, my girl looks awfully adorable when she's annoyed. "Still. I don't think we should rule it out entirely. Maybe we can add it to training once a week?"

The three of us share a look, but I don't even know why we bother. It's not as if any of us will deny her.

A thought grows in my mind until I'm practically vibrating with excitement. "Fine. But we came here to get away from reality for a bit so I was thinking. Now that you've got a good sense of the island, how do you feel about a race?"

She pulls away from the grumpy bastard and looks at me, her eyes lit up and damn near glowing. "I'm in!"

"Winner gets to have whatever they want. A favor of their choosing from the losers. Does everyone agree?"

Zeke looks like he wants to disagree. *Hard.* But he nods along with Hayliel and Theo. Perfect. I'd kill to have that asshole owe me a favor.

I motion everyone toward the starting line we'd drawn on the rocks for Hayliel. "We start here, wind around each of the mountain peaks, and the first angel to touch down back on top here, wins. If no one objects, Theo can count us down."

No one pipes up in disagreement, so I rub my hands together with glee.

"We'll go on three," Theo says as everyone gets into position. "One. Two. Three!"

With a leap and a flap of my wings, I'm in the air, racing toward the first mountain. The others keep up with me easily as we zip around the first peak, but by the second peak, Hayliel and Zeke are pulling ahead.

Fuck!

In a burst of speed, I push myself to catch up with them, but it's no use.

Shit. I didn't think this through enough. I don't want to owe Ezekiel a damn thing.

Theo and I are neck and neck, neither one of us having even the slightest chance of winning, but we don't give up. Even when Hayliel and Zeke, both looking determined as hell, make their final circle around the last mountain peak.

We're watching with fascination, both of us holding our breaths as the pair hurdle toward the top, just about to land, when Zeke pulls back and Hayliel wins. I share a glance with Theo, wondering if he caught the same thing. What the hell is that grumpy fuck up to?

We make it to the top where Hayliel is looking smug as hell. Rightfully so.

"You're fucking fast, beautiful!" I pick her up and twirl her around, dropping a light kiss to her lips.

"Seriously," Zeke adds, looking at her like she's the purest form of treasure. "I'd kill to see you race a few members of the guild."

Theo leans in close, pressing his lips to her hair and says gruffly, "You're a sight to behold."

She bows, taking in our astonishment with a blush on her face.

A question burns in my mind that I can't hold in any longer. Through my bond with only the guys, I say, *Why'd you pull back?*

Zeke's eyes flash to mine, annoyed. I don't think he's going to respond until he shrugs and pushes one word through our mental connection.

Cramp.

He's full of shit, but in this case, I don't care. I'm glad he pulled back for more reasons than just me not wanting to owe him shit. But I'd rather he stop doing these *nice* things that make me hate him less. It's annoying.

"Do you know what favors you want to ask from us yet?" Theo asks, and none of us miss the blush that deepens on her cheeks.

Interesting.

"I have some ideas, but nothing I'm willing to share yet."

I grin wolfishly as ideas for a certain kind of favor flit through my mind. "Take all the time you need, sunshine. These favors need to be *good*."

18

HAYLIEL

We make it back on campus around mid-morning and I haven't been able to shake the aura of bliss. The trip to the island was incredible. More than worth the insanely early wake up call.

Dina left a message on my slate an hour ago, asking—or rather, telling me—that we are far overdue for a girls' day, and she's coming to collect. I don't have a single complaint about that. Besides, I want to fill her in on everything that happened this morning.

Hayliel: I'm jumping in the shower. Meet in the hall between our rooms in thirty minutes?

Dina: Perfect. I'm thinking ... relaxing on the beach with some food. I'll grab everything and see you then!

The grin I've had plastered to my face since arriving on the is-land stays firmly planted while I shower. Having Theo, Raphael, and Zeke get along for an entire morning feels like something to celebrate. Add to that the favor they each now owe me and I'm shivering with the wicked ideas running through my head. I shouldn't let my thoughts wander there, but fuck if I can stop it.

I get dressed in a one piece bathing suit, covering it up with a pair of white shorts and loose T-shirt. I didn't bother washing my hair, knowing I'd want to clean the sand and salt from it later, so I throw it up in a messy bun on the top of my head just as someone knocks on my door.

"I hope you're hungry!" Dina says when I let her in and, as if on cue, my stomach rumbles.

We both laugh. "I'm starving. I'm just throwing my things in a bag and then I'll be ready to go. We definitely needed this girl time."

"It's been a total sausage fest lately. Today will be perfect. And I, uh, kind of invited Mira. I hope you don't mind."

I look up from stuffing a towel in my bag, and Dina's looking almost nervous. "Of course not. She seems cool as hell and honestly, it'll be nice to get to know her a bit more."

"Oh, thank the Archangels. I was worried you'd be upset that

I invited her."

"Really? Why?" I toss my slate in the bag, along with a portable speaker and my sunglasses, before throwing the strap over my shoulder.

Dina shrugs. "I don't know. Seems like she was around Zeke a lot, so I wasn't sure how you felt about that, given the vibes between you two."

I laugh. "Nah, I don't think it's like that with them. Besides, she made it perfectly clear when we first met that she wasn't looking to compete for their attention."

"*Their* attention, huh? Why am I not surprised?" She wiggles her eyebrows at me. "You can't mask the sexual tension with anything, Hayles."

"Oh, shut up." I shove her playfully. "Let's get going."

As we walk to the beach, Dina spills the news that apparently Mira is bringing something for me today, and I can't stop thinking about what it might be. It's not like we've talked a whole lot. The only thing I can think of is that story she mentioned her grandmother reading to her. I definitely wouldn't mind reading that.

We make it to the beach unseen, which is no easy feat on a campus this size, but I'm taking it as a win. Today is all about relaxing with trusted friends. I don't need Seraphina, Cadriel, or any other pieces of shit ruining my high.

Clouds fill the sky, making the day seem darker than it really is, but I don't mind. Hopefully, it'll deter other students from heading to the beach. More sand for us.

Birds chirp, flying high in the sky, and I immediately feel the tension which built in my shoulders as we walked through campus fade away. The moment we step off the grass, I kick off my shoes, and despite the lack of sunlight, the sand is warm between my toes.

I share a look with Dina and that's all it takes for us to drop our belongings, tear off our extra layers, and rush into the water hand in hand. It's a little cold, but I savor the bite against my heated flesh. I thought the hot flashes would go away now that I know what I am, but they've kept steady. Perhaps it's just something I'll have to deal with forever.

It doesn't take long for the cool water to turn frigid and both of us to decide we need to warm up again, so we head back to our towels. I'm eager to find out what scrumptious snacks Dina packed for us.

Mira's waiting when we get back to our things. She lies on her back on a towel, her head propped up by her bag, sunglasses perched on her nose and looking utterly chill. She's clearly aware of the vibes we're going for today.

There are a few more angels along the expanse of beach, but luckily none of them stray too close to us, leaving us in our own little semi-secluded spot.

"Mira! You made it," Dina says, her teeth chattering a little as she grabs the thick towel she brought. Mine isn't nearly as fluffy and cozy, but with whatever heat races through my veins now means it won't take me long to overheat again.

"I did! But there was a crowd of angels headed this way while

I flew over, so if we want to relax, we may want to move this party elsewhere."

"Shit," I say, considering our options. "They just can't let us have one damn beach day, can they?"

Mira looks around and then her face lights up. "Grab your things, quickly. Follow me."

She leads us to the boathouse, but I don't waste any time telling her it's always fucking locked.

"I'm not one to let a locked door keep me out," she says with a wink, then she crouches and pulls out a little kit from her bag. It looks similar to the one Theo had when we followed the lead from Roderick. Where the hell is everyone getting these lockpicking kits from, and when can I learn?

She breaks in easily and we walk inside, quickly shutting the door behind us. I expect to find it musty and desperately in need of fresh air, but instead it's bright and clean. The windows high on the walls let in tons of light, making it seem like we're miles away from campus. Nothing will ruin our day in here.

Despite there being an open area with water access next to a garage style door, it's empty. There are no boats or jet skis primed and ready to go, which is a little surprising. Why keep the door always locked if there's nothing of insane value inside? Sure, a few kayaks hang on the wall and what I think is a canoe held by slots on the ceiling, but that's it.

Tucked in the corner is a couch and a few plush chairs that look cozy as hell. Damn. We probably could have made this work for our secret meeting place instead of the cave. Not that

I don't like what we've created, but this would have taken half the work out of it. I suppose someone must use this space for it to be so clean. I wonder who it is.

My stomach growls loudly, which has both girls looking at me.

I shift my weight from side to side, staring down at my feet. "What? I'm hungry. The guys pulled me out of bed before the sun was up and other than coffee, I haven't eaten anything."

Dina and Mira share a look before they jump into action, motioning me to sit down while they pull out food. Dina's expression tells me I'm not getting away with such little information.

She only lets me eat a few bites before she gives up on waiting. "Alright, alright. Talk and eat, woman."

I swallow the piece of cheese I was chewing on and take a sip of the water Dina packed for us. "All three of them showed up in my room at four in the morning and scared the absolute crap out of me. Then we flew to some random island so I could work on my flight skills to prepare for the big Wingology final. It was incredible."

Dina stares at me, mouth hung open. "Zeke was there too? With Raphael and Theo?"

"Yup."

Mira, looking confused, asks, "Why is that so shocking?"

Dina tucks her legs under her on the couch, looking like she's settling in to offer all the juicy details. "Our girl and Zeke hooked up at the start-of-term party and then he went all possessive, fragile ego on her when she started hanging out with Theo and Raph. Sounds like he's working through his past issues though, and do you smell that?" She leans toward me, sniffing. I follow along, breathing in through my nose, but all I smell is beach.

"I smell a four-way in your future."

I roll my eyes, unable to hold in my giggle at falling for her shit.

Mira laughs too. "So you all haven't fucked yet? From the vibes between you and the guys, I thought for sure you would have."

My cheeks grow hotter than ever, so I stuff a cracker in my mouth to keep from responding. I should have answered her though, because this leaves Dina open to giving her own colorful version. "She hasn't screwed all four of them at once yet, but it's only a matter of time."

I cough, damn near choking on the dry as fuck cracker that's currently stuck in my esophagus. "*Anyway*," I say, throwing them each a look. "We ended the morning with a race. Winner gets a favor from each of them and guess who won."

From the smug look on my face, it's not hard to guess that it's me, and this has Dina squealing with delight. "Well? Do you know what favors you're going to ask for yet?"

I bite my lip and look away, not wanting to give away all the dirty thoughts racing through my mind. Not because I think either of them would care, but because they already fucking know. Apparently, I'm an open fucking book.

Mira smirks, sending me a wink. "Ah, so it's *those* kinds of favors."

"See, I told you it's only a matter of time." Dina lifts her water bottle in the air. "Cheers, to being the Archangels' favorite and getting all that delicious dick."

I don't lift my water bottle right away, but eventually give in. Fuck it. I'll cheers to that.

We eat in silence, welcoming the female comradeship surrounding us. I wasn't sure how things would feel with Mira, but having her here and spending this time with just us girls is exactly what I needed.

"All four-ways aside," I say, throwing a fake disgruntled look at Dina. "This morning was a revelation to me. In class, I've been completely unable to increase my speed regardless of what I do, but this morning I was fast. I felt quicker than the wind. Maybe it's because I didn't have the other students or Professor Uriel breathing down my neck, but if that's true, I'm fucked for the test."

"That unhappy, pompous angel is still a professor?"

"You had him too?" I ask, not really shocked as she isn't too much older than us, but it's interesting to hear her reaction.

"He was my least favorite professor. Always had his head so far up his own ass."

"Well, that hasn't changed. He's conceited *and* has it out for me. It's a fabulous combo," I say dryly.

"Don't let him get to you. Apparently, he lost out on some important position back in the day and hasn't gotten past it.

He's a childish fuck who shouldn't even be teaching, but he's harmless."

I want to disagree, but that bastard doesn't deserve any more of our thoughts today. "Who else did you have as professors when you went here?"

Mira lists a few names, and Dina perks up at the mention of one particular angel.

"Was Malik hot as sin when you attended? The things I'd let that angel do to me." She looks off wistfully, like she's just dreaming up all the scrumptious things she'd let him do.

I laugh and Mira says, "That man was every student's sexual fantasy. Nice to see that hasn't changed."

"I thought you started something with that group from the anything-but-clothes party. What happened to that?"

She sighs. "They were great, but just something to pass the time and keep my mind away from the forbidden professor that haunts my dreams."

"You'll graduate soon, babe," I tell her. "Then he'll be fair game to unleash all of your seductress tactics."

Mira nods. "We sometimes attend the same gatherings. I'm more than happy to start planting the seeds of his Dina obsession if you want?"

Dina claps her hands, looking grateful. "Would you? Yes, please! I don't know what it is about him, but I just can't shake my fixation. Maybe screwing him will get him out of my system." She winks at me and I laugh.

"Oh! Speaking of fixation, I brought this for you." Mira digs into her bag and extracts a folded cloth pouch. When she lifts back the flaps, there are several tiny vials of light blue liquid hooked beneath individual elastics.

"Weird transition, but okay." I eye the little bottles, carefully taking the one she removes from the strap. "What is it?"

"This is an elixir I made that should dampen or mask your power signature from demons."

I stare at her, dumbfounded. "You made this? For me?" Very few angels have made me anything, and something like this requires thought and consideration. I'm honored that she'd offer it to me after our fairly recent introduction. The skeptical part of my brain screams *ulterior motive,* but I'm trying to shut that bitch down ever since the rune showed us she was trustworthy.

"It was nothing. I make all kinds of shit in my spare time, and before I started hanging out with you, I was beginning to go crazy with how much time I had. Besides," Mira rubs the back of her neck, "I haven't exactly tested that it works."

"Dude, this is the coolest thing," Dina says, looking at the small glass bottles.

A million questions race through my head. I want to ask her why she has so much free time. What is it that keeps her from working or doing something she loves? She graduated from the top university in the city so it's not like she wouldn't have any prospects. But instead of bombarding her with personal questions she may not feel like answering, I only nod and focus on the pretty blue vials. "So, how does it work? With how many are there, I'm guessing it wears off?" I want to remove the cork and sniff it, but I damp the urge down.

"Exactly. One dose should last approximately twelve hours, give or take. I tried to make it as tasty as possible but with some of the ingredients ..." she winces, "let's just say it's an acquired taste, but in my experience, the stuff that usually works tastes like shit."

"Even if it tastes like dirt, if this actually works, it'll be such a relief. How did you know they tracked my power?" I hadn't told anyone what the scarred demon asshole had said to me during the attack, so how could she have known?

"I didn't. At least, not for you specifically, but being the daughter of a guild lieutenant gives me certain perks. Access to books and information that others might not have. That's how I knew demons could sense power, and then, after learning that you were chock-full of it, I figured something like that might come in handy. I'd kill to join the guild, but since I'm Pure, they won't take me. So I settle for the next best thing; keeping my eyes and ears open, and snooping around as much as possible."

"I'm sorry," I say, passing the vial back to her so she can tuck it safely away. "The guild would be lucky to have someone like you. Thank you for this."

"Of course. It won't make your power completely invisible, but it'll help you blend in better with the rest of us low level plebeians." She winks.

I stash the leather satchel away in my bag, being careful to position it around something soft so the vials don't break. As grateful as I am to her giving me this wonderful gift, I also hate to think about the day when I'll have to use these.

And given what's been going on between angels and demons, that day *will* come.

We spend a few more hours talking, swimming, and eating. It turns out Mira has made loads of different potions over the years. Some to enhance an angel's natural abilities and gifts, or even one that could make you invisible. Not all of them worked, but from the way her eyes light up whenever she talks about it, I can tell she enjoys playing potion master. Today has shown me that Mira is cool as hell, and I'm really glad she's part of our group.

Dina, being my hilarious best friend, asks Mira about making a love potion, hinting at using it on Professor Malik once she graduates, but there's no way she'd need one of those. Any guy or girl would be lucky to have her without the need of a potion.

By the time the food is gone and we're all feeling blissfully happy, we pack up our little slice of heaven and put everything back the way we found it. Even though I saw the guys this morning, I miss them. It feels like it's been more than just a few hours, so I'm excited to meet up with them in the cave for research in a little bit. I giggle, wondering if Castiel can tell what's going on between the four of us or if he chooses to remain in the dark.

Hopefully, it's the latter.

Opening the boathouse door, I step out into the ocean

breeze, breathing in the scent of brine and sand. I close my eyes and tilt my head up to the sun. Even though it's lower on the horizon, the power of its heat hits me all the same. It's perfect.

The door closes behind me and Mira comes to stand beside me with a smile on her face. "Don't worry, I locked it from the inside so no one will ever know we broke in."

"I want to be you when I grow up," Dina adds, which causes Mira to snort.

We head away from the beach, with Dina on my left and Mira on my right. Something about our little trio feels predestined, like we were all meant to meet and become friends.

Mira doesn't let Dina off the hook for her earlier comment. "You know I'm not *that* much older than you, right? Don't need to give me a complex." She fakes a pout, pointing her best wounded animal look—which is actually believable as fuck—in Dina's direction.

It falls from her face in an instant, and I follow her line of sight, my stomach dropping when I see what caught her eye.

A group of six students, all Fallen from what I can tell, stand between us and the rest of campus. No one says a word as we assess one another. The odds aren't in our favor, and even though I'm happy not to be alone, I fear for my friends.

Mira and Dina might have chosen to be my friends, but they didn't sign up for whatever the fuck this is.

Dina sighs. "These assholes just had to ruin our chill day, didn't they?"

19

HAYLIEL

With more confidence than I should have, I keep walking, doing my best to ignore the six students fanned out and blocking our path.

Honestly, I'm just hoping they'll get the fuck out of our way and not cause a scene, but the closer we get, the more I realize that's not going to happen. They look pissed.

"Does this, uh, happen often?" Mira asks, unsure what's going on.

I frown. "Well, I mean, I'm definitely the butt end of more than one joke and usually have some asshole or another tripping or shoving me, but I don't know what the hell this is. Maybe they just want to talk?" But even as I say the words, I don't believe them.

"I don't think so, Hayles," Dina says, worry lining her voice. Shit. If this turns into something more than just verbal sparring, Dina's father will have a fit.

We make it to a spot where we have to stop because the pissed off Fallen haven't budged. "We just want to get by," I say, keeping my voice neutral. Maybe they'll appreciate a conversation. Though I'm betting they'll appreciate that as much as a kick to the ass.

A guy with a massive forehead leers at me. "And we just want you gone from our school. I wonder which one of us will get what they want first?"

"Seriously? What the fuck is your deal?" Mira asks the group, unimpressed with their bullshit. I want to caution her to be quiet, to not let them bother her, but I can't bury the tinge of joy that she's standing up for me.

"Our deal," a girl with thin lips and even thinner eyebrows sneers, "is that they let this vermin enter our school and expect us to be okay with it."

Fucking hell. This again? I've heard this spiel from Seraphina already. "What the hell did I ever do to you?"

"You live in *our* dorms and take *our* classes as if you're one of us, but you're not," the same girl says.

"You. Don't. Belong. Here," big forehead adds, stepping right up into my personal space.

Six months ago, his words would have caused me pain. Hell, even a month ago they might have, but not now. Now I see this for what it truly is. Weakness.

But it's not mine. It's theirs.

Where I'd normally cower from his nearness, all I feel is strength.

I don't have time to do anything about it though because suddenly Mira is standing between me and this asshole, and she's holding a small, sharp blade to his throat. "It's time you back the fuck up, buddy, and get out of my friend's face."

"Or what? You'll prick me with your tiny little blade?" The smirk on his face might make me believe he's not scared of her, but the glint of fear in his eyes gives the truth away.

The guy I'd seen with Uriel a few weeks ago stands on my periphery. His wounds have healed, but if this breaks out into a fight, he'll have fresh ones to take their place. He stands mostly on his own, a little further back than the other five in the group who have drawn close since our little altercation, but it looks like he'd rather be miles away than confronting us.

Mira smiles, but it's anything but sweet. "I'll use this tiny blade to keep you still while I use this one to cut off your tiny dick." As if she conjured the damn thing, a slightly larger blade rests in her other hand where she holds it to his crotch.

"You're crazy," he says, voice wavering slightly, and hot damn, I'm with Dina. Mira might just be the angel I want to be when I grow up.

"Don't fucking tempt me, you slimy piece of shit." Nothing about Mira's expression can make someone believe that she isn't serious. I wouldn't want to fuck with her, that's for damn sure.

Thin brows steps forward as if to intervene, but that only makes Mira press the blades more firmly into big forehead's body. He whines, voice shooting up a couple of octaves as he screeches, "Stay the fuck back, you idiot!"

Without warning, a Pure angel drops from the sky and I inwardly groan.

"What is the meaning of this?" Professor Uriel looks at the group of Fallen, then at Mira, and finally his gaze shifts to mine.

Not intimidated in the slightest, Mira says, "We were trying to leave when these cockfuckers blocked our path and started threatening us. But don't worry, Prof., we've got it handled, don't we, champ?"

Big forehead nods, raising his hands and backing up slowly. There's a thin cut on his neck, and I don't even want to think about what injuries might be present in his nether regions. Yuck.

"We are a prestigious school and violence among students will *not* be tolerated. I expect to see you all in detention. It would appear, Miss Hayliel, that you are at the very core of all our problems. If it happens again, I will personally see to it that you're expelled."

I suck in a breath, unable to believe the bullshit coming from his mouth.

"You smarmy piece of shit," Mira says, wiping her blades off on her shorts before putting them away.

"What did you just say to me?" Professor Uriel asks, his eyes narrowing to slits.

"You heard me. Hayliel hasn't done jack shit, but you know that already. Don't you?"

If I didn't love Mira before, I certainly do now.

Uriel's jaw drops open. "How dare you!"

"How dare I? You're the professor, asshole. You're the one who's supposed to be taking care of students, but all I see is an arrogant, self-centered jackass with a superiority complex."

Uriel sputters, his face an unattractive shade of red. "That's enough from you. Hand over your weapons and name this instant. We'll see what the principal has to say about your defiance."

Mira only laughs. "Like hell. I'm not giving you shit. And, speaking of Principal Cael, I bet he'd be very interested to know that one of his professors is less than unbiased. Isn't that little tidbit in the school's code of conduct?"

I didn't think Uriel's face could get any uglier, but it does, morphing into something darker. He's pissed. Mira doesn't seem to care that she's just enraged him, though, and to my surprise, he actually backs off.

"I won't tolerate another moment of this. Disperse!" he shouts over his shoulder to the group of Fallen before turning back to me. "My warning still stands. If I catch you causing trouble again, it'll be the last thing you do at this school." Then he turns and walks away.

My heart races, the heavy dose of adrenaline making me shake. Dina's eyes meet mine where she steps forward. She looks sad and apologetic, but I reach out to squeeze her hand reassuringly.

"I see that guy is still a dick," Mira says with a huff. I'm both embarrassed and utterly impressed with the way Mira handled this situation. She reminds me so much of Dina. Confident, headstrong. I know my best friend would have backed me up just as hard if we were anywhere else. But with the amount of pressure that her dad's been putting on her, I don't blame her for keeping silent. I'll have to make sure she knows that.

Before my pulse can settle down, another angel drops from the sky and I almost shriek at the white wings, thinking Uriel is back. But it's Castiel's worried gaze that meets mine. "What in the Archangels mess was that all about?"

"Just another day in the life of a mutant." A heavy weight settles over me. Pushing against it feels insurmountable. I don't bother saying anything about Uriel, unsure if I can bash a professor to another professor, but really, I just don't have anything left in me.

Mira has no such worries, immediately giving him the condensed version of what we just experienced, and with every word she says, I sense Castiel growing more and more pissed off.

"That's unacceptable. I know you'd probably just like to get back to your dorm, but please come with me for a moment. I think it's time we have a little chat with Uriel about the types of punishments he's doling out."

There's very little part of me that wants to be around Uriel again, but I wouldn't mind witnessing the verbal sparring between Castiel and that asshole. "You can head out if you want,"

I say to Dina and Mira, because they sure as shit haven't signed up for any of this, but they don't budge.

I hope someday I can repay their kindness.

We head toward the main hall, hoping to find Uriel in his classroom. Even though it's a weekend, Castiel doesn't think he'd have just gone home after all that. He's most likely having a tantrum in his office, and for some reason, that makes me a little giddy. Serves the asshole right.

With every step we take, I find myself falling deeper into the woman I once was. The girl from before SCU. The one who never fit in. I hate it.

When we're only a few rooms away from Uriel's class, something shakes me from my inner turmoil. Angry, hushed tones come from a classroom up ahead. Uriel's classroom. From this distance, I can't hear what's being said, but they sure as fuck don't sound happy.

With the door shut and the small window covered, we can't see who's inside. It's only when we press our ears to the door that we can hear clearly.

"That wasn't what we agreed to! Do you understand the risks you put all of us in by going off script?" Uriel sounds pissed, and I wonder who he's talking to. Clearly, he doesn't think anyone would dare listen in. Cocky shit.

"You should have all stuck to the plan. Target her when she's alone, make her feel isolated, and keep her preoccupied." Time freezes as I catch on to what he's saying. The Fallen picking on me, his lack of disregard. Is it all part of some elaborate plan they've concocted? I share a look with my friends, but none of us say a word.

I miss what he said next but can easily figure it out when Uriel replies, "I don't care. Find a way to get her alone, but no more causing a scene or you'll ruin everything."

"Why do we need to do this again?" someone else asks, seeming almost bored.

Now that's a question I'd like the answer to.

There's silence for a moment, and I'm worried Uriel won't answer the question. It's only one I've been trying to figure out myself since the Fallen began openly hating me.

"You're not here to know the reasons, you fool. You're here to do as I say. All you need to know is that it's imperative that she's distracted for the next phase of the plan. We need to keep her busy so she can't keep looking into things. And need I remind you she survived a fucking angel blade? No angel can survive that, which only proves she's not one of us."

My eyes widen. How the fuck does Uriel know about that?

"Isn't it true that only demons can survive a hit from one of those blades?" someone else asks, fear present in their voice.

"An angel blade won't kill a demon, no. All the more reason for you to do better or I'll find others who can. And trust me, none of you will like the consequences of failing this task."

It takes everything in me not to barge in and confront Uriel for his shit. Fuck. It kills me that I can't rub it in his smarmy fucking face that I know he hates me, and that now I'll make him pay.

Castiel made a pretty convincing argument though, and that's why, thirty minutes later, our entire group is in the cave.

I'm still fuming, pacing, wanting to go back there and give him a piece of my mind.

"I'm going to ask this, but I don't want anyone to take it the wrong way," Zeke says, and I shoot him an angry glare. I hate those words. It's almost always backed up by some bullshit that you can *only* take the wrong way.

"Is there any chance you misinterpreted the situation?" I open my mouth to chew him out, but he cuts me off. "And before you bite my head off, it's not you I'm doubting. I just can't see Uriel coming up with this shit or executing these types of plans. The guy can't even lie well. We saw that firsthand after the attack on the school."

Theo extends a hand behind me, trailing over my shoulder and up my neck, gently pressing his fingers into flesh until I relax marginally.

Breathe, firefly, he says through our bond, and I do my best to follow his request.

"We didn't mishear," Mira says, then Dina and Castiel nod in agreement.

Zeke's frown deepens. "Fuck. In that case, this is bad. And if he knew about the angel blade, it's not hard to assume where he got that information."

Raphael's eyes grow wide, and I'm still trying to figure out why when he says, "You think he's working with the mole at the guild?"

Mira sucks in a sharp breath.

Shit. He's right. Very few angels know I survived that day. The guild members who showed up to help, and us. I doubt anyone in this cave said anything, so that only leaves the damn guild.

"It makes sense," Raph continues, looking thoughtful. "Principal Cael thought a student was involved in the attack on SCU, but what if it wasn't a student? What if it was a professor?"

Silence falls as we consider his words. Just how far does the web of lies and treachery reach? Angels and demons working together. Professors allowing an attack on school property and directing students to bully others. This can't be the world we live in.

"If what you're saying is true—and I believe it is—things are far worse than we realized. Uriel would have had the means to drop the school's protective shields and let demons just waltz in," Castiel says, looking mortified. "As hard as it's going to be, we can't let on to Uriel or anyone else that we know what's going on. Our only leverage right now is that they don't know that we know. We can use this to our advantage."

I nod. As much as I hate it, he's right. "Uriel ordered the students to get to me when I was alone. I hate to be more of a burden, but maybe that's something we can use in our favor."

"You're never a burden, sunshine. We'll all happily stay at

your side forever."

My cheeks flame, knowing that Castiel is witnessing this, but it doesn't stop the growing hunger in my core. When he says things like that, I can't help but melt into a puddle of goo.

"Then it's settled. I'll see if I can uncover anything that could help us understand what it is he needs you distracted from. For now, lie low and be careful." Castiel turns to me, his eyes softening. "Keep your wits about you."

He turns to leave but I stop him, needing to ask one last question. "Wait. Back at Uriel's classroom, he alluded to the fact that I was a demon. Do you think he truly hasn't figured it out yet and still believes I'm spawned from demons?"

Castiel looks from me to my friends, before his eyes settle back on mine. "It's possible. Miss Hayliel," he says, sighing. Then he adds, "But it's also possible that he knows what you truly are and would rather spread fear instead."

He exits the cave, leaving us with that dreadful thought.

When I finally learned the truth and found out I was a Seraphim, it felt like things were finally settling into place.

Now it just feels like they're crumbling all around me once again.

20

EZEKIEL

I stand outside Hayliel's dorm with a storm cloud of emotion hanging over my head.

Ever since learning about Uriel's devious plan, an anger like none I've ever felt before has taken hold of me and hasn't left. It sits in my gut, simmering until it feels like I'll lose my mind if I don't do anything. But since I can't, not without royally screwing things up, I arranged for something less destructive.

There's not a doubt in my mind that what's happened over the past few weeks has really fucked with Hayliel's head. She tries to hide it behind her mask of happiness and joy, and while I think some of that is real, I see through to the worried, hurt angel beneath.

It's why I invited her to my dad's place where hopefully we can try working on imbuing her sunfire. A nice distraction. Well, that, and because the cave isn't really the safest place for her to practice. Sure, we've warded it and put as many protections in place there as we can, but it's not foolproof.

With dad at work, it'll just be the two of us. No one will barge in, and we're not in a carved out rock on the side of a cliff that might crumble down around us if her power is too strong. Dad's workshop was built for weapon forging and tinkering.

I expected her to put up a fight when I brought it up last night at the cave, or that she'd want Raphael and Theo to come with her, but she agreed without a second thought. As much as I want to assume it's all about me, I'm smart enough to realize that it's likely more about the sunfire and being close enough to visit her parents than anything else.

She opens the door and the breath catches in my throat. Wearing a pair of loose-fitting, high-waisted pants and a cropped tank top, she looks delectable. Her wing jacket hangs just off her shoulders, so I give it the last pull to get it properly in place, though I'd rather she be wearing something else.

As if sensing where my thoughts are going, she smiles and says, "If we weren't flying, I would have worn your jacket."

"In that case, it's not too late to change our minds. We can just practice in the cave."

She laughs, and the sound brings a smile to my lips.

"Hell no. You invited me to your house, Zeke. No take backs. Are you ready?"

I nod. "Let's get out of here."

Principal Cael finally removed the new rule that had us signing out of school whenever we left. Which leads me to believe they either found who they suspected was the inside man or realized no student would be so foolish as to let demons onto the property. Hell, it's not as if we could even adjust the wards ourselves so they're way off base. I hope they found proof that asshole Uriel was involved so he can be replaced. Whatever, I'm just grateful not to feel like a wayward teen trying to sneak out at night.

We leave from her balcony, wanting to avoid as many other angels as possible. The sun is high in the sky, not a cloud to be seen as we make our way to the Fallen district in a peaceful silence. I'm curious to see what she thinks of our house, knowing what she does about the rest of the district.

The entire Fallen district used to be designated entirely to the guild, but over the past few decades, things have begun slowly changing. Now the guild has only one section reserved for lieutenants. Likely a way to keep them close, at their beck and call, but still. Dad lucked out and received a pretty sweet plot of land a while back, and I'm kind of surprised they haven't tried to take it from him yet. If they do, I'll know things have officially gone to shit.

"Holy crap," Hayliel says, stopping to hover over the houses below. "Is this the guild neighborhood? It's so *fancy*."

"Have you not been to Theo or Raphael's family homes yet? This is nothing compared to what the Pures have, but we can't complain."

She shoots me a look, and I know it's because I didn't say anything cruel or harmful about her boyfriends. Look at me, growing up.

"How do you know which house is yours? They all look the same from up here." She scans row after row of black roofs, searching for some distinguishing mark to tell the difference.

"Habit, I guess. When I was younger, I nailed a colorful pair of dad's boxers to the roof so I'd find it more easily, but the guild nearly had a conniption. They only stayed on for two days before they removed them and I got a slap on the wrist."

Hayliel laughs, and I want to tell her more of my childhood stories. I want her to know me, the real me, more than I've wanted anything in a really, really long time. Part of me still fears her rejection, but she hasn't turned me down yet and I'm *trying* to take angels at face value. If she doesn't explicitly tell me she's not interested, I shouldn't put words in her mouth or assume.

"Come on. We're almost there."

We land in front of one of the many houses with white sliding and red doors. The same as all the others and yet so different. The house I grew up in. I watch in fascination as she takes it all in. There's a small wraparound covered porch that goes from the front door around the left side to the back door. Mom and Dad used to spend quiet moments together on this porch every morning. They'd drink their coffees out back, with Dad's arms trapping Mom between him and the railing. I remember looking out and watching them, hoping that one day I'd find a love as perfect as theirs. Now that she's gone, Dad barely spends any time out there. The memories are too painful.

As if sensing the turn of my thoughts, Hayliel grabs my hand and squeezes. "I know we came here to do badass things, but would you mind giving me a tour first?"

"I was hoping you'd ask," I tell her honestly, because I want her in every room of this place. It feels creepy to say, but when I come home to visit Dad, it'll help to know she's been here.

From the entryway she can see most of the first level, including the kitchen with an open space in the wall over the sink that peers into the sunken living room and the informal dining room that Dad and I rarely use since Mom died. I point out small things like the patio door off the kitchen, and the closed door down a short hallway where Dad's room is as we walk by. The garage and workshop are off the dining room and even though I open the door for her to go inside, she doesn't budge.

"Oh, hell no. If you got to see my room, it's only fair I get to see yours." Her eyes twinkle with humor and something else I can't quite place.

"I didn't know you wanted in my bedroom so badly, hummingbird. You should have said something earlier." Tossing her a wink over my shoulder, I head back toward the entrance and continue past it to a set of three doors.

"That's a guest bedroom and bathroom," I say, pointing to the door on the right and the one at the end of the hall. "And that one is mine."

She waits patiently for me to open it, which is surprising

given how excited she seems to check it out, and when I finally do, I motion for her to step inside. I follow her into the tidy room with a bed that looks untouched. I can't even remember the last time I stayed here for more than a few hours. Has it truly been since before the semester started?

Hayliel walks around the room, trailing her finger over my dresser and the shelf filled with medals and awards from my past. She stops at one near the end, glancing at me over her shoulder.

"You were in flying competitions?"

"I was," I say, smiling sadly.

"But not anymore?" Hayliel asks tentatively.

"Not anymore. Flying was something I did with my mom. She was one of the fastest flyers the guild had ever seen, and I had hoped to match her. We were always playing around on her days off, practicing maneuvers or testing for speed, but it never felt like I was competing, if that makes sense. Racing on that island was actually the first time I'd done anything like that since she passed." A sudden pang takes over me. Mom would have loved that island.

"I'm sorry," she says, her body rigid like she wants to come over and comfort me, but she's stopping herself. "If I had known ..."

"It's alright. To be honest, flying with you felt the same in a way. Carefree. Fun. I think it might have been good for me."

She looks like she wants to say more but chooses not to, turning back around to continue her trek around my room. Once again, she stops, but this time she stares at the photo in the frame on my bedside table.

Even though I'm not next to her, I have that picture memorized. It's of me and Mom on the last good day we had together before she was taken. We'd gone to the park and played with the tiny boats on the pond, then grabbed ice cream on the way home. It's been so long now that parts of that day are beginning to fade in my memory, and it fucking hurts. I can't even remember which ice cream flavor we had.

I don't know how long Hayliel has been at my side, but she grabs my hand. "What was she like?"

"The sweetest. Like, eat too much candy and need to throw up, kind of sweet, but everyone loved her. She thought of others in everything she did, always trying to make someone smile or help ease the strain from someone else. She was too good to have gone out the way she did."

"What happened to your mom is a tragedy. I know it doesn't even come close to comparing, but she's always with you. In here." She presses her hand to my chest, right above my heart. "And even though I never got to meet her, I think she'd be proud of the man you've become."

Her words hit me like a sucker punch. Mom would hate how I've treated Hayliel. She wouldn't be proud of me for that. But maybe, if I keep making amends and continue to do better with this incredible angel in front of me, someday Mom will be.

Electricity sparks beneath my skin where Hayliel's hand rests on my chest. The energy in the room builds until it feels like a living, breathing entity, and all I want to do is pull her into me and show her just how much I care for her. But fear of rejection and a worry that I'll fuck things up when we're *finally* making progress has me pulling back. She's with Raphael and Theo, and despite what Theo said to me about sharing, I'm trying fucking hard to respect them.

I think I've caught a flash of disappointment on her face, but before I can study it for too long, it's gone. Probably for the best.

"Come on. Let me show you the workshop."

She follows me across the empty house without a word, watching as I pull a key from my pocket and unlock the workshop door. When she steps inside, she gasps.

"You weren't kidding," she says, looking around. "This place is perfect for experimenting with my sunfire!"

Finally, it feels like I can bring something to the table that the other assholes can't. And yeah, I probably shouldn't keep calling them assholes, but sometimes I can be a bitter, jealous piece of shit. Sue me.

"There's the small forge Dad uses, though he hasn't had much time for it lately. And beside that is his hammer and anvil where he makes the steel sing."

"It must be fascinating to watch." She sounds intrigued.

"It is. Maybe he'll let us both watch sometime." I regret the words as soon as they're out of my mouth. It's not that I don't want her to meet Dad or spend as much time here as possible, but it's just not realistic. And truthfully, I'm not sure that I could handle her here all the time and not get hopeful for more.

She smiles, looking like she wants to say something, but I

change the subject. "There's a foundry there where he can melt down metal and mold it into something else. That's how I made my first dagger. It was pretty much the ugliest thing ever, but I was proud to carry it around with me because I made it with my own two hands."

"Do you still have it?"

"No." I don't elaborate. After Mom died, I was inconsolable. It didn't help that Dad shut himself off from everyone, including me, and it felt like I'd be alone forever. I spent most of my time in the woods, chucking that dagger at a tree and wishing it was the demons who took Mom from me. I lost it out there somewhere and haven't seen it since.

It shouldn't be so hard to share that with her, but the words get stuck in my throat.

Moving on, I say, "Dad polishes the items he makes at that table over there, and this one he uses for filing, bending, and whatever else he needs the space for."

She spreads her hands over the metal table top, stopping at the unused leg vise. "Zeke, this place is cool as hell. What kind of things does he make down here?"

I hesitate for a moment, but decide to open up to her. "Not much these days, but over the years since Mom died, he's tried to figure out how to make his own sunblades. Unsuccessful, of course, especially now that we know exactly how they're made, but he tried all the same."

At my words, Hayliel straightens her spine and looks at me with sheer determination. "If I can learn how to make them,

I'll supply him and the guild with as many as they need to take down the demons hunting our city. And if I can help avenge your mother, I will."

The truth of her words is a tangible thing. How could I have been so wrong about this angel? I thought she was just like all the other girls I've met. Fickle and selfish. But she doesn't carry an ounce of those traits.

"Thank you," I tell her, my voice not as strong as I'd like, but if she notices, she doesn't say anything. Instead, she just walks around the room, picking up tongs and other items with curiosity.

While I watch her, I can't help but think about how glad I am to have kept her from Dad and Azrael. If Uriel knows she survived an angel blade, it's because someone at the guild told him. As much as I want to trust them, I'm beginning to doubt that anyone at that damn place is trustworthy. And if Uriel is connected to whoever the mole is at the guild, then things are dire indeed. Now more than ever, we need to find out who it is so we can stop playing catch up and start making moves.

I grab a small dagger from a rack in the corner and hand it to Hayliel. "We'll start small. When you're ready, I want you to try imbuing this with sunfire."

Her breath shakes when she lets out a sigh. "I'm nervous," she whispers.

"This is a judgment free zone. If it works, great. If it doesn't, we'll pivot and try again. Zero pressure here," I tell her.

"Just the fate of the entire city," she grumbles, but I pretend not to have heard.

A few minutes pass by in silence. Nothing happens, and I can tell Hayliel is getting frustrated already. "Talk me through what happened the first time you summoned it. What were you thinking? Feeling? Explain it to me. Maybe we can find something to use."

She nods, eyes trained on the wall behind me as she relives that moment in her mind. "I was scared. Terrified, actually. I knew the little cocoon I'd made with my wings wouldn't protect me from an entire horde. But then I heard your voice, and the voices of the others, and suddenly I wasn't as afraid. I was pissed. Anger like I've never experienced before overwhelmed me at the thought that those assholes were going to hurt you guys."

I tap my finger on my lip, taking in her words. "It sounds like deep emotions, the fear and anger for your friends and loved ones, is what brought it on that time. If you're up for it—and it's okay if you're not. This won't be easy—but if you are, close your eyes and bring forth that same anger or fear. See if it helps grasp the sunfire within you."

Listening to me, she closes her eyes, holding the small dagger just in front of her chest, and I can't look away from her beauty. She struggles when the emotions don't appear right away, her brow creasing with her mounting frustration.

"Focus on remembering what it felt like at that well, when your friends were so close to death and knowing there was nothing you could do to stop it."

The line between her delicate brows intensifies along with

her determination, and the dagger glows. It only lasts a second before it fades, gone so quickly I could have missed it with one wrongly timed blink.

A grin splits my lips as she opens her eyes, looking at the dagger for any sign that it worked. From deep within the steel, a soft yellow glow emanates. It's faint, but it's exactly what she needed to see to really know what everyone has been telling her. She *can* do this.

Excitement overtakes her until she's jumping with joy and I watch her, half considering joining her. She gently places the dagger on the workbench and throws her arms around me. Hell, we don't even know if what she imbued is enough to take down a demon, but it's enough to give the hope of more. A brighter future. A real chance to take those bastards down and avenge all the angels they've taken from this world.

Her energy fuels my own until I pick her up, her legs wrapping around my waist while I twirl us around. "You did it," I whisper in her ear.

Her hands trail across my shoulders and up my neck, sending shivers down my spine. "I did it," she says, pulling back just enough to grip both sides of my face before diving in to plant a kiss on my lips.

It barely lasts a second, just enough to tease me with what I could have before she jumps out of my arms. She presses her fingers to her mouth and looks at me like she thinks I'm mad at her. "I'm sorry," she says, cheeks turning red. "I know you don't want ..."

Is this what Theo was talking about? And Raphael? Have I truly been such an asshole that she thinks I'm disinterested? But how could she, after everything we've shared? The kiss at her parents' house, that night in my dorm. How can she not see how enthralled I am?

"Fuck it," I say and haul her into me, placing my lips on hers. She gasps in shock and I use the moment to delve my tongue forward, stroking it against hers. The groan that leaves her lips is sultry as she digs at my shirt like she's trying to weld us together, get us as close as angelically possible, so there's not an ounce of space between us. I allow it, feeling like for once we're on the same page.

Gripping her ass, I lift her into my arms. Just like before, she wraps her legs around me, grinding against my erection until I growl. "Feel this?" I thrust against her. "This is what you do to me," I say against her mouth, feeling wild and out of control.

"Zeke," she breathes, making me lose the small ounce of restraint I had to let her take the lead.

If she was unsure how obsessed I am before, she'll have no doubts after today.

I turn toward the workbench and set her down, being very careful to move the blade we imbued earlier out of the way. "I need to taste you, hummingbird." She doesn't protest when I flick open the button of her pants or pull the zipper down. All she does is lift up so I can pull them and her underwear down, revealing her slick heat to me.

I don't waste any time spreading her thighs. Her pretty pink pussy glistens, beckoning me forward until I burrow my face between her legs. She rests them on my shoulders, gripping my hair as I devour her, sucking and stroking, using just my tongue to fuck her until she moans.

Hayliel tastes like a freshly picked peach on a summer day. Sweet and bright. I would gladly feast on her every day for the rest of my life. That thought hits me like a brick, but I don't focus on it now. Not when she's spread out beneath me like this.

"More."

I smile against her and give in to her demands. If she wants more, I'll give it to her.

My tongue laps against her clit while I push one finger, then two inside her wet warmth. She stretches around my fingers, soft gasps escaping her lips, and when I pump my fingers, she tosses her head back.

My dick is rock solid while I watch, but as much as I want to pull it out and replace my fingers with it, I hold back. This isn't about me. This is about her. Her needs and wants, and making sure she feels every ounce of attraction I have for her, even if that means keeping my dick tucked away.

"Zeke," she moans, "I'm so close."

"I know, baby." My fingers pulse, pressing against that special place inside that I know turns her feral, and when her eyes flash open, I'm positive she'll fall apart in mere seconds. I suck her sensitive little nub into my mouth and she shatters, her pussy clenching around my fingers like she'll never let me go.

Slowing my movements, I don't let up, letting her ride out

the orgasm for as long as possible before standing upright. Her eyes are hooded and full of desire as she pulls me up for a kiss, not at all caring that her own juices coat my tongue.

The kiss turns needy, more demanding, right as the door to the workshops opens and my dad says, "Zeke, what—Oh. I, uh, I'll come back."

Hayliel turns to stone beneath me, with her eyes glued to the now closed door. "Oh fuck. Did your dad just …?"

I chuckle. "Looks like he did."

"Why are you laughing!" She swats my arm, pushing me away so she can jump down off the table. "Your dad just caught me in his workshop with my pants around my fucking ankles," she says, keeping her voice low as she pulls the aforementioned pants up.

"Want to meet him?"

She glares at me; her face still flushed from her orgasm and probably from the embarrassment of my dad walking in on us. "Not like I have a choice now, is it?"

Her response only makes me laugh more. I pull her into me, kissing the top of her head lightly. "I'm sorry. It'll be fine, hummingbird. This is just as awkward for him as it is for you. For us."

"Not helping, Ezekiel."

The clock on the far wall tells me he's home earlier than expected, and unless the time is wrong, I'm damn near late for my shift at the guild. I hand her the knife she'd imbued and say, "Tuck that away where he can't see. Looks like we lost track of time, and I need to leave for the guild. I'll drop you off at your parents' place first, though."

Her anger falls away as she looks at me. "Are you sure? I don't want you to get in trouble."

"Don't worry about me. Your safety is more important. Unfortunately, I don't think we're getting out of here without at least an introduction. Think you can handle that?"

She drops her face into her hands and sighs before straightening. It's a little terrifying how easily she puts on a mask of indifference, but I can't deny it'll serve her now.

We exit the workshop and find Dad in the kitchen making a sandwich. He doesn't turn to us right away. "Ah, sorry about that back there. I didn't realize Zeke had anyone over."

"We're sorry too. I didn't think you'd be home this early. Dad, this is my friend Hayliel. Hayliel, this is my dad, Kirach."

"Girlfriend, actually," Hayliel says, and I damn near choke on air. "It's nice to meet you, though I wish it were under less awkward circumstances." She blushes, and it's the most beautiful thing I've ever seen.

I can't say I don't love the sound of it. Her as mine.

"Girlfriend, huh? I didn't know you had one of those." Dad shoots me a soft smile. "I'd love to get to know the girl who finally caught my son's eye, if you have some time?"

I cough. "I'm actually late for a shift, and Hayliel has to get to her parents'."

"But another time, for sure," Hayliel adds, making my dad smile.

"I'd like that. It was nice to meet you, young lady. Son, I'd like to chat with you once you're finished at the guild, if you don't mind."

"You got it," I tell him, pulling Hayliel back out the front door. "Talk later!"

Then we take off in the sky, with my *girlfriend* giggling uncontrollably.

21

HAYLIEL

Mom's reaction to my unexpected visit is exactly what I hoped for. I probably should have let them know I was stopping by, but I kind of wanted to catch them unawares. There's so much happening over here, and I wouldn't put it past them trying to hide the worst of it from me. Showing up without warning them first ensures they couldn't pull something like that.

I trust them. But I also know them enough to understand just how much they want to shield me. It comes from a place of love, so I suppose I can't be too upset. Besides, it's not as if I can really judge them when I'm withholding information, too. Someday I'll tell them I'm a Seraphim. Maybe even soon, if I can get a firm handle on this power.

Dad isn't home yet, but Mom assures me he's on his way while we sit and gab over a slice of pecan pie. It's absolute heaven. I wonder if Mom would consider selling her baked goods to the Sinful Cafe or even any of the bookshops in the other districts. Given the recent issues with Fallen though, I doubt any of the Pure owned shops would consider doing business with her. Their loss.

"So, where's that boyfriend of yours? I hope we didn't scare him off too bad," Mom says, jolting me out of my thoughts.

"No, not yet anyway. He dropped me off but was late for a shift at the guild, otherwise I know he'd have come in to say hi." We've lied to both of our parents now about the aspect of our relationship. I don't know what it was that propelled me to tell Zeke's father that I was his girlfriend. Maybe it's because that's the lie we told my parents, or that I didn't want him to think I was just some random angel putting out for his son.

Isn't that exactly what you were doing? The snarky voice inside my head asks, but I smother her down and focus back on Mom.

"He's a gentleman, that one. I'm glad you have someone that looks out for you, Haylie-bear."

"Me too," I tell her, taking way too big of a bite of pie just to keep from talking.

What would have happened if Zeke's dad hadn't walked in? Would we have taken things further?

Who am I kidding? Of course we would have. I'm so fucking conflicted. In the moment, being with Zeke felt right, but now that I'm back in reality, I don't understand how it could feel that way, knowing everything I have with Raph and Theo. Not that we've labeled anything, but still. I betrayed them, and now my actions might ruin it all.

"Is everything alright?" Mom asks, concern lining the delicate features of her face.

Shit. I stuff everything about Raphael, Theo, Zeke, and my indiscretions into a crate in my mind and tape it shut. I can mull over it all later, but now isn't the time.

"Sorry, Mom. I'm good." I'm preparing to ask about how their telepathy training is going when the front door opens and Dad calls out.

"I'm home! Is she still here?"

"As if I'd leave without seeing you," I tell him, standing to receive one of his infamous bear hugs.

"What brings you to our neck of the woods?" Dad asks, tossing a glance at Mom and the remains of our pie on the table. He doesn't waste a second grabbing a slice for himself.

"I was in the neighborhood and wanted to stop by to see how your telepathy training was going. Mom's been giving me regular updates, but I figured it was time for a test." Tabbris and Yofie really came through for them with their notes, providing enough detail that even a child could probably follow along. Their kindness never fails to astound me.

Dad sits next to Mom, and they both reach a hand out to me while entwining their other hands together.

We're getting the hang of it with physical touch, Mom says through our mental connection.

And we've managed it without a few times, but it takes some practice, Dad adds, his face set in concentration.

Keep practicing. Every day. It's like a muscle. The more you use it, the easier it'll become. I don't push further, not wanting them to hear the fear behind the words, but needing them to take it seriously.

As one, they break the physical connection and close their eyes. Mom speaks through the bond first.

It's part of our routine.

She's better at it.

I smile. "It was tough for me at first, too, but I'm so happy at the progress you're making!"

"We practice every morning during breakfast and at night before bed," Mom says. "More throughout the day, if we can. It's actually quite fun."

"Good. I'd like to experiment with our connection over a distance. Once I get back to campus, I'll test the bond." I stand, happy to see them making progress.

"You're leaving already?" Dad asks.

Sadness seeps in. I wish they could come with me. If they were closer, away from this damn district, maybe I'd stop worrying about them. Maybe I could keep them safe. Though I can't even manage to stay out of trouble, so perhaps it's better they keep their distance.

"I've got to get back, but we'll see each other again soon."

Leaving them is painful, but I take to the sky and do my best to get back to campus in one piece. My neck is sore from constantly checking my surroundings, but I arrive on my balcony without issue. I don't waste a second hiding the imbued dagger and changing into my workout gear. Energy coils around me in waves. I need to let some of it out before I drown in it.

I avoid everyone until I get to Zeke's private training room, where Theo is already working. He's coated in sweat, the muscles on his arms bulging as he pummels a punching bag with a drawing of a demon stuck to it. His eyes hold more determination and anger than I've seen from him before. It's like he's not just fighting an inanimate bag. He's fighting something far more real.

His past.

Not wanting to interrupt him, I turn to leave, but he calls out before I can reach the door.

"Wait," he says, breathless from the beating he'd just given the bag. "You don't have to leave. Come join me."

I hesitate, not wanting to intrude. "Are you sure?"

"Positive. How are you?" He grabs a towel, wiping the sweat from his brow.

"Fine. Happy it's not my face stuck to that bag," I tease, but my heart isn't in it. I can't just act like things are normal when I just had my hands all over Zeke.

He stares at me for a long time, long enough that I start to feel uncomfortable. Shit. I didn't do a very good job at selling that, did I? But, Theo being Theo, he doesn't press me on it and just returns his focus back to the bag.

While I stretch, I watch him. He isn't moving as intensely as he was when I first arrived, but that look of resolve is still on his face. When I feel limber enough, I press a button on the side of the wall to drop a second punching bag, then grab a couple of fake daggers from the shelf of practice weapons. Between lessons with Mira, Zeke, and the others, I'm feeling far more confident in being able to handle myself, but even I'm not fool enough to think what little I know will be enough.

Like with everything else in life, there's always room for growth.

Shoving thoughts of my complicated relationships and friendships into a dark corner of my mind, I get lost in training. Or, at least I try to.

With Theo so close after what I did earlier, my betrayal eats me alive.

As if sensing the maelstrom of my thoughts, he approaches me with two bottles of water in hand. I didn't even notice that he'd stopped punching the stupid bag.

I take the offering, swallowing a few mouthfuls of the cold liquid before setting the bottle on the floor.

"What's really going on, firefly?"

Shit. I don't want to lie to him, but I haven't figured out yet how I'm going to tell them. Can I handle it if they hate me?

The answer is far too obvious. My connection with Raphael and Theo is one I've grown to rely on more than I probably should. I rest my forehead against the cool leather of the bag and take a deep, steadying breath. "I fucked up, Theo."

"Hey," he says, placing a hand on my shoulder. "Whatever happened, it's probably not as bad as you think. Talk to me."

"You say that now, but when you find out, you're going to hate me."

"I could never hate you."

Without bothering to pick my head up, I spill my dirty deed. "You know how I went to Zeke's house earlier? Because his dad has a workshop, we thought might be a great, private, and controlled place to practice imbuing sunfire. Well, I was able to imbue the smallest amount, just enough to cause a faint glow on the blade, and in our excitement, we kissed. Well, a little more than kissing, but his dad walked in before … ya know."

My face feels like it's on fire. Theo hasn't said a word, and even though I've avoided looking at him thus far, I can't help but sneak a peek at him from the corner of my eye. To my surprise, he doesn't look angry at all.

"Come here," he says, holding out a hand for me to take.

I hesitate but take it anyway, following him to the benches along the back wall. We sit, but he says nothing and my thoughts spiral out of control. Is he mad at me? Upset? If he is, he fucking hides it well because it's almost like he doesn't care, which is somehow worse. I wish he'd say something and put me out of my damn misery.

With my hand still tucked in his, he finally breaks the painful silence. "It would have been more than fine if things had gone further between you and Zeke today. Raphael always assumed you had history together."

I look away, focusing on a speck of dirt on the floor. "We slept together at the start of term but, wait. What do you mean, it would have been fine? I hooked up with someone else behind your back. Aren't you mad?"

Theo chuckles, causing my confusion to grow. "I'm sure Raphael will take it a little harder, but it's not like we haven't noticed the tension between you and the Fallen house leader. We knew this was a possibility."

My face falls at his words, and I feel like the biggest asshole imaginable. "You knew I'd cheat on you?"

"No, no. Not that." He squeezes my hand. "And just like kissing me isn't cheating on Raphael, it's the same with Ezekiel. Or at least, it can be if that's something you'd be interested in?"

I stare at him now, completely dumbfounded by the turn of this conversation. And even though I *think* I know what he's saying, I need to hear the words. "What do you mean?"

"I know we haven't put any official labels on our relationship yet, and that's more than fine with me, but have you considered adding Zeke to our dynamic and dating all of us?"

Seconds turn into minutes, and still I keep quiet. I won't lie and say I haven't considered it. Hell, Dina even joked about it on the tower before everything went to shit, but could I even do that?

Theo watches me process his question with an odd look of hope on his face.

Is this what he wants? To share me?

I suppose it makes sense, given how willing he and Raphael

are, but it's different with them. They actually get along.

If he's being vulnerable, then maybe so can I.

"Well, if we're being honest, I have thought about it. But I never considered it an actual option. Zeke doesn't exactly get along with you and Raph, and until recently, I thought the guy hated me."

A soft chuckle escapes Theo's lips, and he nudges his shoulder against mine. "That guy hasn't hated you for a single day in his life. But he has things he needs to work through, same as all of us. When he's ready, I'm sure he'll explain. For now, consider what I said, and if you decide all three of us would make great boyfriends, we can meet up and see about making things official."

"You're serious," I say when I realize he's not pretending or joking in the slightest. When he nods, I don't let myself think about my response too long or I'll lose my nerve. "Okay. I'll think about it."

His smile widens until he's the happiest he's ever looked. I remember he told me once that Raphael was willing to share me because he knew it would make me happy. From Theo's reaction to the small knowledge that I'm even thinking about making things official, I think he must feel the same way.

"Don't worry about what happened with Zeke today. If you want, I can tell Raph and let him know what you're considering."

I didn't miss the fact that somehow Theo knows what it is Zeke's working through while I don't. As much as I want to ask how he knows, now isn't the time. Instead, I shift closer to him. "I truly don't know what I ever did to deserve you," I whisper, welling with tears.

"I ask myself that question every day about *you*, firefly." He wipes away the stray tear that's fallen down my cheek and I lean into his touch.

When I came in here, I was so focused on my own personal shit that I didn't pay attention to what was happening right in front of me. Now that I've calmed down and things don't seem as bleak, I remember how Theo was when I stepped into the room.

As I gaze up at him now, the pain I saw in his eyes at first is still there. "Can I ask you something?"

22

THEO

I stare into Hayliel's dark blue eyes, knowing I'd answer any question she could think to ask me. "Anything. Always."

"How come you're training so hard? You're a talented fighter, so it doesn't really seem like you need the extra practice." She keeps her voice soft, seeming genuinely curious.

I swallow, unsure how to answer, and she squeezes my hand reassuringly, mimicking my actions from earlier. "It's alright if you don't want to talk about it. I understand."

Of course she does. This beautiful, selfless angel in front of me has so much compassion and empathy in her heart. It's shocking for someone who's been through as much as she has.

I don't want her to think that I'm holding back because of

anything she's done, and in truth, I'm not even sure why I am. "I've wanted to tell you for a while now, but I just didn't know how." I sigh, sitting up straighter and preparing to share the horrors of my past. "You know how I sometimes grow a little distant, mostly when demons are around, though sometimes all it takes is just the mention of them, like at the assembly, for me to zone out."

She nods. "Or like at the barn."

I give her a sad smile, not even wanting to think about the way I cowered that day. "Well, those are panic attacks, sort of. Past trauma rearing its ugly head, or so I'm told."

Her brows turn inward. "Past trauma?"

Swallowing takes more effort than it should, but finally I manage to speak. "When I was a teenager, I was best friends with this shy girl who didn't really fit in with my other friends. Serah was beyond kind, and when she was comfortable around someone, she'd be the weirdest angel, but in the best possible way. My cheeks always hurt from smiling so much whenever I hung out with her."

My heart fractures just saying her name out loud, something I haven't done in far too long.

I can tell Hayliel has questions, but however curious she might be, she stays silent, letting me continue at my own pace.

It makes me fall for her even more.

"A friend of mine took an interest in her romantically. He was always hounding me to set them up or invite her to come out with us to the skatepark so she could get to know him. I always refused until finally I just gave in and asked her. I didn't expect her to say yes, but she did. If I had just kept my mouth shut, she'd still be alive." My eyes prick, tears threatening to build, but I hold them back.

She squeezes my hand gently. "I'm so sorry."

Pushing through the hurt, I continue. "The skatepark had always been safe. Rundown? Absolutely. But in all the months we spent there after school, we never saw any violence. Except for that day."

I stare off at the far wall of mirrors but don't notice my reflection. "A demon showed up that afternoon. The asshole killed my best friend, and it was all my fault." Try as I might to hold it together, the words come out fractured. Broken. Just like me.

"Oh, Theo," Hayliel says, tears running down her cheeks. "It's the demon's fault. Not yours."

"No. She was only there because of me! Because I invited her to hook up with that piece of shit coward. Do you know he ran away? He never tried to save her." My hands ball into fists, shaking with the rage flowing through me.

She latches on to me, her strength pulsing into me. "What he did was awful, and what happened to Serah is a tragedy, but neither of those things is your fault. She chose to go. The demon chose to attack. Neither of those are things you could have controlled, Theo."

I finally look at her, my eyes burning with the pain of every-thing I couldn't change. "When we almost lost you, it brought everything back. I couldn't save Serah back then, and suddenly it was happening all over again, and I couldn't save you either."

Remembering that day hurts just as much, if not more. I thought we'd lost her, and I honestly don't know that I would have survived if we had.

She grabs my face in her small hands, staring straight into my eyes. "I'm right here, and I'm not going anywhere. I'll help you train, all of us will. And if you ever come face to face with the demon who took your friend, you'll make him pay, and I will gladly help you do it."

I sense the depth of her conviction through every cell in my body, and suddenly I'm admitting things I should probably keep inside. But life is too short. Nothing is guaranteed, and I need her to know how I feel.

"I love you, Hayliel. You don't have to say it back, but I just needed you to know."

Her eyes widen in surprise, but I don't give her the opportunity to reply before my lips are on hers, my tongue teasing, bolstered with every ounce of feeling I possess for her.

Her touch turns hungry as she pulls me closer still, but it's not enough. Never close enough.

She straddles me as the kiss turns feral, grinding herself against my trapped erection and shooting blasts of pleasure through me. Fucking hell. This woman will be the death of me.

"Theo," she pants into my ear as I trail kisses down her neck.

"I know, firefly. I'll give you what you need."

I tear off her sports bra, tipping her back and sucking a pebbled nipple into my mouth. She gasps as I tease her with my teeth, knowing exactly how she likes it.

When I switch to her other nipple, her moans fill the space around me. The way she grinds down on me, I know she's close to tipping over the edge. As much as I want her to come all over my cock, there'll be time for that after. For now, I just need her to fall apart.

Thrusting up to meet her grinding hips, I pinch one nipple and swirl my tongue over the other before sucking just a bit harder than I'd previously done until she stiffens beneath me for a microsecond as bliss takes control.

Her hips cease their movement but I don't let up, grinding against her and prolonging her orgasm tenfold. She's come so hard, the crotch of her leggings is soaked, and fuck if the sight doesn't make me almost cream my pants as well.

"I need inside of you, firefly, but I can't let you go. I'll never be able to let you go."

She pulls me up so that our lips meet, grinding on me again, and I think I might just lose my mind. With a growl, I stand with her still held against my dick and then slowly lower her to the floor.

"Take them off before I destroy them." I barely manage to get the words out as I pull my own clothes off, tossing them to the floor without a single care for where they fall.

She peels the soaked fabric of her pants down, revealing her drenched panties slick with her arousal and I drop to my knees, desperate for a taste. Her sweet scent fills my nose as I lap up her juices, thrusting my tongue over her clit until she's moaning my name, desperately close to coming again.

"I can never get enough of you," I tell her. She whimpers as I bare her completely and lick her slit one last time. "On your knees on the bench. Face the mirror."

She follows my command without question, and I stare at the beauty in front of me. The soft curves of her hips, her sleek back and plump ass. Without realizing it, I've advanced toward her. I stroke my cock, watching her give up on waiting for me to make a move and reach back to play with the metal barbel at the tip of my dick. Fuck. She turns to me, need filling her eyes, her thighs glistening with desire, and I can't hold back any longer.

I don't want any barriers between us. Not even a millimeter of space. So I step forward until my dick presses against her and groan when it slides easily between her thighs. I thrust a few times, letting my tongue explore her mouth while my hands roam over her body, pulling her hair, tweaking her nipples, and grazing over her swollen clit.

"I'm going to fuck you now, but I can't promise it'll be gentle. Can you handle me rough, baby?"

"Yes," she moans. "Please, Theo. I need—"

Her words cut off as the tip of my cock presses into her tight pussy and I swear the world tilts. I press in further, reveling in her stretching around my thickness, her core pulsing and spasming already.

"Take more of me, firefly. I know you can do it. Fuck. Just like that." As I fully seat myself inside her, our eyes meet and I press a gentle kiss to her lips.

"You are so perfect," I whisper, giving her every ounce of softness I have before my hips thrust forward like I want to destroy her. And maybe I do want to, for as surely as she destroys me, I want to be the cause of her own ruination. I want to bear witness to her crumbling apart by my touch alone.

I'm gripping her hips, probably too tight, but I'm past the point of being able to loosen my hold. I pull her back to meet my powerful thrusts. Her mouth falls open, a silent scream leaving her as each pump of my hips brings her ever closer to yet another release. And when she floods against my cock, I know I won't last long.

My balls tighten. I grunt. But by the grace of the Archangels, I manage to hold off my release a little longer.

"You can come for me again, can't you, baby? Just one more. Please. I need you to fall apart with me." The words sound unhinged, but I don't care.

I shift my hips, and when I sink in again with hard, desperate thrusts, I know I'm hitting that special place inside because her eyes roll back, body tightening for a split second before she loses control at the same moment I do. We're thrown down a tunnel of bliss, the light in the room seeming to expand and shatter all at once as I fill her sweet pussy with my cum, while her inner walls grip onto me like she never wants to let me go.

And I hope she never, ever does.

23

HAYLIEL

Monday started off with a bang in Uriel's class. Despite how fast I could fly on that island with the guys, I was back to being a slowpoke on the obstacle course, and the asshole professor refused to let up on my torture. To make matters worse, a few of the Fallen students went out of their way to shove me against the wall around almost every turn, or corner me into hitting an obstacle.

Fuckers. All of them.

The rest of my day didn't get much better. Harold the Herold put out another article, and if I was under any indication that the tides were turning in my favor, he went ahead and shat all over that idea. It shouldn't have surprised me that the entire article was filled with names I'd recognize as Uriel's little minions, all of whom were vying for my immediate expulsion.

Principal Cael hasn't called me into his office yet, but I won't be shocked when he does. Enough students have mentioned making complaints to their parents, who I'm sure will bring those forth to the principal. It's only a matter of time.

Part of me wishes I could tell them the truth about what I really am, but at this point I'm not even sure it would change anything. Nothing says they'd believe me or even care to alter their opinion of me. Sometimes hating someone gets so ingrained in who you are, it's harder to shake than just continue on as before.

Now that classes are done, Dina and I have tucked ourselves away in the cave to complete our homework while we wait for the others to join us. Her dad's been harping on her to keep her grades up, and I hate knowing that it's my fault they slipped in the first place. As soon as we're done talking about the absolute necessities, I promised her we'd go right back to school work.

Just as I finish writing the conclusion for my Chronicles of Silver City assignment, Mira walks through the cave entrance.

"You know," she says, taking a seat on the rug at our feet. "Sometimes I miss going to school here, but then I see things like this that make me reconsider."

"Girl, don't even," Dina says with a laugh. "I'd kill to be graduated and on my own."

"Yeah, well, I'm not exactly living the dream."

I don't miss the odd tone of defeat in her voice. She always seems so confident and sure. Whatever's bothering her must be big. I want to ask her about it and see if I can help, but before I can pry, Castiel arrives, followed by Raphael, Theo, and Zeke. Shit. I drop my gaze to the table, unsure of how to proceed. Theo was due to talk to Raphael and explain what happened with Zeke and what I agreed to consider. Honestly, I'm a little scared. What if Raphael is upset with me? What if he hates me?

I never even told Theo I love him in return, though I think it would have made things more complicated between all of us if I had.

I'm mentally spiraling when Zeke passes something to Castiel, who takes the item but sends him a questioning look. It's one of the amulets he'd given us.

"Do I even want to know where you got this from?"

Rubbing the back of his neck, Zeke says, "Probably best if you don't ask. Just like it's a good idea not to ask where I got this." He holds up the dark pouch he stole from the guild. "Is there anything you can tell me about this?"

"Right. Well, thank you for this," Castiel says, tucking the amulet into his breast pocket. "May I?"

Zeke hands him the pouch, and I watch in fascination as Castiel opens it and dips his forefinger and thumb inside. When they come back out, he has some sort of grainy substance pinched between them, which he rubs together before letting the particles fall back into the pouch. He smells his finger and gives the tip a small lick, which has Dina gagging.

"If I'm not mistaken, this is the ash from the demon blood

tree, found only on the grounds of the Archangels' Sanctuary."

"Do you know what the guild uses it for? I've never seen it in action before."

"Only rumors. If what I've heard is correct, this can't kill a demon, but it can definitely slow one down. I don't know the exact effect it has, though, so I wouldn't rely too heavily on this stuff."

The demon blood tree? How come I've never heard of this before? I wonder why it's only found on the grounds of the Sanctuary if all it does is slow demons down. Perhaps there are side effects that make it harmful to us?

"I agree with Castiel," I say, looking around the room. "There must be a reason this tree resides only with the Archangels. Without knowing its exact use or any side effects, we should only use it if absolutely necessary."

"It's settled, then." Zeke tucks the pouch back into his bag, surprising me by agreeing. "Now what the hell are we going to do about that bastard Uriel?"

Raphael comes to my side, pressing a kiss to the top of my head that has my chest aching. Oh, thank fuck. He's not mad. "Theo and I were thinking we could poke around his space. Maybe he has items hidden in a drawer like where you stored that silencing candle."

Castiel frowns. "While I agree that idea has some merit, I don't think two students sneaking around would go well. It's better if I go with one of you. That way if we're caught, I can help create a more solid alibi. No one will question me, a long-standing professor, but two first-year students would be quite suspicious."

"That's a good point," Theo says, looking pensive.

"I may have had a similar idea and stumbled upon Uriel's appointment book." Castiel's grin turns mischievous, which is an odd look for him, but I can't say that I hate it. "As you all know, there's no class for students on Friday thanks to some professional development Principal Cael booked for staff, and it just so happens that Uriel will be away in the afternoon."

"You won't need to be there?" I ask, wondering for the briefest moment if Principal Cael is helping us. Having the principal on our side definitely wouldn't hurt.

"I'm attending the morning session, along with half the faculty. Which means Friday afternoon seems like the perfect time to wander through his space."

"If that's the case, it'll have to be Theo that goes with you. My brother is finally back from wherever the fuck he went for work, and my darling mother is using it to get me home. I need to ask him about that special tailor, so if I want answers anytime soon, I have to go." Raphael turns his gaze to me, looking hopeful and a little nervous. "I was actually thinking that maybe you could come with me?"

Emotions zip through me. Joy that he wants to bring me home, and fear that I won't be able to keep my mouth shut against the awful things his family says. But maybe hearing what kind of shit angels they are will jolt them back to reality, because truthfully, I don't care about my relationship with his asshole parents. If they want to treat Raphael like shit, then I don't much care for their opinion.

Glancing at Zeke, images of what happened when we visited his home flash through my mind and heat rushes to my cheeks. I would die if Raphael's parents caught us doing something like that.

"Are you sure your parents will be alright with me coming?" I ask as a distraction. I wouldn't really mind if they weren't alright with it. Raphael needs to understand that he has me in his corner, and if putting up with his pissed off parents is what it takes to prove that, I will.

Besides, something tells me he could use a moderator of sorts when it comes to his brother.

"They will be if they want me to attend dinner. Plus, Raduriel is bringing his buddy from the guild so I don't see why I couldn't bring my girlfriend."

His *girlfriend*. The word sends a bolt of lust through me, along with a flash of my conversation with Theo last night. Could I really be a girlfriend to all three of them? Could I even handle having three boyfriends to myself?

Ah, hell. Who am I kidding? I'd be in heaven.

"If Briathos will be there, just be careful. We don't know who we can trust at the guild yet, though I don't think he's the mole." Shifting his gaze to mine, Zeke says, "For what it's worth, I think you should go with Raphael."

My eyes widen in shock despite my best efforts to remain unaffected. Since when does he think I should spend more time with my "Pure boyfriends"?

"Pick your jaw up off the floor. It's not that shocking," Zeke teases, seeming even more out of character. "If Theo and Castiel are busy, and I'm stuck at the guild, I'd rather know you're someplace safer than on campus."

"Dina would be more than happy to keep me company," I argue, though I don't know why. I want to go with Raphael, so why the hell am I doing this? Ugh. Zeke's attitude change has thrown everything out of whack.

She grimaces. "I would, but Dad wants me home. I leave Thursday after classes finish."

"Then I'll go with Raph, but not because I'm a weakling who needs protection. Because I want to." I squeeze Raph's hand. "And I want updates the moment you have them," I tell Theo and Castiel in my most no-nonsense voice.

"We all know you aren't a weakling, sunshine. But we'd feel better knowing you're with one of us and appreciate that you're willing to follow along. I'm really glad you'll be coming home with me." Raph touches my cheek, thumb brushing over my skin, and all I can do is nod.

Regardless of how awkward or troublesome this meeting might be for me, knowing it's going to help him is all I need to feel good about it.

24

HAYLIEL

It's late, but I can't sleep.

My mind whirls with impossible scenarios and outcomes. So many things have happened lately that I can't seem to shut my thoughts off. It doesn't help that sometimes, when I close my eyes, I see that scarred demon again, his taunting voice ringing in my head.

With a huff, I toss the blankets off and get out of bed. There's no point lying around when I could be doing something useful. I dress quickly, stashing the books I'll need and my slate in a bag, then head downstairs to the Fallen library to work on a project for history class. We're supposed to write a report on an angel of our choosing.

Castiel would probably hate to know that I'm working on it in the middle of the night, especially now that he knows everything else going on, but it's that or drive myself wild trying to sleep.

I don't run into a single soul on my trek down the stairs, and the library is blissfully empty. Being alone used to make me uncomfortable. Insignificant and invisible. But other than the friends I trust, I'd rather be alone than surrounded by angels plotting against me, or onlookers waiting to switch loyalties depending on how the wind blows.

Setting my things down on one of the empty tables, I get comfortable. When Castiel first gave us this project, I struggled to decide which angel to write about. Then it hit me, and I couldn't imagine a better angel. I ended up calling Esther from the photo parlor to ask if she'd mind if I wrote about her grandmother.

She'd been thrilled that I thought of her. So thrilled that the very next day she delivered an old family tome that held a ton of neat information. Each story kept me captivated, enough that I'd honestly probably read through them even without a project.

Despite the late hour, it doesn't take long before her grandmother's epic stories have me hooked. I'm so invested that it takes a moment longer than usual to notice the creepy feeling causing the hair on the back of my neck to rise. A faint scuffling comes from beyond the library doors, but I don't see any light to announce the presence of someone else. Maybe it's only another student grabbing a midnight snack?

I listen for a few more minutes, but the sound doesn't come again. This building might be modern and well built, but it's still fairly old. It could be anything.

I fall back into the story, this one about Esther's grandmother and her innate control over her angelic powers. She'd been known amongst her family to assist all new members in developing their powers. Honestly, her thought process is quite fascinating, enough that I pause my reading to take notes on my slate. Maybe her methods could help me get a better handle on not only the sunfire I'm supposed to be able to wield at will, but also the weather manipulation we're learning.

I don't get far before that scuffling sound is back, but this time it's followed by a steady tapping.

The longer I listen, the louder it gets, until my pulse thrums beneath my skin and I can't shake the feeling that I need to leave.

Now.

I don't waste any time packing up my things, tossing everything into my small bag and scurrying toward the window. Someone whispers from beyond the library doors as I'm climbing out into the cool night air.

Before I manage to fully close the window, the library door opens.

Two students enter the room, followed by a masked figure built like a brick shit house. The students I recognize from our brief altercation near the beach. Fallen.

With the mask on, I can't work out who the other figure

is, but something tells me I've never met them before. Their presence alone makes my heart beat frantically. From the build, I'd guess it's a man, but whether it's an angel or something else entirely, I don't know. They're tall and imposing, covered head to toe in black clothes.

The trio look around the room, searching, but for what?

Something tells me they're looking for me.

Pressing my back into the wall beside the window, I keep still. I know I should run, should move, and get the fuck away from here, but if I stay, maybe I can learn what these fuckers want.

In a voice so deep, it's as if it came from the very night itself, it says, "I thought you said she was here?" Without needing to see with my own eyes, I know this comes from the masked being. Something about the energy has me on high alert.

"She was, I swear it! I—" The squeak of noise from inside has me desperate to look, but I stay put, holding tight to the protection amulet hanging on a chain around my neck.

"Well, where is she now?"

I don't hear a reply, only sharp breaths until a third voice says, "We don't know, but she can't have gone far."

"Then find her!" it growls fiercely, and I jump into action.

I don't know who or what this cloaked figure is, but I know in the very marrow of my bones that I won't enjoy finding out.

I consider flying up to my balcony, but that's too risky. Without my flight jacket, my wings will act like a beacon, and besides, it's the first place they'll look for me.

But where else can I go?

I take off in a run, unsure of my final destination. All I know is I can't stay here.

Keeping off the path, I stick to the forest. It's slower and louder, but my brain isn't working enough to care. I can't get caught. Not when something tells me they weren't coming to find me for just any old reason. Their intent, even if the Fallen students don't realize it, was malicious.

Breaking free of the forest, I push onward. Light from the arena illuminates far too much, so I run parallel to it until I can curve around the back. A twig snaps from somewhere behind me, almost causing me to trip as my heart goes haywire. Fear takes over, forcing my limbs to move faster, push harder. Enough that I almost slip on a few fallen leaves and branches, cutting my pants on the thorny bushes, but at least I stay upright.

It's only when I see the fence that lines the backside of Power house that I realize where my feet have taken me. *Raphael.*

Air escapes me in big bursts, but not from being out of breath. I'm scared. Terrified.

What if Raph doesn't answer?

Once again, I consider letting my wings out just long enough to fly up to his balcony, but it's too risky. If the angels from the Fallen library see them, they'll know where I'm going and it'll put Raphael at risk. I can't do that. I won't.

I'd rather be caught and taken than cause him any harm.

Resolved, I sneak around the far side of Power house and silently enter through the front door. I don't run into anyone on my trek to Raph's room, and by the time I knock on his door, my heartbeat has returned to an *almost* normal frequency.

It takes three knocks before he answers, looking like he'd just rolled out of bed. "Sunshine?" he asks, sleepily.

I feel awful for waking him, but it doesn't stop me from falling into his arms. He catches me, picking me up into his arms and cradling me like a baby.

"What happened?"

A sob escapes me, yet no tears fall. It's like my mouth forgets how to form words because I can't get any to pass my lips.

He carries me into his room, shutting the door behind him and leading us to the bed where he settles us both. We just sit there, his arms wrapped around me, soothing away the fear holding me tightly in its grasp.

"You're safe now. I won't let anything happen to you." He doesn't pressure me to answer his questions or even speak, content enough to just sit with me until finally I pull away.

"I'm sorry," I start, feeling awkward.

"You have nothing to apologize for. Ever."

I chew on my lip, unsure of where to begin.

"What happened, sunshine? Did someone harm you?"

I shake my head. "Not physically." Then I tell him everything. How I couldn't sleep, leaving out the part about my nightmares for now, and how I went to the library to work on a project instead. In a voice that doesn't even sound like my own, I explain what happened in the library, what I overheard, and how I ran straight to him without even realizing.

He pulls me in closer until I can feel his heart banging against his ribcage. It soothes me.

"I'm so glad you're okay," he whispers against my skin. Then his voice turns darker. "The pieces of shit coming after you need to fucking pay."

I nod against him, letting my fear turn into rage. I'm so fucking tired. Tired of being scared. Tired of being targeted. I don't want to run and hide anymore.

"Did they mention Uriel at all? If the Fallen were there, he must be involved."

Shaking my head, I say, "Not by name, but I came to the same assumption as you."

"What about the masked man? Did you recognize him, even a little?"

A chill works its way down my spine just thinking about him. For a second, I can almost hear his deep, smoky voice.

"No. I don't think so." My teeth chatter. When did it get so cold in here?

"You're freezing," he says, pressing his warmth against me. "Come with me."

I follow him to the closet where he tells me to strip down. He rummages through his belongings, and by the time I'm undressed, he's holding out a spare shirt for me to wear. I put it on, loving that it smells of him.

Raphael kisses the top of my head, and I feel a little warmth returning to my limbs. He pulls me back to bed, motioning for me to get beneath the sheets before grabbing a book from his nightstand and joining me. On top of his bedside table sits a new frame with a picture of the three of us at Esther's shop. My heart squeezes at the fact that he keeps us so close to him while he sleeps. I burrow beneath the blankets, a giddiness bubbling beneath my skin and wiping away a little of my fear. His sheets are silken smooth. Far nicer than any I've ever owned.

We rest against pillows, and I snuggle into Raphael's side. "What do you have there?" I ask, curious about the weathered book in his hands and wanting a diversion from the swirling emotions in my gut.

"This is my uncle Isaac's journal. The guy was a bit eccentric, so keep that in mind, but I wanted to show you something I found earlier." He carefully opens the book. Although the page is torn and half of it is missing, one word is unmistakable.

Seraphim.

My gaze shoots to his, and he smiles boyishly.

"Like I said, he was bizarre, so I'm taking everything with a grain of salt. If this is true, though, then he would have spoken with the twins Castiel mentioned."

I try not to snatch the book when he passes it to me, being extra careful with the sensitive paper.

I finally did it. After months of trying, I met with the Seraphim twins. Ingrid and O...From the articles, I would have sworn they looked alike, but...

spot the differences. It's easy to feel just how pow-erful th...stomach. Having been raised in squalor, I expected the...edges. But they were kinder than most of my own fami...I didn't mean to learn their secret. It was purely by acci...I would take it with me to the grave.The information detailed below could change...

I reread the passage three times before finally looking away from it and back up at Raphael. "You don't happen to have the rest of this, do you?" I ask him, though I already know the answer.

He kisses my head, his expression grim. "I'm afraid not. But I refuse to believe that my crazed relative was the only one who discovered their secret. The information has to be out there somewhere. It would be too cruel for it to have ended with this journal and their deaths."

He's right. I don't want to believe that the secret Isaac discov-ered is lost to us now. With everything going on, I *can't* believe it.

Shifting on the bed beside me, he tilts my face up with one finger beneath my chin. "I'm not giving up, sunshine. Not by a long shot. I'll rummage through every book, every cupboard, and every drawer if I have to. You deserve to know as much as possible about your heritage."

Words won't seem to pass my lips, no matter how hard I try. Tears fill my eyes, blurring my sight.

This man.

From the very first day, he's been there. Supporting me. Sticking up for me. Making me feel worthy. I wonder if he understands how much of a difference his actions have made.

When the tears finally fall, he wipes them away. "I think it goes without saying that you're spending the night with me."

25

RAPHAEL

She grins up at me, and even though the smile doesn't quite reach her eyes, I know it won't take long to convince her. It's obvious what's holding her back, and I hate that she fears the angels who came after her. I hate that she's worried about bringing them here.

"Let me protect you, sunshine. And before you say anything, it's not because you're weak. The opposite, in fact. Sometimes I think you might be the strongest angel I've ever met. You don't have to do it alone. Not anymore. So please. Stay."

My words cause a few more tears to fall that I once again wipe away.

She nods, sniffling a little and says, "Alright. I'll stay."

I lean in, placing a light kiss on her lips. "Shoot. I was prepared to do whatever it took to convince you." My kisses carve a path across her cheek, down her jaw until I reach her neck.

"Oh. Well I—" She pulls in a lungful of air as I suck her flesh into my mouth. A moan escapes her before she continues. "I really should be going."

"I don't think so," I murmur against her collarbone. "You're not going anywhere but the magical land of orgasm and bliss, baby. So sit back, relax, and let me take you there."

She snorts a laugh that turns into another moan as my hand trails up her inner thigh. Playtime is over. I've got my girl right where I want her, and I'll only let up once she's completely spent. I want her mind to be a mess of total mush so she can't think about the awful things that could have happened tonight. She won't be able to think at all once I'm done with her.

Wearing only my shirt and her panties, it's easy for me to tease her. I continue kissing a path down her body, lifting her shirt to spend an indecent amount of time on her perfect nipples. They're sensitive enough that she's writhing beneath me already.

I can't wait to delve between her legs and find out how wet she is for me. But first, I need these cumbersome clothes gone. Her shirt goes first, then her underwear, until she's completely bare for me.

"I'm going to taste you now, little sun."

I shift down the bed and she wastes no time spreading her legs, needing this as much as I do. By the Archangels, this girl is perfect.

I tease and taste, avoiding the sensitive nub until she's so close to the precipice that she begs me to let her fall.

"Raph," she whines. "Please."

"Please what, baby? Tell me what you want."

"I want," she pants as I blow air against her clit, "to come on your tongue."

My smile is wicked. "Anything for you."

With only a few deliberate strokes of my tongue and fingers, her back arches, hips quivering as she falls apart. I don't stop, letting her ride the wave into another orgasm. Someday, I want this gorgeous angel to sit on my face and damn near suffocate me for her own needs. But while tonight is about her pleasure, it's also about showing her how safe she is.

The noises that escape from her throat are animalistic. Mewls and cries fill my ears until it feels like my own personal symphony. One I would listen to forever if she let me.

Her eyes are on me as I get off the bed and remove my clothes. Propped up against the pillows, eyes hooded, she's a goddess come to life straight from my fantasies.

She bites her lip as I prowl forward, my cock hard and jutting straight out like an arrow pointing me straight at my target.

I crawl between her legs and plunge my cock into her slick pussy. She moans, digging her nails into my legs. The pain feels good, spurring me on. Grabbing onto her legs, I push them in against her chest and hammer into her like I'm trying to mark her insides as mine. Because that's what she is.

Mine.

Her next orgasm damn near sends me over the edge, but I grit my teeth and hold it back. I'm not ready to end this yet.

When it subsides, I let her legs go and pull back enough to shift her on her side without ever leaving the warmth of her tight pussy. I tap her ass and she jumps a little at the sting of it.

"Raph," she whimpers.

"I know, sunshine. I know. Just one more," I demand as I thrust into her, using her hips as leverage. She feels so fucking good.

Leaning over, I stick my thumb into her mouth and tell her to suck. She does as I command, the sight of it causing my balls to tighten and tremble with the need to fill her with my cum, but still I hold back.

She's almost there.

Extracting my thumb from her lips, I take the wet digit and tease her ass with it. "I need you to come again, sunshine. With me now, can you do that?" My voice doesn't sound at all like it should. It's raw, needy. Desperate. For her, I'm all of those things.

Her mouth is open now, but no sounds come out. The way her inner walls clamp around me, I know she teeters on the edge.

With a little pressure, I push the tip of my thumb into her ass, and that's all it takes.

She screams, her pussy clenching around me until I let the floodgates loose and fall with her into oblivion.

I don't know how long we stay like that, but eventually

I move off her. Shit. I was probably crushing her with my heavy-ass body. Not that she seems to mind, though.

"I'll be right back, sunshine," I tell her quietly. She tries to hold on to me, but her limbs are useless. My girl is bone fucking tired.

As much as I want to let her fall asleep like that, the least I can do is get her some water and clean her up a bit. Someday she'll fall asleep with every part of me still inside her, but not tonight. Not after what she experienced.

She's barely conscious while I clean her up, and it takes great effort for her to swallow even a few sips of water. When I put everything away, I crawl into bed beside her, letting her soft skin soothe my mind. It races with questions and worries, all of my thoughts jumbling into a messy tangle. But one stands out among the rest.

It's not safe for her anymore. Frankly, I don't think it ever has been.

"Hayliel, baby," I whisper against the top of her head. She snuggles into my chest but doesn't say a word. "I don't think you should sleep alone anymore. How would you feel about staying the night with someone from now on?"

Her body grows still, and I can feel her heart rate pick up from where she's pressed into me.

"Sunshine?"

"I ... I don't know," she says groggily, but I don't miss the telltale sign of fear in her tone.

Shit. She probably thinks I mean for her to choose, but that's the last thing I want. I mean, sure, do I want her to spend more time with that grumpy house leader? No. He's been a dick to her most of the time, and while I can appreciate that he's taken his head out of his ass, a leopard doesn't change its spots.

But despite my feelings about him, Hayliel enjoys having him around, and what she wants far outweighs everything else. If she wants to give him a second chance, I won't stand in her way.

Though I may not be there with open arms either.

"You could rotate between my dorm, Theo's dorm, and even Ezekiel's, if you were interested. I doubt either of them would mind. Especially not after tonight."

She lifts her head from my chest, eyes that are no longer sleepy roam my face like she's trying to see if I'm being sincere. "You'd really be okay with that?"

Does she even comprehend the lengths I would go for her happiness? For her safety?

"Baby, I would live with you, Theo, and Zeke in that damn cave for eternity, if that's what you wanted."

Her bottom lip quivers and a single tear falls down her cheek. By the Archangels, she's so fucking beautiful.

"Come," I say, pulling her gently back down to my chest. "Let's get some sleep. Morning will be here far too soon."

26

THEO

We meet in the cave before school. It hadn't been the plan, but when the usually quiet house leader asks everyone to go somewhere, you show up. It would be a lie if I said I wasn't intrigued. All he'd said was there'd been a new development, which could mean anything. Good or bad.

I was about to stop by and escort Hayliel. Want to join? I press the message through my private bond with Raphael, curious what he'll think of Zeke's summoning.

His cheerful voice enters my head with a response. *I'm actually with her now. We'll be at the cave in five minutes.*

Give her a kiss for me. Smiling, I imagine him doing just that. I shake my head, not needing to get lost in the lust fog that Hayliel is so good at dragging me into without even trying.

Before I leave my room, I shoot off a message to Castiel, letting him know of Zeke's request. We really should open up a path to communicate with our entire group instead of having to send different messages to include everyone, even if it's frowned upon by the university to have private mental connections with students.

It takes me no time at all to arrive at the cave, but only Dina is here. Castiel still hasn't responded to my message, so I have no clue if he'll show up. Dina says she's having lunch with Mira and Hayliel, so at least they can loop the girl in on anything important.

When Hayliel and Raphael arrive, I expect a happier pair than the two angels in front of me. Something must've happened. As hard as I try, I can't help but worry it's about the odd sort of relationship we've formed. I push those thoughts aside, though. They would tell me if something was wrong.

Zeke is the last to arrive, and the man looks furious. I don't think I've ever seen his scowl so deep, and I've seen it pretty damn fucking deep. If I was wondering before whether this news was good or bad, I now have my answer.

This shit is *bad*.

"Sorry I'm late. Have you updated anyone yet?" he asks Dina. When she shakes her head, he continues. "Then I'll cut to the chase. The Fallen library was vandalized last night. So far, there have been no witnesses, but we're still looking into it and searching for the culprit. I haven't ruled out Uriel's little Fallen minions, but the thought that Fallen ruined their own fucking library pisses me off more than if it were a Pure."

I consider his words, but the motives don't line up. What would tearing apart an entire university house library prove? That wouldn't just harm Hayliel. It would harm the entire Fallen population at Silver City University and the school itself. From what we've seen of Uriel, he wants to keep shit contained to just Hayliel.

My gaze travels to the woman I can't seem to shake, and I catch her and Raphael sharing a look that has unease curling through me.

"What do you know?"

Raphael's usually happy persona turns dark as he says, "Hayliel couldn't sleep last night, so she went to the Fallen library. Instead of studying, she had two Fallen and some cloak-wearing psycho coming after her. She ran and ended up at my dorm, where she spent the night."

An unnatural silence falls over us as we stare dumbfounded at the pair.

"What?" Zeke growls, his fury growing rapidly. My own builds right along with him. If this is Uriel's doing, I swear I'll make him regret ever coming at the girl who owns my heart.

She frowns. "When I left the library, nothing was out of place aside from whoever was inside looking for me. The two Fallen seemed terrified of the masked being, though. Maybe he got so mad they took it out on the books?"

An angry cloaked figure? Just what the hell happened last

night?

A memory hits me straight in the chest. The nightmare I'd had last night woke me in a pile of sweat and fear. I thought it was about Serah being chased by a demon, but what if it was something else? I didn't think too much about it at the time, but now I take a second look. Could my body tell Hayliel was in danger? Is that what truly woke me up?

No. Most likely, it was just an unrelated nightmare. Even as I think it, something nags at my mind, refusing to let me drop it. I need to decipher the implications a bit more before I bring it up to anyone. For now, I'll focus on figuring out how to keep Hayliel safe.

Clearing my throat has all eyes turning to me. "I think it goes without saying that even more than before, we need to ensure that you're never alone. If the Fallen and this cloaked figure are working with Uriel and they were trying to kidnap you in the middle of the night, then who knows what lengths they'll reach to get what they want? We can't be too careful."

"Castiel should be here. Maybe there's something he can do at the faculty level," Zeke adds darkly. I get the sense he would like to do several things to the likes of Uriel that our professor and the rest of the school wouldn't agree with. I'm right there with you, buddy.

"I did text him and asked about coming to the cave, but he hasn't responded yet. When he responds, I'll fill him in and see what he can do."

"Should we consider looping in Principal Cael?" Dina asks,

chewing on her top lip.

It's a decent question, but we already have enough angels in the know that I'm not sure how I feel about adding more. Especially someone as powerful as the head of the school. Still, we're not at a point where we can completely turn down the idea.

Raphael answers before I get a chance to. "Honestly, I'd like to know what Castiel thinks about that before we make any decisions. He'd know more about the man than we would."

"Agreed," Zeke says, "But let's not rule it out yet. For now, we'll double our efforts to make sure Hayliel is never alone. Ideally, we'll even have as many as two angels with her at all times, though that may not always be doable."

"I hate this. I don't want to be a burden to any of you, but that's exactly what it sounds like I'll be." My sweet, gorgeous angel drops her head into her hands, and my heart hurts at the sight.

In a second, I'm at her side, gently pulling them down. "Hey. You are never a burden to us. Ever. Each angel in this room cares about you, so much so that we would all be devastated if something bad happened to you. It's not a burden to help keep you safe. It's an honor." I lean in and press a soft kiss to her lips, and when I pull away, her expression is a little less dark.

"Fine." She checks her slate and sighs. "So, who wants the first shift of walking me to class?"

I ignore the lunchtime rush of students heading to the main hall to grab a bite to eat and instead make my way back to the cave. Raphael is with Dina and Hayliel, who are planning to eat their food in Dina's dorm room with Mira. When he's done, he'll join the rest of us here. He never said exactly what it was we needed to talk about, but it sounded important.

The shit just keeps piling on.

Zeke arrives next, looking worried. "Did something else happen?"

I shrug. "I don't know, but I'm getting tired of these fucking surprises."

Just as Zeke nods his agreement, Raphael walks through the cave entrance, his usually cheery face just as grim as it was this morning.

"What is this about? Is Hayliel alright?" Zeke asks him, and I have to hand it to the guy. He's made great strides in his behavior since the little talk we've had. I just hope he's showing her this side of him too, instead of just us.

Raphael, who usually would have taken Zeke's gruff tone as an attack, only nods. "She's fine right now. Mira and Dina will keep her safe through lunch, anyway. I wanted to talk to you both about last night. I don't think she should be left alone, even then."

"What did you have in mind?" I ask. Zeke doesn't say anything, but he looks a little uncomfortable, and I can't quite understand why.

"She agreed to spend her nights between the three of us,

assuming we all agree."

Relief floods me at his words. I hadn't even realized I'd been worried about what he would say until now. "Well, shit. You won't hear any complaints from me."

Zeke has basically stopped moving at this point, looking eerie as hell where he stands like a stone statue. Raphael has to say his name twice before he snaps out of it.

"Sorry. What did you say?"

I can't stop the grin that spreads across my face, but Raphael rolls his eyes. "I said, are you cool with having Hayliel spend her nights between the three of us, or are you too much of an asshole to make it work?"

Ugh. Raphael and I talked about this. He agreed to be nice to Zeke and give him another chance, since he'd been making an effort not to suck.

Zeke narrows his eyes at Raph, but I butt in before things take a turn. "I think what he means it that Hayliel would like to spend a few nights with you each week. Is that something you're comfortable with?"

"She said that?" he asks Raphael.

"More or less, yes."

He's silent for a beat, then says, "If it's what she wants, and neither of you have issues with it, then I'd like that very much."

"It's clear to us—*both of us*—" I shoot a look at Raph, "that Hayliel has feelings for you. We know what went down between the two of you over the weekend—"

His head whips toward me with guilt written all over his face.

"Look, I'm sorry. It's not like I planned for it to happen, it just did."

This poor guy. Who would have thought the prickly Fallen angel would be so damn dense?

"Archangels, will you just shut up? We're trying to include you," Raphael says with a huff, causing Zeke to promptly close his mouth.

More gently, I add, "We just want to see her happy, and you're part of making that happen."

He swallows, a slight blush lining his cheeks. I never would have imagined seeing this grumpy ass dude blush, but I guess stranger things have happened.

At seeing Zeke soften, Raphael's annoyance fades. "Then it's settled. She'll bounce between our rooms at night. I considered setting a schedule, but I think it might be better if we keep things sporadic and unpredictable in case anyone is watching us closely."

"That's a good idea," Zeke says before I can.

"I agree. We can't be too careful," I add, then bite the bullet and bring up the other item that won't seem to leave my mind. "Did either of you have nightmares last night?"

They both look at me like my face has been replaced with an ass. It's not like it was *that* weird of a question.

Zeke grimaces, but eventually nods. Raphael does too, and my stomach sinks.

"And were they about a woman being chased by a dark figure? I thought it was just my past, the usual images that haunt me while I'm sleeping, but now I'm not so sure."

Raphael's face pales. "All I heard was an angel screaming, begging for help, but I was surrounded by darkness and couldn't find her."

"I..." Zeke starts, then stops. He takes a breath before he says, "I thought it was my mom, but the location didn't make any sense. It wasn't at home or the barn. It was here."

"Maybe it's nothing ..." I say, unsure of my thoughts.

Raphael laughs. "When angels say that, it usually *is* something. What is it, Theo?"

Swallowing hard, I blow out a hard breath and share my thoughts. "It's just ... sometimes it feels like my connection with her is stronger than anything I've experienced before. I assume it's the same with you guys, but the fact that all three of us had strange dreams on the night where she was almost captured by some weirdo in a mask makes me think it's not just in my head."

Zeke, who I expect to scoff and tell me I'm an idiot, actually looks like he's considering it. "I've never heard of an angelic connection being so strong that dreams were shared, but that doesn't mean it's never happened. Hell, Hayliel's entire being is proof that we don't know shit about fuck."

"Add it to the list of things for us to dig into," Raphael mutters, though I know he's thinking the same thing I am.

Our connection with Hayliel seems to strengthen on the daily, and if it were up to us, we'd make it as deep as fucking possible.

27

HAYLIEL

I haven't seen the masked man again since that night in the library. At least, not in real life.

Sometimes I catch a glimpse of something black from the corner of my eye, but when I turn to look, there's nothing there. It's probably just my imagination playing tricks on me, but I can't shake the fear that he's out there somewhere. Watching. Waiting to pounce.

I spent the night wrapped in Theo's arms, and the nightmares that usually plague me never surfaced. It was my first full night's sleep in so long that today it feels like I can conquer anything. It's wild to me how much getting the right amount of sleep can change things for the better.

While it's nice having someone with me at all times, I feel bad. My friends are showing up late to their own classes and leaving early to ensure that I'm never alone. They're harming themselves to protect me, and I hate it.

I don't want to be that friend anymore.

Professor Sofiel talks about our final exam, and I try to listen, I really do, but with only fifteen minutes left of class, I can't force myself to pay attention.

Someone knocks on the door, interrupting her. She opens it just enough to have a hushed conversation with whoever it is before turning back to the class. "Miss Hayliel. There's someone here to see you. Please gather your things and head to the hallway. I'll send the rest of the examination details to your slate."

My heart skips a beat. If it were another student, I doubt she'd let me leave early. It could be Castiel, but that would mean something happened, and it's big enough for him to pull me from class. Shit. I hope it's not that. I can't handle more bad news.

Under the watchful eye of my classmates, including a death-filled glare from Temperance, I walk toward the front of the class, and as I pass through the doorway, my stomach plummets from what I see there.

Professor Uriel waits for me in the hall, a manic glint in his eyes.

"What do you want?" I ask, folding my arms across my chest as the door closes behind me. I probably shouldn't be so brazen with this lunatic, but I'm just so fucking angry. First, he instructs fellow students to bully me, and now he shows up to pull me out of class early for Archangels know what.

Whatever it is, it's nothing good. I know that for a fact.

"You've got detention with me today. I didn't want you bailing or using your friends to get out of it, so I made sure neither option would be a problem."

His words cause panic, but I keep my expression neutral. He's clearly been watching us if he knows someone always escorts me to and from class. In my mind, I press into my mental bonds and send out one message to everyone. *Uriel pulled me from class early. He's personally ensuring I don't miss my detention.*

He smiles, but it's far from comforting. "Come with me. And don't bother fighting, it'll only make things worse."

Raphael's cheerful voice, now full of anger, pops into my head. *That fucking piece of shit.* He's followed by Theo's smooth, reassuring one, *We're coming for you, firefly.*

My legs feel stiff, but I force them to move. It helps to know that my friends are aware, and I trust they'll come quickly to my aid. Besides, his classroom is in the main hall, so we'll have to leave the tower. Someone will see us.

The farther I follow him, though, the more I realize he's not taking me out of the tower. I halt mid-step. "Where are you taking me?"

He turns, one side of his mouth tilted upward. "To detention, as I said. The room we're going to is just around the corner. Will you continue willingly, or do I have to use force?"

A shudder runs through me, one I know he sees because

it only adds to the glee on his stupid asshole face. Something terrible crosses my mind that has panic lodging itself in my throat. Could Uriel be the masked man who tried to take me from the library? Logically, I know it can't be. His voice is no match for the deep, ominous timber of the cloaked being. But it doesn't stop the trickle of unease coursing down my spine.

"No," I say belatedly, not wanting to find out what his idea of force is. Moving my limbs is a struggle, but I manage. When we round the corner, Uriel opens a door and beckons me inside. Through the bond, I say, *Get Castiel. Uriel isn't taking me to his office. I'm in the—*

But as I pass through the doorway, a heavy weight presses against my conscience, cutting off all access to my mental connections. I whirl around, hoping to flee, but the bastard stands in front of the closed doorway.

"Sit down. Detention starts now."

The room is empty except for two desks. His and mine. It would appear no one else is joining us.

I can't decide if that makes me calmer or more nervous. Uriel alone is something I'd rather not deal with, but the mental and physical gymnastics I would have to endure in order to survive Fallen students, along with Uriel's bullshit, is too much to think about.

Maybe this is a good thing.

A self-deprecating laugh threatens to bubble up from my throat, but I swallow it down. Whatever the fuck this is, it's definitely not a *good* thing.

Grabbing the slate from my bag, I unlock the screen, hoping that whatever it is that's blocking my telepathic ability isn't also affecting electronics. If I can just get a message out to my friends, they'll know where to find me.

I fucking hate needing them to rescue me, and it seems like it happens every other god's damn day, but I'd rather deal with that than this man.

Before I can click any more buttons, though, Uriel stands over my desk with a scowl. "Put your things away. You can do your homework on your own time. We need to talk."

I sigh, feigning a strength I don't feel, and tuck my slate back into the top of my bag, hitting a button before I pull my hand back. "If you wanted to talk, Professor Uriel, all you had to do was say so."

"Oh really? Is that all I had to do? You insolent child. Don't speak to me as if you understand the world." He moves back to the large desk at the front of the class, but doesn't go behind it. Instead, he rests his ass against the front and stares at me. "Since you've been avoiding your mandatory counseling sessions, why don't we use this time to catch up, hmm? Unless you have something better to do for the next three hours?"

He laughs at his own joke, but I don't make a sound. Three hours? How the hell am I to survive so long with this crazy man?

My silence only seems to piss him off, but as scared as I might be, I remind myself of what Castiel said. Normal angelic or demonic weapons can't kill me. And while we may not know exactly what *can* yet, other than the fabled God who's no longer around, I'm confident that anything this asshole has won't do permanent damage.

Hopefully, it won't come to that.

"The last time we spoke, you didn't notice any changes within your body resulting from your golden wing emergence, but that's not the case anymore, is it?"

Outside, I'm unaffected by his words, but inside I'm screaming. What does he know and how does he know it? "I'm not sure what you mean," I say, acting confused and not giving anything away.

He slams his fist on the desk, causing me to jump in my chair. *So much for unaffected, Hayles.*

"Don't play dumb with me, Miss Hayliel. It will not end well for you."

I sit up straighter in my chair, not liking his tone. "I'm not playing at anything. You watch me struggle on the obstacle course every week, Professor. I'm slow and disoriented. Nothing has changed."

He clucks his tongue and strolls around the room. My gaze follows him, not wanting to let him out of my sight.

"Your inability to improve there is quite worrisome, and as your counselor, I must caution you that failing to pass the test will result in you not moving forward with your friends."

"I'm trying," I grit out, but I know we aren't just talking about the stupid obstacles anymore. If I fail, it'll only make his plan of getting rid of me that much easier. I wonder what Castiel will think of his threats, or even Principal Cael. Would he really not allow me to progress if I don't *do better*?

I'm so lost in thought, I don't realize that Uriel has moved until I feel his presence behind me, along with the cool touch of a blade against the base of my throat.

"My gut is warning me there's something you're still not telling me." He presses the tip of the blade down until I feel a pinprick of pain and the amulet beneath my shirt warms against my bare flesh. "Let me ask again. What other changes have you noticed besides the golden wings?"

I freeze, unsure how to answer him. From where he holds the weapon, I can't tell if it's a regular blade or an angel blade. We already knew he was working with the mole at the guild, so it's not a stretch to assume he's also working with the angel supplying those awful blades. Neither will kill me, of course, but if it's anything like last time, it would still incapacitate me for a while.

A shudder runs through me. I don't even want to think about what he'd do with my unconscious body. *Focus, Hayles. What is he searching for? And what can you give him that will make him believe you're playing along?*

"I'm always hot," I tell him, playing up the tremble in my voice in the hopes he'll back off.

"What do you mean?" he asks, not relieving the pressure on the blade.

"I don't know. I can't find anything about it, but I'm always so fucking warm. That didn't happen before."

He takes a step back and begins pacing again. This time he

doesn't speak to me, but he isn't exactly silent. Is he arguing with himself? I strain to hear the muttered words.

"Is it possible she really doesn't know anything? No, I know what my task is, but if she hasn't discovered—of course I haven't forgotten what's at stake, but how do I steal her knowledge if she has none?" On and on he murmurs. It's enough that I'm beginning to wonder if he even knows I'm still here.

When the room grows silent, all the hairs on my arm stand on end.

"You think you can fool me, missy? Trick me into believing that you don't know precisely what you are? That you don't know the exact reason you survived that deadly blade?" Even though he's behind me, I keep my face as calm as possible and wait to see what happens next.

I feel his movement first, the air whipping toward me from behind in a flurry, but he never reaches me. Someone pounds on the door, two hard knocks that have Uriel halting, weapon raised and glinting in the low light of the room.

The handle has runes etched onto it, but from my vantage point, I can't see if the end holds a glittering soul stone. If he's carrying an angel blade now, things are bleak indeed.

The knock sounds again, harder this time.

Who could it be? Clearly not someone Uriel is expecting, but that doesn't rule out the Fallen he's working with.

Have my guys found me? Do I want them to, if this lunatic might have an angel blade?

"I'm in the middle of something right now. Please come back

later," Uriel calls through the door, sounding less crazed than before.

"Open the door, Uriel," Castiel replies. I keep the relief at his voice tucked inside. The feeling doesn't last long though. Uriel shoots me a death glare over his shoulder.

Does he know Castiel is working with us? Would he harm a fellow teacher? Shit, shit, shit.

Castiel doesn't wait a moment longer, somehow managing to unlock the door without breaking it, and even Uriel looks shocked. Cool as ever, like he didn't just barge into my makeshift mental torture chamber, Castiel says, "Ah, there you are, Miss Hayliel. When you didn't show up for our meeting, I began to get worried. Thankfully, someone saw you headed here with Professor Uriel. Come on now, we have much to discuss."

I get up to leave, but the asshole stands in my way.

"Can't you see we're in the middle of something, Castiel? As her school counselor, I really must insist—"

"No need. I spoke with Principal Cael and he's agreed to transfer counselor-ship of Miss Hayliel to me."

Uriel sputters, but Castiel only feigns confusion. "I thought you'd be happy to have a little time free on your calendar. It's no bother to me, and with her thinking of changing her focus of study away from Wingology, this makes the most sense."

Wait. What? I am? Sure, I've thought about it, but it's not like I mentioned it to anyone.

Either way, I'm grateful to Castiel for this ingenious idea and rush to his side with a nod. I don't bother looking over my shoulder, not needing to see Uriel's face to know he's pissed as hell.

As I follow Castiel down the hallway, I can't help but worry, though.

Have we just made everything worse?

28

HAYLIEL

The walk back to Castiel's office in the main hall is more tiring than it should be for the distance. I can't stop looking over my shoulder every few seconds, wondering if Professor Uriel is following us with his blade.

It's foolish to think he would. That man lives behind a carefully crafted facade, one that appears righteous when really he's just a slimy bug beneath it all. If others knew the truth, he'd hate that almost as much as he hates me.

Castiel doesn't say anything to me, even when we pass through the threshold to his classroom and he shuts the door. He wastes no time pulling out the silencing candle and lighting it. Only then does he speak.

"Are you harmed more than what can be seen?"

I don't even realize what he's talking about until I look down and notice the small line of blood from where Uriel's blade pressed into me. The wound is already healed and only the crimson stain remains. I barely even felt the wound. Is this what the protection amulet does?

I nod. "More shaken than anything." The heat that usually races through my limbs is gone now, leaving behind a chill. I know it's my body coming down from the high of adrenaline, but it doesn't make it any easier or stop my body from shaking.

"Do you feel comfortable enough to tell me what happened, or would you like a moment?"

I consider his question before answering, realizing quickly that I need to get it off my chest as fast as possible. I don't want this to fester inside for any longer than necessary. Quickly, I tell him about Uriel showing up early to pull me from class, the weird sensation that pressed against me when I stepped into that room and how it cut off my mental connections. He seems concerned at that, but waves me on.

I begin to explain the interrogation, then recall the recording I took. I didn't even turn the damn thing off, so I stop recording and press play, letting it speak for itself. Hearing it again so soon after it happened has acid bubbling in my stomach. Even my own voice sounds foreign, as if it comes from someone far stronger than I ever could be.

Castiel doesn't interrupt even once, letting the video play through until he showed up. "Honestly, I don't know what would have happened if you hadn't come. How did you know where to find me?"

"Your friends wasted no time finding me after your distress call. They tracked you to just outside the door and wanted to bust the damn thing down themselves, but I asked them to let me handle it."

My heart soars at knowing what lengths my friends would go to in order to protect me, but I'm glad they didn't. Deep in my soul, I know the only reason Uriel let me out at all was because of Castiel. Another professor and the not so veiled threat of the principal. If three pissed off students had shown up in his place, I don't even want to think about what might have happened.

Oblivious to my internal thoughts, Castiel continues. "Uriel's behavior concerns me, so I don't want to push him more than necessary until we know more. I hope you understand."

I nod. He doesn't know just how fully I do understand. The less involvement they have, the better, though I know they wouldn't agree. As much as I want to do everything on my own, solely because then it's only myself at risk, I understand that it's not feasible. Still, they don't need to be going off, making silly decisions that put them in the line of fire any more than they already do.

Especially not when they can die and apparently I can't.

I'm the entire reason for this shit storm. My gray wings, then gold, and now with rumors spreading about the incredible things I've endured. It's my fault. My mess. My problem. And once the truth gets out, there's not a doubt in my mind things will get worse.

"Do you think Uriel knows what I am?"

"I'm afraid I don't know. His questions make me think all he has are suspicions, but we can't know for certain." He motions for me to join him behind his desk. "Come here. I have something that might help take your mind off everything, at least until our pretense of a counseling meeting is done and you can get back to your friends."

My eyes light up curiously at the book Castiel pulls from the same hidden drawer where the candle was, but instead of questioning him about it, I take the conversation in a different direction. One that has hope blossoming inside me. "Did you really talk to Principal Cael about becoming my councilor?"

"I did. And what I said about you changing your major isn't something you need to decide on now, but it worked to move the switch forward."

"Thank you," I tell him, wondering what it is I did to deserve someone as kind as him on my side.

"No need for all that." He waves a hand dismissively. "Now, do you remember the friend I spoke to about you before we knew you were a Seraphim? He retrieved this from his old family estate and agreed to lend it to me as long as I kept it in my care and promised to be gentle with the ancient pages."

"On my life," I promise him, reaching for the book with careful movements. It's bound in a soft, supple leather, slightly worn down with age. On the cover, sits an indented sun, painted a brilliant gold that almost seems to shine on its own. It's stunning.

Carefully, I flip open the cover. The next image is a simple drawing of a woman standing in front of a fiery orb, a subtle glow seeming to emanate from her. Or maybe it's from the sun behind her. Either way, she's ethereal.

With every page I flip, the more engrossed I become. Something about it seems familiar, though I can't directly name what. All I know is that I'm eternally grateful for it. I read through information on all types of angels. Our strengths, weaknesses, and powers from generations before.

The item in front of me is rare indeed, and it shocks me to my core that Castiel's friend not only had this in his possession, but allowed him to borrow it. If he's caught with it, I fear what may become of him.

No. I won't think about that. I can't, or else I'll waste what precious time I have with it. Because as interested as I am in reading this tome front to back, I know my time with it is limited, so I flip straight to the section on Seraphim and begin to read.

The Seraphim are the highest ranking angels, and their existence is quite rare. These divine beings are known for their ability to dispel and destroy the shadows of darkness by harnessing the powerful fires of the sun. Using this method, Seraphim have the power to smite their enemies.

The more I read, the more it all seems like a fairytale instead of real life. Is this what I did to those demons near the well? Did I *smite* them? I skim a little, utterly fascinated, until I find what I'm looking for.

> *Through extensive research, we discovered that Seraphim sometimes struggle to wield the sun's fire. The vessel must be solid and true in order to receive such power. Without it, the fire will become unpredictable and, in the worst cases, fatal.*

Fatal. Nothing but God could kill me, or you know, my own damn ineptitude. Great.

I read it again, getting stuck on the part about a vessel. Am I the vessel, or does this text refer to something else, something we're missing in order to make it work? I glance at Castiel, wanting to know what he thinks.

"Have you read this?" I ask, even though I know the answer.

"I have. Ask your questions, Miss Hayliel. I fear we will soon be out of time."

"This mentions that the vessel must be solid and true. What does that even mean?"

He scratches his chin, looking over the passage I just read. "I believe it refers to the Seraphim itself, as they are the vessel for the sun's fire. May I speak frankly?"

I laugh. "I think we're well past the point of you not being able to do so. You never need to ask."

He nods, the smallest smile curving his lips. "You are an angel who's been through a lot in your short years. I think it's helped you become exactly what you needed to be."

Exactly what I needed to be? I almost snort at the thought but hold back, letting him continue.

"You could have turned bitter and jaded, but instead you're kind. Accepting. Strong. You didn't let that treatment break you like it has so many others in your position. For that reason alone, I already believe you to be the solid and true vessel this book says you need to be. The only one who needs convincing of that is *you*."

I can only stare as the weight of his words settles around me like a warm blanket.

Is he right?

Am I the obstacle I need to overcome to wrangle this power?

It hits me then just how much I've grown in the few short months I've attended Silver City University. Just because I'm scared now doesn't mean that progress should stop. In fact, it's even more reason to pull my big girl panties up and find a way to accept myself, just as my friends have already done.

Maybe then I'll be able to not only help fight this upcoming war, but end it without anyone I love getting harmed in the process.

29

EZEKIEL

I'm being summoned.

My stomach twists as I fly the distance from school to guild headquarters and ponder what it is I'm getting called in for. Try as I might, there's too much unsaid between Azrael and me that it's impossible to pinpoint.

He's waiting for me when my feet hit the ground. Azrael stands off to the side, near the front entrance. This can't be good.

He spots me quickly and approaches, his expression unusually blank. "Zeke. Thank you for getting here so fast. Please come with me." Like a rocket, he shoots up into the sky, not bothering to wait for me. The move is so out of character, it

268

takes me a moment to gather my thoughts and follow.

Azrael is acting strange, and now he's taking me to some undisclosed location. This can't be good. It's only when I see the familiar street that I realize where he's taking me. His house in the Fallen district. A little of my worry falls away. Before all of this, I never would have considered that this man, the lieutenant I've grown fond of and learned so much from, would be up to anything shady. But if the last few months have taught me anything, it's that I let my emotions cloud my judgment.

As much as I don't want to believe anything negative about Azrael, with the way he's acting, I can't be too careful. Something is either horribly wrong or I just found the mole.

We land outside his house, an exact replica of the one my dad lives in, and Azrael unlocks the door. Once inside, he pulls out a bottle of whiskey and two glasses. "Want one?"

I stare at him for a moment too long before realizing he's serious. "Uh, no. Thanks."

"Suit yourself." He pours himself half a glass, downs it, and then fills it up again. In all the time I've known Azrael as my commanding officer and even before that as someone who worked with my dad, I've never seen him like this.

Suddenly, Hayliel's panicked voice filters through my mind. *Uriel pulled me from class early. He's personally ensuring I don't miss my detention.*

Shit. Using my mental connection with Raphael and Theo, I fill them in. *I'm stuck with Azrael right now. Can you make it to Hayliel? I'll wrap things up here as quickly as possible.*

On it. Raphael replies.

Theo follows that up with, *Everything alright?*

I think so. Will update once I know more.

"So, Zeke, why don't you sit?" Azrael's voice startles me from my mental conversation. It takes a moment for his words to register, and then I'm just pissed.

"Your summons insinuated that this was important, so why the hell are we playing tea time at your house, Azrael?"

I swear, from the look he's giving me, I must have punched him in the face. He lets out a long breath, but my mind is filled once more with Hayliel's voice that I can't concentrate on Azrael anymore.

Get Castiel. Uriel isn't taking me to his office. I'm in the—

My back straightens as all the blood in my veins turns to ice. I have to go. I need to get my girl away from that fucking piece of shit, then make sure he never goes near her again. I'm about to turn when Azrael's words have me halting in my tracks.

"You've been pestering me for information for weeks. If you want to know what I've learned, then get comfortable and listen."

I'm so fucking torn about what to do. My heart tells me to fly as fast as I can to help Hayliel, but my head tells me to stay here and let Raphael and Theo handle it. A few months ago, I'd never have left anything to them. My ego and pride wouldn't allow it, but now ... now I realize I don't always have to be the knight in feathered armor.

As if he knows my dilemma, Theo's voice echoes in my head.

We've got Castiel and we're on our way to her now. Will update soon.

Thank fuck. I drop instantly onto the sofa, causing Azrael to chuckle. He thinks it's about what he's just said, but really, it's relief at knowing Hayliel is protected, and always will be in my absence. As much as I hate to admit it, I'm learning that sometimes it's okay to rely on others. Necessary, even. Raphael and Theo have proven themselves worthy of Hayliel, and as much as I might have hated it at first, I know they'll keep her safe and keep me in the loop. What more can I ask for?

"I'll start by apologizing," Azrael says, pulling my focus back. "I know you hated that I didn't loop you in, and I hope you know I took no joy from it either, but at the time, I felt it was necessary."

I understand what he means. I've kept so much from him too, but I say nothing. It wouldn't help anything if I were to shout what I was actually thinking. I am not the enemy. Maybe we both need to learn to trust each other more. Shrugging, I ask, "And now?"

"What I've discovered has grown into something bigger than just myself, but I'm not ready to let the rest of the guild in yet."

"Why not?"

"Well, for starters, I want to see what you think. This tip originated with you and the friend who wanted to be anonymous. Once I bring this up officially, they may not be able to stay anonymous."

Damn. I didn't even think about that. Having Hayliel's identity revealed won't do us any favors. "I'm all ears," I tell him.

"After going through the deceased's belongings, I recovered a deleted message from his slate that mentioned a name. Roderick. This led me down a rabbit hole about a Fallen angel who's built quite the reputation as a man for hire. He and his crew will work for anyone, as long as the cause piques his interest and the coin pads his pockets. From what I can tell, your dead angel was working for him. I haven't been able to uncover who Roderick's working for now, but I'm hoping you'll know something. Otherwise, I doubt it'll take long to figure out once we make this investigation official."

I watch Azrael for several minutes. He did exactly what I hoped he would when I brought him news of the body. He found Roderick. But does that mean I can trust him? I want to. Just like my father, he's done nothing to make me think otherwise. "You can't."

Azrael looks at me like I've lost my marbles. "What do you mean?"

Taking a deep breath, I say, "You can't make this official with the guild. Everything you just told me, I already know."

"Ezekiel Oren, what the hell have you gotten yourself into?"

I ignore his more than valid question. "Roderick is the one who killed that angel, using an angel blade he got from his current employer."

"How do you know this?"

I have to play this carefully. If I slip up, Azrael might look into my friends. "Someone I trust witnessed it. I even have the blade in my possession." He opens his mouth to speak, but I cut him off, knowing exactly what he's going to say. "No. I won't give it to you. It's safer with me, somewhere only I know about."

Azrael stands, and for a moment I'm worried he's angry, but he just swallows the rest of his whiskey and pours himself another. "Would it be safe to assume that you also know who Roderick is working for?"

I wince. "Yes, and no. I don't know exactly who, but I do know some. You may want to sit."

"By the cock of God," he mumbles, grabbing the entire bottle and bringing it with him.

"Roderick is working with a powerful angel, one I'm unable to identify." Azrael nods like he expected that, but I'm about to shatter his world. "That isn't the worst part. The angel he's working for has partnered with demons. They're collecting angel blades and are certainly not afraid to use them."

Azrael's eyes widen, his glass of whiskey completely forgotten on the coffee table between us. "For what purpose? And do I even want to know how you came to find all this out? By the Archangels, Zeke, this is some deep shit you've gotten yourself in."

"We aren't sure of a purpose yet. As for how I know, let's just say it's been a crazy few months."

He taps his fingers on his leg but eventually gets up to pace his living room. "It concerns me that the guild hasn't uncovered anything about this. Yes, we knew demons had gotten a bit more riled up than usual, but things have been quiet these last few weeks. Honestly, I just assumed they'd given up and gone back into hiding. Now I'm worried what it means that we haven't discovered this group of rebels before now."

"I'm afraid there's a reason for that, and you're not going to like it."

"To be fair, this conversation hasn't exactly gone how I expected it to. I thought I had news for *you*. Turns out you're the one with all the information. What else is there?"

"We have an unidentified mole in the guild. I mean, shit. It's likely we have more than one at this point."

Azrael halts in his tracks, turning slowly to look at me.

"I know you don't want to believe it, but it's true. Whoever it is helped them break into the armory and steal our sunblades. Making any of this official will tip them off that we're aware, and who knows what kind of landslide that will create."

"Bloody fucking shit," he mutters. "You don't have the clearance to know about the armory, but I won't bother asking how you found out. There's not enough time in the day for you to catch me up on all the shit you've gotten into, is there?"

"No, sir."

He sits back on the couch, elbows propped on his knees, and looks into my eyes. "Are you absolutely sure, without even the shadow of a doubt, that we have a mole?"

All I do is nod, because what else is there? He knows the truth if he only thinks about it.

"Damnation." Azrael reaches for his drink again.

"The demons are growing bold, and I think having the guild

in their back pocket is the cause. Why else would they attack us so close to the guild?"

"What do you mean? There was an attack near the guild?"

I can only stare at him, my mouth opening and closing like a damn fish because I thought he knew.

"My friends and I were attacked almost a month ago between the Fallen district and guild HQ. We were severely outnumbered and barely survived. Someone from the guild saw the fight on their way in for their shift and brought a crew to us. At least five showed up, probably more, but I wasn't exactly focused on counting them. Lieutenant Atlas was supposed to tell you, but they left to hunt down the demons who fled, so I'm not surprised he forgot." I don't bother mentioning what happened to Hayliel. Maybe that's the wrong choice, but it's not my story to tell.

"This has gotten far too out of hand. Is that why you kept all of this from me? Because you thought I was the mole?"

I consider lying to him, but I know he'd hate that more than the truth. "I never wanted to believe you were involved, but we couldn't risk it. If it helps, I haven't shared this information with my father either. There's too much at stake."

"While I wish you would have come to me with this earlier, I don't blame you for keeping this close to your chest. Your instincts are solid, Zeke. The guild is lucky to have you and so is Silver City."

A vise I didn't realize was wrapped around my chest, loosens. I thought Azrael discovering I not only kept this from him, but even briefly suspected him, would ruin the relationship we had. Instead, he's supporting my choices and even complimenting me. "Thank you, sir."

"For what it's worth, I think you should tell your dad. Give it some thought and maybe we can talk to him together. For now, I have a plan for a little trap to lure out the snake."

On the flight back to campus, with a plan in place to lure out the bastard mole, I finally allow myself to think about Hayliel and that bastard Uriel. Castiel saved the day, and it sounds like he even went a step further with his saving. He's now her counselor instead of that piece of shit trash bag. It sure helps to have him on our side. Hopefully, it's the same with Azrael.

Where are you? I push the thought to Hayliel, hoping to find her and see how she's doing.

She doesn't make me wait long. *In my room. Everything alright?*

Of course she asks me that, as if I'm the one who just got locked in a room with a crazy angel. I swoop down to her balcony, knocking at the same time I push two little words through our connection. *It's me.*

Within seconds she opens the door, looking freshly showered and absolutely fuckable. I move without even thinking, wrapping her up in a hug so tight it cuts off all the oxygen to my lungs.

She's hesitant at first, but eventually hugs me back just as tight.

"Fuck. I want to track that piece of shit down and take his wings for being such a shit. How are you? Did he hurt you?" I pull back, needing to see for myself.

A small smile plays on her lips like she's enjoying my brief moment of freaking the fuck out. That's when I notice the cut on her neck.

Rage simmers as I trail my finger along the raised red line. "He did this?" My voice is dark, oozing every ounce of the destruction I feel when thinking about someone else touching her. Harming her.

She nods, chewing on her bottom lip like she's scared to admit it. But I don't want her scared of me. I want her to use me. To make me her blade and point me toward the enemies she wants to annihilate. I turn to leave, but her small hand on my arm halts me in my tracks.

"Stay. I'd rather you be in here with me than out there defending my honor."

The truth of her words is easy to read in her eyes. "I nearly left Azrael to come for you. I would have if it wasn't for Theo and Raphael assuring me they'd take care of you."

"I'm glad you stayed. I wouldn't want you to get in trouble because of me." Before her words wound me too deeply, she adds, "But I'm glad you're here now."

"You don't understand," I whisper.

"What do you mean?" Her eyes search mine, and I wonder what she sees in them. Three months ago, hell, even two, I would've just stayed quiet and hoped she figured it out, then probably get pissed off when she didn't. Now I'm not leaving anything up to chance.

"Don't you get it, hummingbird?" I cup the side of her face, trailing my fingers across the curve of her cheek. "Watching you nearly die almost broke me. I will risk life and limb to make sure that doesn't happen again. My place at the guild means nothing if you are not safe somewhere to annoy me and drive me absolutely wild. It's all worthless compared to you."

Her eyes turn glassy. But I'm not done.

"I'm sorry. For what I put you through after our first night together." The next words are hard to get out, but the girl in front of me needs to hear them, so I force them past my lips. "My ex-girlfriend was a Pure. She only dated me as some sick joke with her friends and dumped me for the guy she really wanted to be with. Another Pure asshole, just like her. She did enough damage that I couldn't see past my own fears to realize that isn't what you were doing. I know it doesn't excuse my behavior, but I hope in time you'll learn to forgive me."

"Oh, Zeke," she says, "I'm sorry she hurt you. Whoever she is, she lost out on a great guy. One of the best I know."

I bring my hand up to cup her cheek and grin wickedly. "One of them, huh?" I only mean it as a tease, but it's too soon. Our issues might all be out in the open now, but they're too fresh.

Hayliel reaches up to stroke my forearm, mimicking the way my thumb moves across her skin. "I don't want to choose, Zeke. You or them. Them or you. I won't do it. I'd prefer to choose *us*, but I'm prepared to only choose myself if that's what it comes down to."

There's a knock on the door and Hayliel calls out, "Just a second!"

This moment feels like an edge, one I've been precariously balanced on for far too long. It's time to decide. Do I step back to safety, or do I allow myself to fall? When I wipe away all the gunk of my past, it's a simple decision to make. "I'm still trying to understand how I fit, but I don't want you to choose, either. Despite my earlier misguided thoughts, Raph and Theo are far better for you than I could ever be. They make you laugh and learn and grow. They make you happy and take care of you. I want all of those things for you. I need you to be happy."

Her hand trails up my arm to cover the hand resting against her cheek. "You do all those things for me, too. Sure, you're a little grumpy and rough around the edges," she giggles, "but you make me smile. With you, I feel emboldened, like I can do anything in the world without consequence. Safe, because I know you'd move city and earth to protect me. Raphael and Theo see it just as I do."

I close the space between us, needing to feel her body pressed against mine as her words settle around me. "This is unfamiliar territory for me," I whisper.

"We'll explore it together. All of us."

My lips hover mere millimeters from hers, but I wait. Giving her the option to pull back if this isn't what she wants. My heart might shatter, but I'd accept the pain if that's her choice.

She lifts on her tiptoes, melding her mouth to mine. I thought the kiss would be soft, gentle, but it's the opposite. Need and desire fuel the movement of my lips, my tongue, and she matches me for all of it.

Knock. Knock. Knock.

We pull apart, chests heaving and my cock as solid as marble. Our eyes lock, electricity zapping through me when I find the same desperation matched in hers.

"That's Theo. He's coming to get me for the night." Hayliel's eyes drop briefly to my lips, and I can't stop the smile from spreading.

"I'll take a rain check on the rest of this conversation then, hummingbird," I say, cupping her chin and running my thumb along her bottom lip. She bites it playfully and I groan.

She kisses the spot where her teeth just were, then smiles. "You can count on it."

While she's heading toward the door, I adjust my erection enough so that it's hopefully not visible.

"Hey man," Theo says, his smile wide like he knows what he's walked in on. Ugh. I might not hate him anymore, but he's too damn nosey. Like yes, I'm glad he talked some sense into me, but for fuck's sake, let me enjoy this moment before sucking all the fun away.

"Hey. Thanks for getting her away from that psycho."

"Of course. You'd have done the same. How'd things go at the guild?"

Shit. I totally forgot about that. "Azrael finally offered an update on the body we found. Went off about Roderick and how he wanted my thoughts before going to the guild."

"He can't!" Hayliel says while she slings a bag on her back.

"That's exactly what I said. I had to tell him a few things, but I excluded any mention of you, the blade you survived, or Seraphim."

"Thank you. I know it won't stay secret for long, but I'd prefer we keep it to ourselves for a little longer."

"I'm confident he's an ally, but it might not hurt to get him out to the cave to be sure. And now that he's aware of a mole, we have someone else on the inside looking out for evidence of who it might be."

Theo nods. "Let's do that. Having him fully on our side is a win for us. Even your dad too, if you trust him."

I consider it. From the start, I never thought Azrael or Dad were involved, but part of me is a little scared to learn the truth just in case I'm wrong. "Maybe," I reply instead.

Time is ticking down for the asshole that wants to take down his own kind.

Whoever it is, we'll find them.

30

HAYLIEL

The closer we get to Friday, the more worried I become.

For Theo and Castiel. For Raphael and meeting his family. It feels like we're making big moves. I just hope they're going in the right direction.

Despite my woe-is-me attitude, the sun beams down on us with not a cloud to be found like it's mocking my inner thoughts. My usual bodyguards are withheld elsewhere, so I'm having an early dinner with Gagiel, Yofie, Tabbris, and Sidriel. We sit on the benches around an unlit fire pit. Sidriel talks between bites of food, telling us the grand love story of her mom and dad. Gagiel is enraptured. He's barely chewing what little food he's managed to put in his mouth.

I take another bite of pasta to hide my smile. Someone has a crush. But are his affections returned? I'll have to find out, then maybe do a little matchmaking to see if I can help speed their growth along.

"Well, well, well, what do we have here? The mutant away from her guardians?"

The same group of Fallen dickwads we know are working with Uriel close in on us. There are six of them surrounding the benches and smiling like they've finally succeeded in getting me alone. If it were anyone else here with me, I might say the odds were fairly even. There are five of us and six of them. But these angels with me today aren't guild-trained. They're victims of previous bouts of bullying and are now about to experience it again. Shit.

Since this whole 'get shit on for sport' thing isn't exactly new for me, I've gotten damn good at multitasking. *Fallen bullshit happening at the firepit. Any chance one of you could come back me up? I don't want the others to get hurt.* I push the message through the mental pathways with my friends, hoping at least someone is now free. At the same time, I lock eyes with the big foreheaded guy who must be the leader of this little band of misfits. "Your obsession with me is growing tiresome, dude. I get it. You don't like me. I'm different. Don't you have better things to do than ruin our meal?"

"Don't you have better things to do than dirty this school with your filth?" Thin eyebrows glares at me.

"Good one," I say, deadpan. I'm so fucking sick of these

assholes. Sick of their taunts. Their games. And I won't stand by for a second if they try to harm my friends. "Look. You wanted to get me alone, right? Well, let my friends go and you've got me. Deal?"

"What?" Gagiel and Sidriel say at the same time.

"Hayliel, no," Yofie and Tabbris echo.

I stand and set my food down on the empty bench behind me. "I'll be fine. I'm enjoying having you on campus too much to risk you going back to virtual studies, so really you'd be doing me a favor. Please."

"Alright, the nerds can leave," big forehead says. "Then we'll make you regret ever thinking you could come here and pretend to be one of us."

"Yeah, yeah, yeah," I mutter. To my four friends, I say, "Go. I'll message you later, okay?"

The Fallen group disperses enough to let my friends out, but quickly closes around me once they're gone. I watch them walk away slowly before finally turning back to the fuckers ruining my day. "Well? Let's get this over with, then."

They all move as one, stumbling over each other in a bid to grab me. It's almost laughable. I avoid getting caught by everyone except for thin eyebrows. She looks more than pleased to have caught me, but if she thinks I'm giving up easily, she has another thing coming. Catching sight of my half-eaten bowl of pasta, I lift it with my mind and dump it on her head.

She shrieks as creamy white noodles slide off her head, half of it getting caught in her hair. "You bitch!"

"Oops." I giggle and dart away from them, my back toward Power house. I don't want to fight these assholes, not on school property and certainly not after I've been warned oh so many times of my imminent expulsion should I get caught 'at the center'. Running away feels like the coward's move, but it's better than falling into a trap and getting kicked out.

"Come on, demon spawn. Why don't you show us your little tricks, hmm?" big forehead taunts.

Seriously. Who taught these assholes to trash talk?

I take another step back, noticing at least two of them holding what looks like a needle in their grip. They want to drug me? But why?

"You want to see some tricks?" Gagiel says, coming up to stand at my side.

"What are you doing?" I whisper. Sidriel, Tabbris, and Yofie stand with us now, too.

"You're our friend, Hayliel. We would never leave you," Gagiel replies, making my heart squeeze.

The usually quiet Sidriel raises her voice until it booms loud and strong around us. "Hayliel is a guardian of angels. A protector for all. Drop your hunt for her removal from this school or you'll find out just what *nerds* can do when given the chance."

Then, as if her words were a signal, Yofie and Tabbris lock their hands together and create a powerful storm between us and the six Fallen. Rain and lightning crash down on the ground separating our two groups, while a powerful wind blows against them, not allowing them passage forward.

My mouth falls open. Holy fucking shit.

I don't realize I've said the words out loud until Gagiel says, "Aren't they amazing?"

Our little moment is ruined when an angel drops from the sky just outside the storm. Principal Cael. Oooh shit. Behind him I find Raphael, Theo, and Zeke. All four of them look pissed as hell.

Tabbris and Yofie let out a yelp and allow their storm to dissipate. No, no, no. I can't let them get in trouble for me.

"Principal Cael, it's not their fault," I begin immediately.

"Silence. You six," he says, pointing to the disheveled looking Fallen students. "In my office. Now!"

"But Principal, she—" thin eyebrows is cut off.

"I don't want to hear another peep from the lot of you. Go, before I do something you'll regret."

They rush off, and Principal Cael turns to us, his face stern and unreadable.

"Please let me explain," I try again, stepping to stand in front of my friends.

"There's no need, Miss Hayliel. These three gentlemen already alerted me to the issue, and I watched it all unfold. I appreciate that you all stayed on the defensive. It will make my job much easier. Perhaps it's best if you all go back to your dorms for the night. Take this weekend to let the dust settle and by next week, this should all be blown over. Understood?"

We all nod our agreement. When he leaves, I turn back to my friends. "Thank you for sticking up for me, even though I told you not to. And that show of power with weather manipulation? Holy hell!"

"She's right," Zeke says. "Makes me think maybe the guild should start utilizing it more."

"Is everyone alright?" Theo asks, his eyes straying to the group before coming back to land on me.

"Yup! Though that's about enough excitement for me, I think," Gagiel says with a laugh. "Maybe we'll do what the principal suggests and retire for the night. Dinner next week?"

"I'd love that."

To my complete and utter shock, all three guys follow me back to my dorm room. Theo and Zeke take off before coming inside. Both of them promising to be back soon.

"I'll be right back, sunshine," Raphael says, placing a quick kiss to my lips.

"Aww, you too? What is going on?"

"You won't get a single thing out of me." He mimes zipping his lip. "Shower. Get into some comfortable clothes. I'll be back before you know it."

I do as he says, grumbling to myself as he leaves, which only causes him to laugh. Rude.

While I shower, I can't stop thinking about what it means to have all three of them here with me. I'm honestly not sure what to make of it. It feels like a big step, but maybe with everything that's happened, we're all ready to get along. I fucking hope so.

After today, I don't think I can handle any more confrontation.

In record time, I'm clean and freshly dressed in a pair of sleep shorts and tank top when there's a knock on my door.

"Open up, firefly," Theo calls, and I rush to answer it.

Raphael hands me a bag of snacks, then opens the door as far as possible for Theo and Zeke to carry in a mattress. A fucking mattress. What the hell?

I laugh. "What is even happening right now?"

The three of them share a look, but it's Zeke who responds. "We thought it was a good idea if all of us hung out. Are you down for a group movie night? We'll even let you pick the film."

"To be totally honest, sunshine, the options are limited, but you still get the final say."

This feels like an alternate reality. The last time I watched a movie was at the park when Raphael did delicious things to my body. Alone in my room with the three of them, I'm not sure I'll be able to keep my cool.

"What's that for?" I ask, my voice coming out squeaky. Fuck. I bet they know what I'm thinking already. But it's too soon. We don't even know if everyone can get along, let alone if they'd all want to be naked at the same time. *Get a grip, Hayles.*

"I figured we'd crash here tonight, if that's alright with you. Your bed is way too small for all of us to sleep on," Theo says.

"Why?" Raphael teases. "What were you thinking it's for?"

"Uh ..." Heat rises to my cheeks.

"We're all here because we want to be near you, firefly. Don't get me wrong, we want the other stuff too, but it's just to make sure this can work first before removing any clothes."

"Right," I say breathlessly, already picturing them naked. Shit.

"See?" Theo elbows Zeke playfully. "Told you."

"Movies!" I blurt like an idiot. "For the love of the Archangels, someone show me the damn options so we can move on from this awkward conversation."

"You mean the one where the three of us fuck you?" Raphael says with all the nonchalance of a news reporter. "Because we will, sunshine. But tonight is just about bonding and relaxing. The ravishing will come later."

"I'd like that," I whisper, locking eyes with Zeke. Theo hands me a list of movies, and I skim over the titles. They all sound romantic except for one called *John Wick*. Probably best not to add any more fuel to the raging fire that is my desire for these guys.

While they're setting it up, I mention how I'm surprised Seraphina and Cadriel have been acting mostly civilized lately. Weird that it's the Fallen giving me more trouble than those two. Oh, how things have changed.

"I heard their parents threatened to cut them off if they made another scene," Raphael says, snorting a laugh at my bewildered expression.

"No fucking way!"

"I'd have loved to witness those conversations," Theo says, and I nod in agreement.

The movie begins, and we all keep our distance. Slowly, we

gravitate toward one another until Raphael rests his head in my lap, while Theo and Zeke sit on either side of me. We all share occasional soft touches that have my heart singing with joy.

This is what I was missing. All of us in the same room getting along. Laughing and talking like nothing in the world could harm us as long as we stay together.

31

THEO

Last night feels like a dream.

Zeke was on his best behavior, and so was Raph. The two of them got along far better than I expected for our first official hang out as a group. I know they're only doing it for Hayliel's benefit, but it's nice to see that we can all put aside our differences.

All morning I've thought about how we can keep this momentum going and push forward. Not that I want to rush anything, but seeing how happy Hayliel was to have us all together really put things into perspective.

I consider our options while I wait for Castiel in the cave.

Raphael and Hayliel left earlier and have likely already arrived at his family's home by now. Part of me wishes I could be there to witness what she thinks of his family. At least I know he has her there as backup if his mom goes off the deep end with her shit. I don't imagine our girl will put up with much disrespect, not when it comes to our charming Raph.

The entire purpose of the visit is to ask Raduriel for something, which will cost Raphael a lot more than he's let on to the others. I just hope his brother doesn't let him down. We need as much protection and strength as we can get, and having runes stitched into our clothing is exactly the benefit we need.

We never fully discussed it, but they'll likely wind up stuck there until tomorrow, so it'll at least be another day before we can test out our newfound group dynamic again.

Castiel arrives, looking stressed out and holding a small duffel bag that immediately captures my interest. "What's in the bag?"

Instead of answering, he brushes me off. "I'll explain once we're there. Unfortunately, I just learned our time to sleuth through his things has been cut in half. Let's go."

Shit. Half the time? No wonder Castiel's acting different. Our carefully laid plan is disintegrating around us. Let's hope Uriel left enough breadcrumbs for us to discover his secrets quickly then.

We exit the cave, our strides long as we make the trek toward the main hall. Besides a few students still mingling about, the campus is pretty empty, which is what we were hoping for. The fewer witnesses who see us creeping about, the better.

As we walk down an empty hallway, Castiel raises his fisted

hand to stop me. Footsteps sound from up ahead, causing my heart to beat faster. I look around, trying to find a place we can sneak into and hide until they pass, but just as quickly as they came, the footsteps recede. Perhaps whoever it was forgot something and had to turn around?

Finally, we make it to Uriel's classroom with no further surprises. The door is locked, but Castiel must have expected it because he somehow has a key. It's impressive to me how he always seems prepared, though that might just be a product of his old age.

Once we're inside, Castiel shuts and locks the door while I look around. Nothing looks out of place. The bookshelf on the far wall appears the same as it did when we helped clean up the books that had fallen during the attack. The student desks are lined up neatly, and no garbage or other paraphernalia line the floor. A typical classroom.

Uriel's desk is fairly empty. On top is a planner that's almost half the size of the entire flat surface, a cup filled with pens and pencils, and nothing else.

Castiel looks through his bag of tricks, pulling out a weird-looking flashlight. When he catches me watching, he says, "This will detect traces of someone's power, so if Uriel is hiding things in his desk like I do, then we'll follow the trail and find them."

I stare at the object quizzically, unable to look away when he turns it on. I want to ask him how he protects himself from anyone finding his own hidden items, but I don't. As curious as I am, it's none of my business, so instead I ask a different question. "And what exactly are we looking for?"

"Illegal objects. Names. Dates. Anything that looks suspicious or even hints at his motives." He purses his lips, meeting my gaze. "I'm hoping we'll also discover if he knows about Hayliel's true heritage or not."

"You think he doesn't know she's a Seraphim?" I give the idea some thought, but every point leads to him knowing. He's the Wingology professor, after all.

"Honestly? If he's working with the same angels Roderick answered to, I wouldn't be surprised to find out he's been kept in the dark. For now, though, it's all speculation."

Nodding, I turn back to Uriel's desk and pick a starting point while my mind wanders. Castiel isn't wrong. From what we heard in the barn, the angel who gave Roderick that blade regretted it and had planned to be more selective about who received such a boon in the future. Perhaps they would do the same with knowledge.

It's possible that whatever he's been tasked with doing is what will prove his loyalty to whoever he answers to. If that's the case, we can't underestimate him. Not with Hayliel on the line.

I empty the cup of pens, hoping to find *something* hiding at the bottom. For a moment, I get excited, until I realize it's only an oddly shaped eraser. I sigh. As if the answer to "What's Uriel's end game" would be found among a pile of writing utensils.

Putting everything back in the cup, I glance at Castiel from the corner of my eye. He doesn't seem to be faring any better than I am right now, either.

I move on, flipping through the planner. Not that I think he's dumb enough to put anything incriminating right there on his desk for anyone to gaze upon, but he *is* a cocky asshole. Who knows what he'll do? With every page I flip, the only thing I'm closer to understanding is that this guy has terrible handwriting. Some of his words look more like something a five taloned griffin would have made, and those creatures haven't existed in over a century.

There's nothing incriminating in here, and the appointments I find only have initials which make it impossible to glean if these are regular school meetings or something more nefarious.

I huff out a breath, dropping the pages, and am about to move on when something catches my eye. Peeking out from beneath the planner is a strange-looking contraption. It almost looks like a ruler, except it's not quite the right shape and there are sections missing from it.

"Do you know what this is?"

Castiel looks up, his eyes widening. "I'm guessing that's a decoder for this." From within a hidden drawer, he pulls out a folded piece of paper. When he opens it, we both stare. In the center is a plainly drawn map of Silver City, along with a string of gibberish next to several marked points.

"You think you can figure it out before we have to leave?" I ask him. He doesn't respond, snapping a photo of the map with his slate as he checks the time. "Likely not, but I'll try."

Leaving him to that is harder than I care to admit, because I'm intrigued. Decoded messages, marked up maps. If this wasn't real life with actual danger involved, I might even enjoy myself.

Shit. I'm fucked up.

Shaking my head, I make my way toward the bookshelf. When we were last in here, I didn't pay much attention to the things I'd been putting away. Even now, the books I pull out don't seem important at all, and besides, Uriel asked us to clean up the books himself. If he'd been hiding something, he wouldn't have wanted us so close.

Castiel's slate beeps a few times, and I know it's bad when I watch his lips turn down, brows drawing together as he reads.

"Shit. We have to go," he says, folding up the paper and placing it back in the drawer. "Find the book on flight tactics and push it in as far as it'll go."

I waste a precious second just staring at him; the request more than a little odd, before jumping into action. When I find the book, I realize it's one I'd already pulled out and put back in, but I follow Castiel's instructions and push it in further. Behind me, stone grates against stone, creating an unpleasant sound and revealing a hidden door opening in the wall.

What the hell?

Jovial voices reach us from the hallway. The first voice I recognize clearly as Uriel, sounding far too happy for my liking, but the second is too soft for me to make out any distinct features.

We need to leave. Now!

I spare one more glance at the shelf and the top of the desk, wanting to make sure I didn't leave a single thing out of place.

Castiel ushers me through the door we just revealed, but I don't get a chance to take in my surroundings or enjoy the fact that I'm in a secret fucking passageway.

He pushes on a stone, and the door slides closed. Just as it finally slots into place, I swear I can hear Uriel's key turning in the lock just outside the classroom.

We don't stick around for him to enter.

32

HAYLIEL

I spent last night cuddled with three gorgeous angels, and even though I *know* it happened, it still doesn't feel real. My mind hasn't felt this rested in a long time, or at least it feels long.

It was a little awkward at first, but I expected that given the guys and their history with me, and I guess with each other. But we made it work.

Okay, so we more than made it work, but that's beside the point. Waking up to them sprawled around me on the bed, while the spare mattress they hauled in lay completely forgotten on the floor had angel wings fluttering in my stomach. I want us to do it again.

And I want everything else they promised, too.

Now, though, I've got other things to worry about. Like spending the afternoon with Raph's family.

Wind roars against my ears as we fly to the housing district, but I barely hear it. My thoughts and fears drown out everything else.

I've talked to his mom only once, and to be honest, the experience wasn't something I've been clamoring to repeat. The woman is nasty. Part of me worries they won't like me, while the other part says good riddance, because angels like that aren't who I strive to impress. The opposite, actually.

No, I don't care what they think. I'm only here as support for Raphael.

The man in question sends me a shy smile, his blond hair caught in a vortex of air and making him look even more attractive.

We lower in altitude, breaking through the cover of cloud, and the wind steals away my gasp. Below us, directly in our trajectory, is an enormous property that looks nothing like the single-family homes I've seen.

As we land just outside the gate, my mouth hangs wide as I take it all in. I'm about to tell him how stunning his house is when I catch the look on his face. He's more nervous than I've ever seen him.

"Listen, I should warn you about my family," he begins, but I cut him off by placing a finger against his lips.

"Screw your family. I'm here for you, Raph. I'm on *your* side. Not theirs."

He pulls me against his chest and we just stand like that for several minutes. When his breathing has calmed down a bit, he breaks the silence. "I just want you to be prepared. I can't guarantee they won't say or do something offensive. You put up with enough shit from everyone else, sunshine. I don't want you to have to deal with it from my family as well."

I pull back, needing him to look into my eyes and see the truth of my next words. "I can take it. What I can't take is them being asshats toward you. I promise you don't have to worry about me. There's nothing they could say that would change how I feel about you. And as long as you want me here, I'm staying."

"You are not from this world, I think," he says, placing a soft kiss against my lips. When we break apart, he turns to face the gate he'd clearly rather not enter.

As much as I'd hoped my words would soothe away some of his worries, he still isn't himself. Gone is the usually happy, funny, carefree guy that I'm used to. The man before me is sour and nervous. He reminds me more of Zeke in all of his grumpiness than the Raphael I've come to care for. And as much as he tries to plaster on a smile and hide it, I see through it as easily as breathing.

A butler greets us at the door, which is far larger than any door truly should be, and ushers us inside. With Raphael's hand in mine, I follow him into a large entryway with closets lining one wall and row after row of mirrors on the other. When I catch sight of myself, eyes wide and full of wonder, I try to school my expression into something more neutral.

It'll be as clear as day to these angels just how much I don't fit in here. I won't do anything to encourage them to make things more uncomfortable for Raph.

The butler announces to Archangels-know-who that we've arrived, and it takes a moment for me to realize that this is how I'm being introduced. Weird, but okay. Not exactly how I envisioned Raphael's parents meeting me as his girlfriend, but with these angels, I have a feeling my expectations will be found lacking all around.

A man and woman sweep across the floor to meet us. Or rather, she sweeps, moving like she's the epitome of importance. He moves like he's being pulled here by the ear trapped in his grandmother's grip.

"I'm so glad you both finally made it. A little late, though, isn't it?" the woman says, causing my hackles to rise.

Raphael's smile looks pained. "Nice to see you too, mother. Is Raduriel here yet?"

"No. Your brother is far too busy with work. We can't expect him to be everywhere at once, can we?" Her eyes travel from Raphael to me, taking in my windswept hair and the way I'm holding on to Raphael. "And who are you again, dear?"

I want to tell her that Raphael is just as busy but since I'm trying to make a good first impression, I keep a lid on that topic.

Raph replies for me, his tone implying just how proud he is to call me his. "This is Hayliel Gracelin, my girlfriend. Hayliel, this is my mother, Karena and behind her is my father, Andras."

"Gracelin, hmm?" Karena says, contemplating. "I don't

think I've heard that name before."

"Likely not. We don't have too many Pure angels among our ancestors."

"Pity."

This damn woman is getting under my skin, and we haven't even left the front of the house.

"Oh, I don't think so." My voice comes out tight, but I try to calm the rage bubbling inside me. "But it's quite nice to put a face to a name, and a pleasure to meet you as well," I add the last bit for Raphael's dad, who's kept silent through this entire exchange.

"What do you mean, a face to a name? Raphael, I do hope you aren't boring this poor young lady by talking about your mother at every given opportunity."

I grit my teeth and can almost hear Raphael's grinding to dust. "Oh, no. It's nothing like that. I was simply referring to the time we spoke on a call not too long ago. It was a brief conversation, so I won't blame you if you don't remember."

She stands straighter. "Of course I remember. Since the meal isn't ready yet, there's still ample time to change, dear." Her last dig is directed at Raphael, but she doesn't stay to make sure it hit its target before she's whipping around and leaving us, taking Andras with her.

Raphael doesn't waste a second pulling me through the house, pointing out little things as we pass by, but never linger. I can't believe this is the house he grew up in. There's far more space here than any family of four needs.

He said his parents were always throwing parties, which might be fun if his parents weren't as they are, but overall it just sounds lonely.

We finally make it to his room and it takes almost no time at all to realize this was never a place of peace for him. There are no photos or knickknacks, nothing of substance but the necessities. It hurts my heart.

An outfit is laid out on top of his bed, and it seems to bother Raphael. "If I don't change into that, she'll only berate me about it while we eat."

It really shouldn't surprise me how awful this woman is, but it does. How could anyone treat others, least of all their child, like that? "Has she always been that way?"

"Since I can remember, yea. Though it's always to me and never to Raduriel, which just makes me want to say no even more." Raphael only stands there, staring out the window. Something about his stance makes me think this isn't the first time he's been like this.

"And your dad?"

His jaw clenches. "He married into wealth, so he keeps his mouth shut instead of pissing off his cash cow."

Hearing that explains a lot about the man I just met. "I'm sorry. That's not the home life anyone should have to endure." I walk to his side and wrap my arm around his torso as we both stare into the field beyond the house. "Has Theo spent much time here?"

"He has. Actually, Mom would even make little jabs comparing me to him too, but for some reason, they didn't sting as much as the ones about Raduriel. Which sucks because there was a time in our lives when we were close. I even looked up to him. Why my parents had to ruin that is beyond me."

A heavy fist squeezes my heart, tempting me to march right back to Karena and Andras to give them a piece of my mind. But even I know better than to assume someone like me can change things for Raph. Unfortunately, what he has to endure at home is more than likely never going to change, but what I can help with is how he views himself.

I pull him down onto his bed and just hold him, running my hands through his hair and down his back. A contented sigh leaves his lips, but neither of us speaks.

Whatever happens tonight, I want him to know that he's not alone anymore. Not now, and hopefully not ever.

I don't know how much time passes before there's a knock on the door and a voice calls out to Master Raphael, requesting our presence in the dining room. I feel Raph's sigh all the way to the marrow of my bones. He's trying to fortify his walls.

I grab his hand, squeezing once before we head downstairs.

Raduriel is already there, along with his friend Briathos from the guild. Raphael told me on the flight over that he and Zeke are old friends, which I find fascinating, but keep it to myself.

Karena frowns when she notices Raphael hasn't changed. "Was there something wrong with the outfit I laid out for you? Why you insist on wearing such garbage is beyond me."

Garbage? He's not wearing rags, for fuck's sake. "I think he looks very handsome in what he's wearing now."

He offers me a soft smile, but it's wiped away before it reaches his eyes when his bitch of a mother responds. "Well, of course you would, dear. But Raphael grew up in a wealthy Pure family and should dress the part."

I ignore her barb, following Raph to our seats. He mumbles something under his breath, which sends his mother into a tailspin.

"What was that? How many times have I told you that you need to speak clearly if you want angels to understand you? Do I need to book another appointment with your speech thera-pist?"

Is this woman for real? I look around the table, absolutely floored to find no one else saying a damn thing to protect or stick up for Raphael. If this is what it's always like for him, no wonder he doesn't want to come home.

The first course arrives, and a blissful silence falls over the table as we all dig in.

Raduriel lets out a happy sigh as the staff takes away our empty plates to make room for the next course. "I didn't realize how much I missed the taste of this food."

His mother beams. "If you're called away again in the future, we'll serve your favorite to make the return even more special." She turns to me, a curious look on her face. "So, how did you go from tutoring my son to dating him?"

It catches me so off guard that I struggle to keep the annoyed look off my face. She thought I was his tutor the first time we spoke too, and even though we corrected her then, it seems she's forgotten.

"It's the opposite, actually. Raphael was *my* tutor. I wouldn't have been able to ace my midterm without his determined and focused guidance." I shoot him a warm smile before continuing. "As for how our relationship evolved, it was natural. As easy as breathing."

I can tell Raphael appreciated my kind words by the way he presses his leg against the outside of my thigh.

His mother looks like she wants to speak, but Andras makes the first comment of the evening to me then. "What subject was he helping you with, if you don't mind my asking?"

"Our angelic powers class. Coming from a Fallen family, it was my first experience with using any type of powers, and unfortunately it took some getting used to. But Raph never judged me or made me feel weak, which I appreciated."

His father appears pleased by my comment, but the look is wiped clear off his face the instant his wife speaks.

"My youngest, helping the less fortunate? Now that is a surprise indeed."

My smile is tight as I say, "Not to those who know him well."

Surprisingly, she doesn't clap back with anything and allows us all to focus back on our meals. Raduriel still hasn't said much or spoken up for his brother, but the closer I watch him, the more I notice the small twitch in his jaw whenever his mother speaks. Interesting.

Briathos looks just as uncomfortable as I am, though Karena

doesn't seem to realize a damn thing.

Clearing my throat, I say, "The food is delicious, Mrs. Adams. Have you always known how to cook?"

The bitch scoffs while Raphael squeezes my leg under the table.

"The lady of the house does not do her own cooking, dear. The kitchen staff prepared the meal, as they always do, though I find it rather dry myself. I'll have to speak with them again about expectations."

There's not a chance in hell that I'd want this angel as my mother, boss, or anyone else near me at all. I can just imagine what *speaking* to them about expectations would be like. I bet she adopts the same tone she uses when speaking down to Raph.

We make it through to the next course with only a few more incidents. Raduriel became animated while talking about his work, and of course Karena couldn't pass up another opportunity to compare and belittle Raphael. As if he's not a completely different angel. I truly think she expected having kids would be like making a batch of cookies, where the mold is the same and all cookies turn out exactly perfect.

What she fails to realize is that Raph *is* perfect. No thanks to her.

"You should take this as a learning opportunity, Raphael," his mother begins, heading on yet another tirade. I've had enough.

I set my drink down a little too forcefully; the sound drawing everyone's eyes my way. Then, without even a second thought, I stand and look around the room. Raphael stands beside me, not saying a word but letting me glare daggers at everyone else as I try to keep my cool.

"Whatever are you doing, child? Sit down, Raphael. You're causing a scene," Karena starts, looking annoyed. And I snap.

"Thank you for dinner, Mrs. Adams. While the food was lovely, the company was anything but."

Karena sucks in a sharp breath while the rest of the angels sitting at the table only wince. "Excuse me? I—"

"No. I'm not finished." My hands threaten to tremble, so I fist them until I feel my nails press into flesh. "You treat Raphael like he's less than everyone else when, in fact, it's the opposite. Your youngest son has a brilliant, sharp mind. He's caring and funny, and one of the best angels I've ever met. It's a pity you can't see past your own nose to witness it. And I'm sad to see the rest of you aren't any better, either. I never really understood why he avoided coming home, but after sitting through just one dinner with you, I get it now. If I were your child, I'd avoid you too."

I stalk from the room, not bothering to wait for a response. From the corner of my eye, I see Raph say something to his brother, but I'm shaking with a surplus of emotions and can't focus enough to hear what he says.

Shit.

I hope I didn't just make things worse for him with his family, but fucking hell. Someone needed to say something. And if Raphael's father and brother were too chickenshit to do so, then I am more than happy to speak up. Every. Damn. Time.

Raph catches up to me, tugging me along and pulling me into a room so fast, I don't even have a chance to see where we are before his mouth descends on mine. The kiss is different from any we've shared before now. Those were demanding and all-consuming, but this one, something about it makes me want to cry.

He holds my face in his hands, his lips caressing mine tenderly.

Love.

That's what I feel in this kiss.

His utter devotion.

After a few minutes, he pulls away, letting his forehead rest against mine as he stares into my eyes. Into my very soul. "Thank you," he whispers, running his thumb over my cheek.

"I meant every word," I tell him, needing him to know that I'm on his side. I need him to believe that he's not the disappointment his family treats him like.

He kisses me once more before slowly backing away. When my senses finally return, I realize where he brought me.

A library.

My jaw hangs open as I gaze around the room, taking in the shelves and ornate spiral staircase in the center of it all. If I grew up with something like this, I'd never leave the house. Though, I guess if I shared that same house with a mother like Karena and a mentally checked out father like Andras, then maybe even this library wouldn't be enough to keep me here.

Raph pulls a key out from his pocket and points toward an

empty cabinet. "That's where I found Isaac's journal. It looks empty, but that's only a ruse."

He unlocks the door, revealing the hidden contents inside. We pull everything out, cataloging what we find in case it's helpful. And as much as I'd like to take all of these books with us, we don't want whoever is clearly trying to hide them to know we've discovered them.

I'm flipping through the last book when a piece of paper falls out and flutters to the floor.

My gaze flicks to Raphael's before we both crouch to pick it up. The paper is faded, creased in places, but there's no denying I've seen this exact shade of beige before.

It's a missing piece of Isaac Adam's journal.

33

RAPHAEL

I stare at the torn paper in Hayliel's hand, wondering if it's too much to hope that whatever's written on this page makes sense and isn't just nonsensical jargon. It would be a miracle, given the state of that damn journal, but I reckon we're overdue on miracles. It's time for something to go our way.

She turns it over, giving us the first glimpse of text.

Can it really be?

Pulling out my slate, I bring up the photo I'd taken of the missing entry. When I first took it, I was worried it was a bad idea. If this got into the wrong hands ... even if there are no true answers in the photo, it brings light to enough things that we'd rather stay in the dark. Right now, though? Now I'm grateful for the foresight.

We hold up the paper, trying to place it where the torn edges are. Even with all the words now in front of us, it takes effort to read the shredded, worn paper.

I finally did it.
After months of trying, I met with the Seraphim twins. Ingrid and Octavius.
From the articles, I would have sworn they looked alike, but seeing them up close, it's easy to spot the differences. It's also easy to feel just how powerful they truly are. It's almost hard to stomach. Having been raised in squalor, I expected them to be different. Harder. With sharper edges. But they were kinder than most of my own family members.
I didn't mean to learn their secret. It was purely by accident. But I vowed to them upon my life that I would take it with me to the grave.
The information below could change everything if it winds up in the wrong hands.
These unbelievable twins weren't both born Seraphim. In fact, they weren't even twins at all. Only Octavius was born with the Seraphim gene. Ingrid was born Pure. Looking at them now, though, I almost don't believe it. I wouldn't if they hadn't admitted it to me.
A bond. That's what made it possible. Octavius

and Ingrid shared such a strong bond that their essences merged, and once they performed the bond ritual, it was irreversible.
One Seraphim turned into two.

The moment I finish reading, my eyes race to meet Hayliel's. She looks just as surprised as I am.

"There's a ritual to bond angels?" she asks sheepishly.

You'd think being angels ourselves would mean we'd know the answer, but this is unchartered territory. Or at least, I thought it was. "Honestly? I have no idea. Before this note, I would have said absolutely not. Our special ceremony to wed is as close to a bond ritual as I thought we had. And even so, knowing that my crazed uncle wrote this makes it hard to believe, but ..."

"But what?"

I try to decipher the look that flashes behind her dark sapphire eyes. Whatever it is, it spurs me to speak the truth. "But what if it's real? The connection I've felt with you is unlike anything I've experienced before. Maybe there's some merit to what's written on this page."

"Maybe."

I watch as she thinks, and as much as I want to ask her to share, I keep my mouth shut. Glancing at the antique clock on the shelf beside us, I inwardly curse. Shit. Raduriel likely won't be long now. I don't want him to know that we've found this hiding spot.

Without knowing who taped the picture to the back of that glass, it's better if we keep this between our trusted group for now.

Once everything is back in its place, I close and lock the cabinet door before beckoning my silent beauty up the stairs and into my old study room. At least here we can talk privately, and when my brother does come, we'll hear him before he arrives.

She chews on her lip. "I wonder how things went with Uriel today. Has there been any update? I left my slate in your room."

I nod. "Just that they have news, though, not to get our hopes up too high. We'll call them once we're done with my brother, and then hopefully we'll have a clear plan of action."

"Hopefully. Do you think Castiel will know more about this? Or maybe his friend that lent him the book about Seraphim?"

"It's possible. That man knows far more than I would have expected from a history professor. At this point, I refuse to cross anything off without at least trying."

She chuckles, smiling sweetly. "My parents will like you."

Heart beating fast, I look at the gorgeous angel sitting on the top of my desk and grin. "Of course they would. I'm charming as shit," I tease. "At least with a stomach full of food."

Her hands move to cradle my face, eyes boring into mine. "Always, Raph."

She pulls me closer and I kiss her hard, unable to stop imagining how she would look sprawled naked across my desk, her legs spread like the pages of a textbook. I could taste her right here. Feast until I'm ready to burst before making her moan so loud that it filtered through the whole damn house.

As I trail kisses down her neck, fully intending to do just that, the door to the library opens and Raduriel calls out, "I'm entering the library."

Hayliel covers her face, cheeks reddening behind her hands, and I curse. Fucking Rad. Like yes, he's coming here because that's what I asked him to do, but dammit. Couldn't he have kept busy for at least another half an hour? My brother seems to have no issues droning on and on about his accomplishments, so why must he choose now to stop?

I'm slowly pulling away from the delectable woman in front of me when my brother adds, "And now I'm climbing the stairs."

My sunshine groans softly, and for a second, I worry she's in pain until she whispers, "How does he know what we were about to do?"

Not pain at all then. Mortification. Fuck, she's cute.

I laugh, my sour mood turning lighter as I pull her into my arms. "Well, that's obvious, babe." I tuck her head under my chin. "With the way you stood up for me at dinner, it's a wonder I didn't clear the table and claim you right there in front of everyone. You can thank me later for my discretion."

Before she can respond, Raduriel raps his knuckles on the open door, a smirk on his stupid face. "I hope I'm not interrupting."

His words cause Hayliel's face to redden further and now I'm just getting pissed. Making her blush is my job. And Theo's.

And fine, Zeke's too. But not him. *Remember, you need his contact. You can't flip out at him yet.*

Putting on a fake smile, I say, "Is Briathos downstairs?" I didn't think to get approval from the group on whether we could loop him in on what's been happening. Not that I'm giving my brother all the details either, but he's bound to demand at least some information before he helps us. If he's even willing. But with Briathos and his position at the guild, I'm not sure it's such a good idea. Zeke hasn't even told his own father anything yet, or his commanding lieutenant.

"No. I came alone, like you asked. What's going on?"

Hayliel and I exchange a glance, and despite the earlier outburst or the embarrassment from a few short moments ago, she must see that I haven't managed to fortify my walls yet.

She turns toward him, drawing her shoulders back. "We actually have a request, and we're hoping you'll help us without asking too many questions."

He looks almost stupefied. If this moment wasn't important as hell, I'd be laughing my ass off at the sight.

"That's not cryptic or anything." His gaze jumps between us, assessing. "I'll help you with whatever you need, but I can't promise that I won't need more information. Does that work?"

I sigh. It's not ideal, but we expected this would be his response. Besides, nothing says he needs to know all the details, at least not before we can get him to the cave and have his intentions checked. I want to smack myself. Why the hell didn't we think of that before? That's the only way I'll truly trust him at this point.

Hayliel waits for my nod before she agrees, but the clever minx adds a little loophole. "We can agree to that. Though we may not always answer your questions. We've been burned before," she adds when he seems hurt that we wouldn't trust him.

The entire exchange baffles me. First, that he's willing to help without even knowing the full story. And second, that he'd be shocked that we—or I—don't trust him. Has he been living in a fantasy world all these years? He's never once done anything to make me trust him. Not in a long, long fucking time.

Feeling annoyed, I blurt out, "We need that contact you have for rune stitched clothing."

He turns wide eyes on me. "Fuck. The rune weaver? What the hell have you gotten yourself into, Raphael?"

An angry retort rests on my tongue, but Hayliel places her soothing hand on my arm, stopping me.

"By the Archangels, everyone in this damn family sure likes to blame Raph."

"That's not what I—"

"His only misstep is that he's associating with me. We need the special clothes for protection because a whole host of shit is about to rain down on us and we're trying to stop it."

I take her hand from my arm and pull it to my cheek. "For the record, getting close to you is the furthest thing from a mistake, sunshine." I didn't think I could love this woman even more, but here I go. To my brother, I say, "She's right about one thing, though. Bad things are coming. Hell, they've already happened, and we're just trying to stop it before it's too late. Can you put me in touch with this rune weaver or not?"

Instead of answering, Raduriel closes the door. Hayliel and I stiffen, unsure why he's acting strange. Honestly, as sad as it is to admit, I wouldn't even be surprised if my shitty brother attacked us right here.

He doesn't, which only causes curiosity to flow through me like the tide.

"I'm going to ask you both a question, one that I probably shouldn't given it'll ruin my career if it gets out, but first I need you both to promise that if the answer is no, you won't breathe a word of it to anyone. Can you do that?"

"Of course," Hayliel says, then both sets of eyes turn to me where I hesitate. I give in after a moment, agreeing to his terms.

My usually controlled and perfect brother runs a hand through his hair, messing up the strands. "The bad things that are coming. Does it have anything to do with demons?"

Shit. Fuck. Is this a trap? I wouldn't put it past Raduriel, not if his job is on the line. But even as I think those words, I realize that's not quite right. He's putting his career in jeopardy just by talking to us about it. It's so wildly out of character for him that I can't wrap my mind around it.

I think we can trust him, at least with the demon part, Hayliel says through our mental connection.

I stand up straighter and prepare to do the one thing I never thought I'd do again. Put my faith in my older brother.

"Yes."

Raduriel curses and begins to pace. He's frazzled, and my earlier comfort at seeing him so bent out of shape vanishes. If he knows about the demonic happenings here, things are bad.

"Wait," Hayliel says, confused. "How do *you* know about it? I thought you had an office job?"

Her question makes me realize I never really told her much about my family or what they do. The less I talked about my brother or parents, the better. But looking back, maybe that wasn't the best choice.

"I work closely with the governor and city commissioner, which usually consists of pompous, self-righteous pricks gathering to complain."

I snort a laugh, which has Rad smiling briefly before it falls.

"Lately, though, things are a lot more serious. I just returned from a sequestered meeting with all the city's higher ups to discuss the rise in demon attacks, whispers of a Fallen rebellion, and a note from the Archangels."

I blanch. "They're aware? The Archangels, I mean."

He nods. "I read the note myself. They're planning for war."

"Against the demons or the Fallen?" Hayliel's voice trembles, and I know his answer has the power to shift her entire world.

He looks away, unable to meet our eyes. "For anyone who stands against them."

If they're talking about an all out war, things are way bigger than we expected and happening on levels we never even could have imagined.

My slate pings and Raduriel says, "I've just shared the rune weaver's contact details with you, and I also let her know she'd be hearing from my brother. I know you might not trust me right now, but I'd like to be kept in the loop and assist however I can with what you're planning."

"We'll have to talk with the others first to make sure they're on board, but I'd like that," Hayliel says, and I realize that as much as I thought I'd hate the idea, I don't. My brother has been more helpful in the last half an hour than he has in over a decade.

I don't think anyone will disagree with him helping, especially not once we get him to the cave and test his intentions.

We got what we wanted in coming here. The rune weaver. We still have to convince her to help us, or at least fund the clothes, but that won't be a problem. I just have to hope Theo and Castiel had as good of luck as we did.

Raduriel shifts to face me, his expression solemn. "I've been open and honest with you both today because I trust you." He turns to Hayliel, a small smile lifting his lips, "And your outburst at dinner was glorious and long overdue. It put a lot of things into perspective for me, so thank you for doing what the rest of us should have. Raphael, I'm sorry I haven't been there for you like I should have. It shouldn't have taken her speech for me to realize how shitty I've been, but I hope you'll let me make it up to you."

His words cause a crack to form in my carefully built walls. I've waited years for him to have this revelation, and I honestly thought it was past the point of any reconciliation. Yet I can't ignore the blooming hope cautiously spreading through the seams. On the outside, I keep my expression neutral despite the war raging inside me.

"That said," he continues, "I'd appreciate if what we discussed today didn't leave this room, or at least doesn't go beyond the trusted friends you mentioned."

The space between us fills with a pregnant pause charged with possibilities for the future. One not filled with the constant pain and betrayal of having my only sibling turn their back on me, and instead stand at my side.

With a nod to my brother, I say, "You have our word."

34

HAYLIEL

Raphael brought me back to his room after his brother left. With the bomb he'd just dropped, neither of us wanted to just sit around and do nothing.

A war.

Have things gotten that bad already? In truth, the war against demons is long past due, but the Fallen? Even after all the things I've witnessed from Roderick, I wouldn't wage war on them. Growing up with Fallen parents, I knew they were unhappy with the way of the world, but I never could have imagined this happening.

Raphael calls the rune weaver, who surprisingly answers on the second ring, despite it being a Friday evening. While they hash over the details of our rune-stitched clothing, I test out the long distance connection with my parents to see how they're doing.

The possibility of an attack on the Fallen, especially those who are innocent like my parents, makes me physically ill. But the Archangels are smart. They're our rulers for a reason. I doubt they'll go into any situation without all the details and a foolproof plan to protect those who've done nothing.

They didn't win a war against God, or survive as rulers for this long, without the brains to show for it.

I don't expect to reach my parents. Not on a random Friday night without prior warning, but they must have been practicing hard because Mom answers almost immediately.

All good! Baking as always. You okay?

I smile as her choppy words fill my head. *All good here. Proud of your progress, Mom. Love you.*

Love you, Haylie-bear.

I'm relieved just knowing they're alright. War will take time, and we'll use every second to figure out a way to keep my parents as far from it as possible.

A thought strikes me so suddenly, I'm a fool that I didn't think of it sooner. I should give my protection amulet to them. It's only one, but it's better than nothing, and as a Seraphim, I'm far more protected than they are already. I could never choose which of them would get it, and I already know how it would play out. Dad would refuse to wear it and insist that Mom use it. Even if they made a schedule, he'd find some way to get it around her neck. Maybe Zeke or Mira could steal me another one?

Fuck. I need to get better at thinking ahead.

I check my slate and see a few missed messages in the group chat.

> **Theo**: How was family dinner? Was Raduriel helpful? Hoping we can talk soon.
> **Zeke**: My shift is done, so I'm available anytime, too.
> **Hayliel**: Eventful, to say the least. We'll call in a few minutes to explain. Wish you were both here.
> **Theo**: Me too, firefly. Me too.

The little typing bubbles pop up several times from Zeke before eventually fading. I'm desperate to know what he was going to say, but I don't let myself dwell on it. If he wants to be part of this, he'll need to let down his guard and say so. I'm done trying to read his mixed signals.

When Raphael ends the call a few minutes later, he turns to me with a small grin that tells me everything I need to know. The rune weaver has agreed to help us. At least we have *some* good news.

"Theo and Zeke are ready to chat whenever we are," I tell him, trying to keep the panicked thoughts from returning.

He must pick up on it because he takes my hand in his. "We'll call now, but first, were you able to reach your parents?"

"I was. They're fine. Bless the fucking Archangels for that."

He pulls me into his arms, pressing a kiss to the top of my head. "Good. That's good."

We settle onto his bed and spare no more time before connecting with the group. While we snuggle up among a mass of pillows and blankets, we prop the slate up on a lap desk that Raphael pulled from his closet, and I immediately want one for myself.

For a second, I worry maybe we shouldn't sit so close together but then chastise myself for even thinking it. If last night taught me anything, it's that I need to give angels the chance to react or not. I can't keep trying to predict the future, worrying about what-ifs. We have far worse things to worry about.

Theo and Zeke immediately pick up on our moods, asking us to explain what went down.

Raph shakes his head. "You go first. What did you learn from Uriel's classroom?"

Zeke rolls his eyes, clearly annoyed with Raph for putting off the sharing of what we learned, but in this instance, he's right. Once we tell them about war, everything else is going to feel a hell of a lot smaller in comparison.

Theo shrugs. "Nothing substantial. His planner had a few appointments, but it's not like he wrote out the names or any incriminating details. Other than that, we found a decoding tool that went along with a map of the city. There were several marked areas on it, but we weren't able to decode the notes before we had to leave. Castiel took photos, though, so he's not giving up."

"Marked areas? Those don't sound good," Raphael says, and I frown.

Zeke sits forward, getting closer to the screen. "Do you remember where they were?"

"Let me guess," I say before Theo can respond, "One was in the Fallen district?"

"No, actually. That's what was so weird about it. The marked places almost seemed random. If there's a rhyme or reason to them, we don't know what it is yet." He frowns. "Why did you think it would be there? What happened?"

"The good news is, Raduriel agreed to help us, and I've already spoken to the rune weaver. She needs our measurements and a list of runes we want sewn into the fabric. Given the next bit we have to tell you, we should give her this information as fast as possible so she can get started right away."

A message from Zeke flashes across the top of the screen. His measurements and rune selection sit there for a few seconds before disappearing.

"Do you just have your body measurements saved to your notes or something?" Theo asks, voice teasing.

"Ha. Ha," Zeke replies, his tone annoyed, but I see the slight tilt to his lips. "Those are from getting fitted for the guild uniform. Now, what is it you aren't telling us?"

We explain what Raduriel told us, sparing no details, and the further we get into it, the more jittery I become.

Zeke huffs out a derisive breath. "That's extreme, isn't it? A war against demons I can understand, but Fallen? Don't they remember what happened the last time we had a war among our kind? It didn't end well."

"Not to mention, because of the ridiculous rules of the guild, the entirety of our angelic fighters are Fallen. How the hell do they plan to handle that?" Theo adds, and holy shit, he's right. If the Archangels declare war on Fallen, will they force the guild to attack their own?

All of this is too much.

The need to see my parents face to face and make sure they're alright is an itch I need to scratch. I won't be able to sleep tonight without knowing they're safe. "I'm going to the Fallen district. Tonight. If the Archangels truly are planning to declare war, my parents won't stand a chance. Maybe we can ward their house like we did the cave? Or at the very least, I can try to convince them to take a vacation somewhere far away. I hear Earth is beautiful."

My breaths come fast, my mouth dry as I try to take in more air than my stiff lungs will allow.

"Breathe, sunshine," Raphael murmurs, soothing me.

I take a few deep steadying breaths, filling my lungs with the citrusy scent of Raphael, but the terror in my belly never fades.

"If you go, we all go," Zeke says. "We're in this together."

We don't waste a second in heading to see my parents, only stopping to meet up with Theo and Zeke on the outskirts before flying in together.

Something heavy weighs me down, settling like river stones in my gut.

This damn fear will be the death of me. I have to shove it aside and remind myself that we have time. Time to finish training my parents. Time to make a plan for their safety, and time to figure out what the fuck is going on so we can handle it.

When we land, it takes a moment to recognize the sounds around me, and then another second more to realize it's coming from within the walls of their house.

Someone is inside, tearing the place apart.

I rush forward, but before I make it past the threshold, I'm knocked clean off my feet.

Zeke is closest to me, and he kneels down to check that I'm alright while Raphael and Theo focus on taking down the asshole who threw me to the ground.

"You should help them," I tell Zeke, standing up and wincing as my tailbone twinges.

"It's only an angel. They can handle it. Besides, I know you're about to rush inside."

"I have to make sure my parents are alright," I tell him, preparing to fight him on it, but he surprises me.

"I know. That's why I'm going with you."

My heart crashes against my ribcage, beating wildly as we head through the open doorway and into the ruin that is now my parents' home. The air is tinged with the scent of fear and something metallic. It burns my nose, threatening to make me throw up.

This is all my fault.

The words repeat in my head, but I try to push them back. Now isn't the time for a meltdown. I have to focus on finding them.

At the end of the hall, a hulking figure turns to us.

Demon.

As if matters could get any fucking worse.

Zeke moves into step beside me, not giving the beast a moment to anticipate our movements. He attacks with brutal precision, and for a moment I'm lost in awe of him.

Claws wrap around my shoulder, tossing me against the kitchen wall. The protection amulet around my neck warms, but my side still aches from where I hit the side of the counter.

I've never let pain keep me down before though, and I sure as fuck won't start now.

The demon snarls at me, revealing its sharp teeth and swiping its claws through the air between us, but I duck and manage a blow to its right knee that has it stumbling.

I take advantage of the moment of weakness, trying desperately to summon the sunfire I'm supposed to be able to harness.

Nothing comes. Not a single drop.

We parry a few more times before the demon's next hit sends me sprawling past the kitchen table. I flip over backwards; the amulet taking the brunt of the pain I know my body should feel right now.

My hair has come loose from the braid I'd tied it in before

we left Raphael's house. It blocks my view, but when I move the strands off my face, I finally notice where that awful smell is coming from.

Blood.

Pools of it lie on the floor. Streaks line the walls.

No!

Rage and sorrow build inside me like an inferno. It might not be their blood. But if it is … I turn back to the demon stalking toward me, oblivious to everything else around us.

What was it Castiel said? I'm the only one in the way of my power, and I need to accept that I alone am enough.

Closing my eyes, I let those words flow through my limbs, echoing inside my very soul.

I am a true and solid vessel. My parents knew it. My friends know it. And it's about damn time I know it, too.

When I open my eyes, I sense a chasm of heat growing in my chest. It's familiar, reminding me of the hot flashes I've experienced ever since the shift, but now I know where it's coming from.

My essence of sunfire.

The demon must sense something in the air because it stalls in its advance.

Is that fear I see lining the ragged edges of its face? Good.

I push every ounce of belief in myself, along with the rage and fear, toward that pool of heat inside me, stoking the fire and forcing it through my limbs. The demon snarls, swiping a powerful claw-tipped hand exactly where I stand. Except, I'm no longer there. As if I can dance on the winds of time, I'm now staring at the leathery wings tucked against its back.

I reach out. Time seems to slow down as the demon turns its head to face me, his features etched in surprise. When the tip of my finger touches the demon in front of me, time stops, just for a moment, and then the demon disintegrates into nothing more than dust.

Air leaves my lungs in big breaths as I finally glance away from the pile of ash in front of me, only to catch sight of all three of my men watching on in fascination.

"You all saw that, right?" Raphael asks, watching me like I just pulled the moon from the sky.

Theo's laugh is incredulous. "You can teleport. Holy fucking shit. You can *teleport!*"

His words unlock a memory inside me of that night we nearly died in our quest to confront Roderick. I teleported then too, though I didn't realize it. But how?

At Zeke's feet, I notice a familiar patch of dust. "What happened there?" I ask, confused. Did I somehow manage to kill that one, too?

He smiles triumphantly. "I tested out that blade you infused. It wasn't as instantaneous as your touch appears to be, but it did the job all the same."

"That was ... you're incredible," Raph says, unable to look away from me.

"It was," Theo adds. "I'm glad we knocked that asshole out in time to watch."

The happiness from basking in their wonder diminishes when I breathe in the scent of iron again and remember what it is we're doing here.

My parents. The blood.

"Has anyone seen them yet? I don't want to believe—" A sob escapes me before I can continue further.

"I'll check your room," Zeke says, asking the guys to stay with me, but I'm too busy staring at the bloody handprints by the back door to hear how they respond. As much as it kills me to see it, it brings a bit of hope to my chest. At least one of them was alive enough to grab the wall, and right now, with grief and rage sitting heavy on my shoulders, it's enough.

Zeke comes back, but he doesn't say anything. All he does is give me a small shake of his head. But I already knew they wouldn't be down there.

My heart thumps erratically in my chest, yet the new reservoir of heat reminds me that I will find them, and I'll make whoever thought to take them from me pay for what they've done.

The blood is fresh. It has to be given I spoke with my mom through our mental connection not too long ago. Maybe she can tell me where they are now.

"I'm going to—" I begin, but I'm interrupted by a dark, commanding voice that stirs fear in my belly.

"Hayliel Gracelin," the deep voice booms from outside.

I force saliva down my dry throat, swallowing past the lump of terror.

I'd know that voice anywhere. That dark tenor seemingly fathomless.

The cloaked figure is here.

35

HAYLIEL

"Who's that?" Raphael asks, like he can tell just from my expression that the answer isn't a good one. It's not.

It takes a few tries before I can make the words pass my lips. "I can't say for sure, but his voice is almost identical to the masked man from the library. It doesn't vibrate with power like it did that night, but the way it makes me feel like I've stepped into utter darkness is the same." A shiver races down my spine, all the way to my toes.

Raphael's gaze sharpens, and I wonder if he can tell how afraid I am. "What the fuck is he doing here, of all places?"

Outside, the voice booms again. "I know you're in there.

Come out and greet me. I have an offer for you."

The more he talks, the more something itches in mind. But what? Where else have I heard him?

"There's no way in fucking hell you're going out there, hummingbird," Zeke says, looking angry.

Raph nods. "For once, I agree with him."

I expect the same from Theo, but he surprises me. Stepping forward, he grabs my shoulders and stares into my eyes. "Tell us what you're thinking."

Internally, I smile at how well he knows me. Even through this terrible situation, he's thoughtful. "His voice. Is it familiar to you?"

My three guys share a glance, and I know they hear it, too. "From the barn," Theo goes pale.

"Oh, shit." Raphael says.

"This is the boss, the angel who ordered demons to nab Roderick."

Pieces slot into place in my mind at the revelation. If this asshole has my parents, I have to go outside and face him. "I'm sorry," I whisper, locking eyes with each of my guys. "We need to know who he is and what he wants. If he really is who we think he is, then he has plenty of angel blades and I can't just—"

"We're coming with you," all three of them say in unison. My supporters. My protectors. They'll back me until the very end. I fight back the tears threatening to consume me. I can't let them out yet. Not now. Not when my parents' lives sit on my shoulders.

On legs that don't feel like my own, I walk through the now unfamiliar house, past demon dust and broken furniture, until I reach the front door. It's open, but not wide enough for anyone to walk through. My heart pounds in a sporadic rhythm as I push the door all the way open.

There, standing on the edge of the street, is a figure so magnificent it puts all the drawings I've seen before to shame. Four white wings stretch wide behind a massive frame, with his signature flame-topped staff held loosely at his side. He'd be handsome if the manic look in his eyes wasn't so prominent, or his smile wasn't so gleeful. If I weren't seeing this with my own eyes, I'd never believe it.

Archangel Auriel stands in front of me on a nameless street in the Fallen district, and I'm pretty sure he took my parents.

"It's so good of you to join me, my little seraph. I was beginning to think we'd never get a proper introduction."

Now that my initial shock at seeing a fucking Archangel has worn off, I walk past the threshold, feeling my guys disperse around me on the front step. I don't miss the fact that somehow this guy knows my secret. While few of us know it, the pool of angels who could have blabbed is still too large to know who it is without looking into it.

Raphael, Theo, and Zeke say nothing. Likely sensing that it's me who has to run this little game. "There were other ways to meet me, Archangel Auriel. You didn't have to harm my family. Especially not after all the offerings we've given in your honor over the years."

His joyful expression darkens slightly. "Except for this year, isn't that right? Besides, I rather like this method. It promises a more, shall we say, obedient partnership."

I can't halt the derisive laugh bubbling out of me. "Partnership? You expect me to work with you after what you've done?"

"Well, yes." He says it so matter-of-factly that my jaw falls open. "It's that or watch everyone you love die before meeting the same fate. You can laugh all you like, but over time I believe you'll come to see things from my perspective."

Pain threatens to drown me, but in that moment I feel the mental connection with my guys warm, like a silent offering of comfort. I do my best to keep my expression as neutral as possible, not wanting Auriel to see just how much his words affect me. "And what would this partnership entail, exactly?"

His deep laughter sounds like a forest of trees falling in a storm. "So eager! All will be explained in due time. You've certainly got my friends in a tizzy, little seraph. They're all worried about the powerful angel who can't seem to die. They can sense your power, smell it even, but you know that. It's only dead little angels who don't have power, isn't that right?

Anger flares in my chest as he throws the words of that scarred demon back at me. The only way he could know what was said that day was if that damn demon survived to tell him about it. I guess the guild never managed to track them down after all.

Zeke steps forward, but I hold out a hand to stop him. Through our shared mental connection, I warn them all off about making a move. *Please don't. I couldn't handle it if he hurt you, too.*

"How cute. Listen to the powerful woman at your side, boy, and stay down. I have no intentions of harming you. At least not today."

"Then why are you even here? What do you want?" I grit out, my jaw locked.

"You, of course," he answers, like there's nothing else he could possibly want.

"But why?"

"Well, for starters, a Seraphim would do wonders for my cause. You could help keep my friends in line and build a brighter city. Besides, you're rather pretty. You might not know this yet, but I like to collect pretty little things."

The shine in his eyes makes me uncomfortable. The smart thing would be to back down, but I can't seem to force my tongue to behave. "So that's what you want me for? Why you took my parents? Not for a partnership at all, but to be my employer?"

He rolls his eyes, laughing like he would at a toddler attempting to make a joke. "I never did like that word. Join me and help me cleanse the city of those who are undeserving."

"I think we might have a different idea of *cleanse* and *undeserving*," I say, deadpan. The only one undeserving right now is him.

His entire demeanor changes. Before now, a devilish smile lurked behind his every word, but every trace of it is gone. Wiped away like it never existed. All that's left is a poisonous rancor that turns my stomach. "I see. Fine. You want time? Have it. Don't say I was never gracious and giving."

I doubt this guy has ever been either of those things a day in his damn life. How could he be when he's killed so many, with plans to do it again?

"Returning my parents will help me decide. It'll prove I can trust you. No partnership survives without trust," I say, like I might actually work with this psycho.

As expected, he isn't fooled. "No. They stay with me. Though of course you can see them. This very moment, in fact. You only need to come with me."

"Hummingbird," Zeke growls beside me, like he knows I'm considering it. How could I not? Archangel Auriel has my fucking parents. A headache builds behind my eyes, threatening to take me down.

This is all too fucking much.

"The next move is yours, little seraph. Join the cause, or prepare for war. You have seven days to give me your answer." His wicked smile has returned, warning me I won't like his next words. "While you contemplate, I'll do my best to keep your parents alive. Comfortable, even. You have my word."

Then, so quick I would have missed it with one poorly timed blink, he taps his staff on the ground once, and he's gone. Leaving me with an impossible choice to make.

Agree to his disgusting plan to cleanse the city while saving my parents in the process, or work against him and lose them forever.

Hayliel's story will continue in Wings of Valor, the final book in the SCU series.

Acknowledgements

I've had an absolute blast writing this book. Witnessing the characters grow makes me happy, and I hope it does the same for you. It's hard to believe there's only one more book left in Hayliel's story!

Thank you to my editor, proofreader, formatter, and cover and graphic designers for putting up with me and helping make this one hell of a book.

A massive shout out to Completely Booked PR for beta reading and hyping me up.

To all the friends who have kept me sane these last few months, I'm so grateful the book world brought us together. I adore you and hope that someday we'll meet in real life!

And finally, thank you to all the readers who took a chance on me. Without you, this wouldn't be possible. I hope you'll stick around for the final installment in this series.

About the Author

Victoria is a Canadian girl with a love for travel, music, books, games, and mayonnaise. She spends her mornings writing before work, and hopes to one day write full time. Friends say she gives the best hugs and you can usually find her laughing at her own lame jokes.

Facebook Group: /victoriasvillainousqueens

Facebook: /victoria.pauley.506

Instagram: @victoriapauley.author

TikTok: @victoriapauleyauthor

Website: victoriapauley.com

Also By Victoria Pauley

Standalones

Caged (*MF Gang Romance*)

A Night of Indulgence and Sloth *(MFM, Office,
Dark Romance)*

Series and Duets

<u>Silver City University</u>

*(RH/Why-Choose, Academy, Paranormal Ro-
mance)*

Wings of Deception

Wings of Torment

Wings of Strife

Wings of Valor

<u>Creating Destiny Duet</u>
(Double MF Fantasy Romance, Greek Mytholo-
gy)
Guided by the Stars
Fighting for the Stars